THE PASSENGER
LISA LUTZ

TITAN BOOKS

THE PASSENGER
Print edition ISBN: 9781785651731
E-book edition ISBN: 9781785651748

Published by Titan Books
A division of Titan Publishing Group Ltd
144 Southwark Street, London SE1 0UP

First Titan edition: March 2016
3 4 5 6 7 8 9 10

A CIP catalogue record for this title is available from the British Library.

Printed and bound in Great Britain by CPI Group Ltd.

TO MR. B & MR. D

FOR MS. C

CONTENTS

TANYA DUBOIS

I

When I found my husband at the bottom of the stairs, I tried to resuscitate him before I ever considered disposing of the body. I pumped his barrel chest and blew into his purple lips. It was the first time in years that our lips had touched and I didn't recoil.

I gave up after ten minutes. Frank Dubois was gone. Lying there all peaceful and quiet, he almost looked in slumber, but Frank was noisier asleep than he was awake. Honestly, if I had known what kind of snorer he was going to turn into, I never would have married him. If I could do it all over again, I never would have married him even if he slept like an angel. If I could do it all over again, there are so many things I would do differently. But looking at Frank then, so still and not talking, I didn't mind him so much. It seemed like a good time to say good-bye. I poured a shot of Frank's special bourbon, sat down on Frank's faux-suede La-Z-Boy, and had a drink to honor the dead.

In case you were wondering, I didn't do it. I didn't have anything to do with Frank's death. I don't have an alibi, so you'll have to take my word for it. I was taking a shower when Frank died. As far as I could tell, he fell down the staircase all on his own. He had been suffering from vertigo lately. Convenient, I know. And I doubt he mentioned it to anyone. If I had waited for the police and told them the truth, maybe life could have continued as normal. Minus Frank.

I poured another drink and contemplated my options. My first thought was to dispose of the body. Then I'd tell the authorities that Frank left me for another woman. Or was running from a loan shark. It was well-known that he had a love for cards but no talent for it.

I decided to test my strength to see if it was even possible. I tugged on Frank's bloated and callused feet, feet that I had come to loathe—why do you have to tell a grown man to clip his toenails? I dragged the body about a foot from his landing site before I gave up. Frank had put on weight in the past year, but even if he were svelte I couldn't see depositing him anyplace where he'd never be found. And now there was a suspicious trail of blood in the shape of a question mark just above his head. I might be able to explain it away if I called the police and stayed put. But then they'd start looking at me real carefully and I didn't like people looking at me all that much.

I tried to imagine my trial. Me, scrubbed clean, hair pulled back in a schoolmarm bun, wearing an innocent flowered sundress with a Peter Pan collar, trying to look *not guilty*, with my hard-edged poker face dry as the desert. I couldn't imagine how I'd summon tears or sell that shattered look of loss. I can't show much emotion anymore. That was something Frank always liked about me. There was a time I used to cry, but that was another lifetime ago. My heart was broken just once. But completely.

As I sat in Frank's chair, nursing my drink, I pretended to be weighing my options. But there was only one.

Frank kept his gambling stash in his toolbox. A little over twelve hundred dollars. I packed for a short trip and loaded the suitcase into the back of Frank's Chevy pickup.

I was only leaving two people behind, if you don't count Frank: Carol from the bar and Dr. Mike.

Dr. Mike was the top chiropractor in Waterloo, Wisconsin. There were only two, so it wasn't much of a competition. He'd taken over the practice three years ago, when Dr. Bill retired. Ever since the accident, my back hasn't been right. Dr. Bill used to fix me up once or twice a month. I saw Dr. Mike more frequently. The first time he put his hands on me, I felt an electric jolt, like I had woken up for the first time in years. I came back the next week and it was the exact same thing. I came back the week after that. I missed a week and Dr. Mike dropped by the bar to see how I was doing. Frank was on a fishing trip and Dr. Mike offered to give me an adjustment in the back office. It didn't go as planned.

I couldn't trouble Carol at this hour. I'd wake her kids. Maybe I'd send her a postcard from the road.

My chiropractor worked out of an office on the first floor of his three-story Queen Anne–style house in the nice part of town. The smart thing to do was to get out now, run during those precious hours when the world thought Frank was still in it. But I had few real connections to this world, and Dr. Mike was one of them.

I drove Frank's Chevy truck to Dr. Mike's house and took the key from under the rock. I unlocked the door and entered his bedroom. Dr. Mike made a purring sound when he was in a deep sleep, just like a Siamese cat I had as a child. He kind of moved like one, too. He always stretched his lanky limbs upon waking, alternating between slow and deliberate, and fast and sharp. I took off my clothes and climbed into bed next to him.

Dr. Mike woke up, wrapping his arms around me.

"Do you need an adjustment?" he said.

"Uh-huh."

That was our little joke. He kissed my neck and then my lips and he turned onto his back, waiting for me to start. That was his thing; we never did it unless it was my decision. I had started it, I'd continue it, and today I was ending it.

Dr. Mike and I were never a great love story. He was the place I went to when I wanted to forget. When I was with Dr. Mike I forgot about Frank, I forgot about running from the law, I forgot about who I used to be.

When we were done, Mike was massaging the kinks out of my back and trying to straighten out my spine.

"You're completely out of alignment. Did something happen? Did you do something you shouldn't have?"

"Probably," I said.

Dr. Mike turned me over on my back and said, "Something has changed."

"It's about time, isn't it?"

I'd felt like a speck of dust frozen in an ice cube for far too long. I should have done something about this life I had long before Dead Frank made me do something.

I looked at the clock; it was just past midnight. Time to leave. I got dressed quickly.

Dr. Mike studied me with a professional regard. "This is the end, isn't it?"

I don't know how he knew, but he did. There was no point in answering the question.

"In the next few days, you might hear some things about me. I just want you to know that they're not true. Later, it's possible you'll hear more things about me. Most of them won't be true either," I said.

I kissed him good-bye for the last time.

I drove thirty miles before I gassed up the truck. I had one ATM card and one credit card and withdrew the $200 maximum for each. I drove another twenty miles to the next fuel stop, got a strong cup of coffee, and withdrew another two hundred on each card. Frank had always been stingy with our money. I had one credit card and a small bank account and neither provided sufficient funds to set you up, if you decided to take an extended vacation. I made one more stop at a Quick Mart, got another four hundred dollars, and dropped the cards in the Dumpster out back. I had $2,400 and a Chevy truck that I'd have to lose before long. I should have been tucking money away from the moment I got the key to the cash register. I should have known this day would come.

The truck smelled like my husband—my ex-husband? Or was I a widow? I'd have to decide. I guess I could have never married. Either way, I drove with the windows open, trying to lose the scent of Frank.

I merged onto I-39 South, leaving Wisconsin behind. I drove through Illinois for some time until I saw a sign for I-80, which I knew would take me somewhere. I had no destination in mind, so I headed west, mostly because I didn't feel like squinting against the morning light. And I planned on driving through dawn.

I hadn't brought music for the drive, so I was stuck with local radio and preachers all night long. I hooked onto a station while speeding along the rolling hills of Iowa. It was too dark to see the denuded trees and murky snow marring the barren February landscape.

The Iowa preacher who kept me company for the first half of my journey was listing the seven signs of the Antichrist. One was that he'd appear Christlike. I listened through the static of the fading station and noted a few more clues. He'd be handsome and charming. He was sounding like a catch. But then I lost reception. So it's quite possible I'll run into the Antichrist and never know it.

I toggled through the stations to another minister preaching about forgiveness. It's a subject that doesn't interest me. I switched off the radio and drove to the sound of wind swishing by and wheels on asphalt while headlights of people on a different path blinked and vanished in my peripheral vision.

I remembered the day I met Frank. I had only been in town a few weeks, hoping to land work somewhere. I was drinking at his bar, which was named after him. Dubois'. Sometimes I think I married Frank for his name. I never liked Tanya Pitts. Didn't like the first name, didn't like the last name. No doubt, Tanya Dubois was a promotion.

Back then, Frank had some life in him and I had none, so it worked out just fine. He gave me my first real job. I learned how to pull pints and mix drinks, although we didn't get too many requests for cocktails in our humble establishment. There wasn't much more to my life with Frank. We didn't have any children. I made sure of that.

After driving all night, I found myself just outside Lincoln, Nebraska. It was time to take a break and lose the truck. I found a used car dealership and traded in Frank's two-year-old Chevy Silverado for a seven-year-old Buick Regal and seventeen hundred in cash. I knew I was being fleeced, but it was better not to draw attention to myself. I wouldn't be keeping the Buick for long, anyway. I drove another ten miles to a small town called Milford and found a motel called Motel that looked like the kind of establishment that wouldn't mind an all-cash transaction. When they asked for ID, I said I'd lost mine. I paid a surcharge and signed the register as Jane Green.

I slept for eight solid hours. If I were guilty, could I have done that? I woke with a hunger so fierce it had turned to nausea. I opened the door of room 14, on the second story of the stucco building, and leaned over the balcony to catch a glimpse of the town where I'd landed. I don't think that balcony was up to code. I took a step back, spotted an unlit red neon sign for DINER.

I returned to my room, washed up, and headed out, giving myself a quick reminder: *You are Jane Green for now. Forget who you used to be.*

It was eight in the evening, well past the dinner crowd, so I took a seat in a booth, figuring the counter is where everyone talks. I probably wouldn't be very good at that, since I had no identity. That would come later.

A waitress named Carla dropped a menu in front of me.

"Can I start you off with anything?" she asked.

"Coffee," I said. "Black."

"Try it first; then decide." She poured the coffee. "I'll give you a minute to look over the menu."

She was right. It wasn't the kind of coffee you drank straight. I drowned it in cream and sugar. Even then it was hard to keep down. I perused the menu, trying to decide what I was in the mood for. It occurred to me that Jane Green might be in the mood for something different than Tanya Dubois. But since I hadn't yet changed my clothes or my hair, I could probably last another day eating the food that Tanya liked. Jane Green was just a shell I embodied before I could be reborn.

"Have you decided, sweetheart?" Carla asked.

"Apple pie and French fries," I said.

"A girl after my own heart," Carla said, swiftly walking away on her practical white nurse's shoes.

I watched Carla chat with a trucker who was hunched over a plate of meatloaf at the end of the counter. He grumbled something I couldn't understand.

Carla squinted with a determined earnestness and said, "Sunshine, I think you need to go on antidepressants. Yes indeed, you need a happy pill. The next time you walk into my house I want to see a smile on that handsome face of yours. Do you hear me? See that sign there? We have the right to refuse service."

"Carla, leave the poor man alone," some guy in the kitchen yelled.

"Mind your own business, Duke," Carla said. Then she filled more cups of coffee, called customers *honey* and *sweetheart*, and belly-laughed at a joke that wasn't funny at all. I thought it would be nice to be Carla, maybe just for a little while. Try her on and see if she fit.

I devoured my pie and French fries so quickly even Carla was impressed.

"I haven't seen three-hundred-pound truckers put food away that fast. You must have been famished."

"Yes," I said. Short answers. Always.

I paid the check and left, walking down the dull drag of the small town, which hardly deserved a name. I walked into a drugstore and purchased shampoo, a toothbrush, toothpaste, hair dye in auburn and dark brown, and a disposable cell phone from behind the counter.

The clerk, a middle-aged man with the name Gordon on his name tag, rang up my order and said, "That'll be fifty-eight dollars and thirty-four cents."

I paid in cash. As I was leaving, the following words escaped my mouth: "Thanks, sweetheart. Have a nice day."

It felt so wrong, I almost shivered in embarrassment.

I found a liquor store on the way home and purchased a bottle of Frank's favorite bourbon. I figured I could drink away all my memories. I paid in cash and said a mere "thanks" to the clerk.

Back in the hotel room, with the heating unit rattling out of time, I spread my bounty on the bed and tried to decide my next move. I'd known it all along, but I didn't yet have the courage. I took a shot of bourbon and plucked my phone book from my purse. I inhaled and practiced saying hello a few times. Then I dialed.

"Oliver and Mead Construction," the receptionist said.

"I'd like to speak to Mr. Roland Oliver."

"May I ask who is calling?"

"No. But I'm sure he'll want to talk to me."

"Please hold."

A click, and then Beethoven blasted over the line. Two full minutes passed and the receptionist returned.

"I'm afraid Mr. Oliver is very busy right now. Can I take a number, and he'll call you back?"

I didn't want to say the name, but I didn't see any other way of reaching him.

"Tell Mr. Oliver that his old friend Tanya is calling."

This time I got only a few bars of Beethoven before Mr. Oliver's deep sandpaper voice came on the line.

"Who is this?" he said.

"Tanya Pitts," I whispered.

He said nothing. I could hear his labored breath.

"I need your help," I said.

"You shouldn't have called me here," he said.

"Would it have been better if I left a message with your wife?"

"What do you want?" he said.

"A favor."

"What kind of favor?"

"I need a new name."

"What's wrong with the one you've got?"

"It's not working for me anymore. I think you know someone who can take care of these things."

"I might."

"I want a clean identity, a name that's prettier than my old one, and if possible, I wouldn't mind being a few years younger." Tanya Dubois was about to have her thirtieth birthday. But I didn't want to turn thirty before my time.

"You can't get identities served to order," Mr. Oliver said.

"Do your best."

"How can I reach you?"

"I'll reach you. Oh, and if you wouldn't mind, I'm going

to need some cash too. A couple grand should do it."

"You're not going to become a problem now, are you, Ms. Pitts?"

He used my name like a weapon, knowing it would feel like a stab in the gut.

"Make it five grand," I said.

I knew I could get more, but I had gone years without asking Mr. Oliver for a dime, and I found a point of pride in that.

"Where are you?" he said.

"I'll be in touch."

"Wait," he said. "How have you been?"

I could have sworn the question was sincere, like it mattered to him. But I knew otherwise.

"Good-bye, Mr. Oliver."

2

The next day I took 81 South to I-35 South, bisecting Oklahoma. I stopped in a town called Norman just after three thirty and checked into the Swan Lake Inn. I didn't see a single swan or lake during my two-night stay. I gave Mr. Oliver exactly forty-eight hours before I made my second call.

"Do you have it?" I said.

"Yes, I have what you requested," he said.

"I don't want to wait. Tell me now. What is my name?"

"Amelia Keen."

"Am-me-li-a Ke-en." I sounded it out slowly. Then I said it again, trying to decide whether it suited me. I thought it did. "That's a good name."

"I'm so happy you're pleased," Mr. Oliver said in the tone of an automaton.

"Who was she?"

"Just a girl who died a year ago in a house fire. No one is collecting death benefits. She wasn't married and didn't have any children. She was twenty-seven when she passed, which makes you twenty-eight now."

"You got the age right. Form of ID?"

"Social security and a passport without a photo. Do you have an address for me?"

"Overnight the documents care of Jane Green to the Swan Lake Inn on Clyde Avenue in Norman, Oklahoma. Then wire five grand to Amelia Keen at the Western Union office on Clyde Avenue. I'm going to ditch my phone after this call, so everything better be in order."

"You—Ms. Keen," he said. "I suppose you should start getting used to it."

"I suppose so."

"Ms. Keen, be careful out there. If you get caught, you're on your own."

"Wasn't I always?"

"You'll have what you need tomorrow. I don't expect we'll need to speak again."

"I have one more favor I need to ask of you."

"What?"

"Don't try to kill me."

Amelia Keen. Amelia Keen. It was a name you could make something of. Maybe Amelia Keen had some ambition. Maybe she would go to college, learn another language. Amelia Keen could become a teacher, a businesswoman. Maybe she could fly airplanes, maybe become a doctor. Well, that was probably a stretch. But Amelia Keen could be educated. She could take up tennis or skiing; she could mingle with folks who did more than play pool at a bar every Saturday night. She could marry a man for more than his pretty last name.

I walked down to the lobby of the Swan Lake Inn. I almost wanted to meet the misguided soul who'd named it, just to ask if he or probably she had bigger plans that had fallen through the cracks. It tried harder than the last fleabag motel, which made it somehow seem even more forsaken.

I spoke to the desk clerk. She couldn't have been older than nineteen. This didn't look like a stop along the way— she was doing hard time at Swan Lake. You could tell from the way she clamped her mouth tight over her teeth that whatever dose of ambition she was dealt as a child she'd already squandered on booze and meth. She had checked me in without an ID, no problem. Her name tag said "Darla." I've always been fond of name tags, since I'm terrible at remembering names. Or maybe I don't see the point of learning someone's name when I'll just have to forget it later.

"Hi, Darla," I said. "How's your day going?"

"Good, Ms., Ms. . . ."

"Jane Green."

"Right," she said, pupils as unfocused as a blind man's.

"I'm expecting a package to come for me tomorrow. It's really important. Can you call my room as soon as it arrives?"

"Yes, ma'am," Darla said, writing herself a note.

I gave her a twenty-dollar bill, even though she'd called me "ma'am."

I turned off my disposable cell, trashed it in a Dumpster outside the Swan Lake, and bought a new one at the corner convenience store. I strolled down the main drag, found another diner, and ordered a burger and fries. I made it clear to the waitress that I wasn't into small talk. I avoided eye contact with every person who passed my way.

Having no name is dangerous. One false step, someone discovers that you're no one, and eventually they find out who you really are.

I spent the night in the motel room, watching people on television pretend to be someone else. I realized I had to have a new personality, new mannerisms, inflections, likes, dislikes. I picked up the scratch pad and the cheap ballpoint pen by the bed and began jotting down character traits that I might try to shake.

Tanya hated broccoli and avocados. She called everyone a bastard, even in a friendly way. Sometimes she just used it as a replacement for a name that had slipped her mind. Tanya had a tattoo on her ankle. Something stupid she got in high school. Tanya was always twisting her back or rubbing her shoulder, trying to align herself between adjustments. Every once in a while, she stole Frank's pills—he had a bad knee. Unfortunately, Frank wasn't much for sharing narcotics and was very good at basic math.

I looked at the piece of paper on Tanya and thought how fucking dull this woman was. How lucky I was to be able to leave her behind. I found a book of matches at the bottom of my purse. Tanya's purse. I ripped the page off the pad and set the corner on fire, dropped the ashes and last bit of flame into the toilet, and let her go.

Then I scribbled some ideas for what Amelia Keen might be like. She'd have good posture. She'd look like someone who read books. She'd read books. Amelia was a good swimmer, but so was Tanya. Maybe Amelia should take up running. It might come in useful sometime. Maybe she was the kind of person who made friends easily. No, that wasn't a good idea. One thing I knew for sure about Amelia Keen: she was a single woman and she was going to stay that way.

Darla called me in the morning. The package had arrived. I tossed a sweater over my pajamas and rushed into the lobby, trying to swallow my adrenaline.

Darla held out a large brown envelope. I forced a warm smile, said thank you, and made a swift departure.

I got a paper cut rushing to unzip the seal with my index finger. A small dot of blood landed on my new birth certificate. Amelia Keen, born 3:32 a.m. on November 3, 1986, to George Arthur Keen and Marianne Louise Keen at Providence Hospital in Tacoma, Washington. A Scorpio. Powerful, magnetic, jealous, possessive, compulsive. My mother used to read charts obsessively. I never bought into it, mostly because I was a Pisces, which always sounded a lot like a jellyfish without the sting. But looking back, maybe that's exactly what I was.

Now I could change all of that. Change everything about

myself that I didn't like, starting with my hair. I had become a blonde a long time ago when I realized that men look at you differently when you burn the color out of your hair. I wondered how they'd look at me as a brunette. Maybe they wouldn't look at me at all. It would be nice to be invisible for a while.

I took the shears into the bathroom and took inventory of what I saw. A cheap dirty-blond dye job, hair too long to style, light brown eyes shaded by dark circles. I sliced a few inches off the bottom, into one straight even line. I had been cutting my own hair for years. Not because I was cheap or particularly good at it, but sitting in that chair, the hairstylist asking all those questions, always gave me a knot in my gut.

I gave myself bangs, even though I knew the hair would tickle my forehead and drive me mad, but I already looked less like Tanya and more like Amelia. I mixed the auburn and brown together with the developer and began drawing lines on my scalp with the plastic bottle. After my hair was soaked in product, nostrils burning with chemicals, I checked my watch, slipped off the gloves, and turned on the television.

There was a movie playing, set in a college. One of those old campuses, stone buildings with pillars and staircases everywhere. Students reclining lazily on the grass under the shade of hundred-year-old oak trees. I liked the way this one girl looked. She was trying to get people to sign some petition. I didn't catch what it was all about. She was wearing faded blue jeans that seemed as soft as an old T-shirt, a white tank top, and a green army jacket; dog tags and a house key hung from her neck. She looked like she didn't care what anyone thought of her. And she looked really comfortable. At the bar I always wore dresses or skirts and impractical shoes that took bites out of my feet. Amelia Keen wasn't going to wear anything that hurt her.

I washed out the sticky dye and dried my hair, leaving dark stains on the sandpaper-rough motel towel. I combed out my new 'do and sharpened the flat line of the bangs, snipping a few wayward strands. I slid into an old pair of blue jeans and a navy blue sweatshirt, stuffed the rest of my clothes into my suitcase, and left Swan Lake a different woman. A brown-haired, brown-eyed woman. Five foot six, one hundred and twenty-five pounds, mid to late twenties. I looked like so many women you've seen before I doubt you could've picked me out of a lineup.

I drove to a photo shop and had my passport photos taken.

"Don't smile," the photographer said. It was the first time I could remember that I wanted to.

While I was waiting for the photos to be developed, I drove to a stationery store and bought a laminating sheet. Then I went to a drugstore and bought a razor blade, a baseball cap, red lipstick, black eyeliner, and mascara. No blush. Amelia Keen didn't have a rosy glow. I returned to the photo shop to collect my pictures. I set to work on my passport in the backseat of my stale Buick. I used a tiny dot of glue to keep my photo in place on the blank passport. I placed it on top of my hard-shell suitcase for the next step. I took a clear sticky laminating sheet and poised it over the page. My hands shook some and I waited until I got my nerves in check; I had one chance to get this right. I laid down the laminate in one clean, even motion. I used the back of the razor blade to sweep away the air bubbles. Then I sliced around the edges until the passport lifted up from the suitcase.

I looked over my handiwork and was satisfied. Probably wouldn't pass customs, but I had no intention of flying anywhere.

Next, I found a thrift store. Bought more denim and plain button-down shirts. One checked, one plaid. I tracked down an army surplus store and got a green jacket like I saw that girl in the movie wear. While I was there I picked up a pair of size-eight combat boots. I bought cheap underwear. Amelia Keen would spring for something nicer when she had a job. I tossed Tanya Dubois's suitcase in a Dumpster behind a gas station. For a moment I let myself reminisce over the last time I threw away my life. It hurt back then; I didn't feel it much the second time around.

I slid back into the Buick and checked myself in the rearview mirror. I painted my lips bright red. It was my one indulgence in vanity.

I drove to the Western Union office and parked across the street. Maybe I could just walk into the money store, flash my shiny new ID, and get out clean. But I'd just committed light extortion and my victim, so to speak, might have had other plans besides a simple payoff. I'm not a cop, a private investigator, ex-military, or a mercenary. I'm an almost-average civilian with no special surveillance skills to speak of. I don't know how you evade a pursuer. I only had basic logic and a strong survival instinct, and the feeling that maybe this transaction wouldn't go down as seamlessly as I would like.

I scoped the vicinity around the Western Union storefront. Behind the glass doors there appeared to be three people besides the employees—two men, one woman, as far as I could tell. My Buick was parked between a Range Rover and an Audi. A middle-aged man was smoking a cigarette in the black Range Rover. The Audi, I noticed, had out-of-state plates. In an old Thunderbird in front of the shop, a man, maybe in his twenties, leaned back in his seat, sunglasses on. Looked maybe like he was sleeping, but that would be a good cover.

I could sit and wait and see what happened next. But if they were professionals they'd probably outlast me. And I couldn't stomach sitting in this sour, musty car much longer. If I looked a man in the eye, I'd know his intent. I wasn't always like that, but I'd learned over time. I shoved my hair into the baseball cap, put on a pair of sunglasses, and walked right over to the Range Rover.

The man saw me as I approached. He rolled down his window when he realized I wasn't moving on.

"Hello, sir."

"Good afternoon . . . miss?"

I think the boy's clothes, hair tucked in the baseball cap, and lipstick threw him off.

"Are you planning on killing me?" I asked.

"Excuse me?"

"I think that was a pretty straightforward question," I said.

"Why would I want to kill you? Is this some kind of joke?" The Range Rover man was clearly taken aback, scared even.

"Relax. Just asking a very simple question. All you have to do is answer it and then I'll be on my way."

"No, I don't want to kill you."

"Thank you," I said. "That's very good news. Have a nice day."

I strolled past his car and walked up to the corner. I heard his engine turn over and watched him angle out of the parking spot and drive off. There was only one other possible attacker. The sleeping sunglasses guy. I walked across the street and knocked on his window. Either he was an excellent actor or I woke the man from a deep slumber.

He rolled down the window, tipped his sunglasses onto the edge of his nose, and looked me over with tired, hooded eyes.

"Can I help you, miss?" he said, a frog in his throat.

"Do you know me?" I asked.

"Huh?"

"Do I look familiar in any way?" Surely my would-be killer would have a photo to go by.

"Did Clara send you?" the recently awakened man asked. He was not my killer.

"Excuse me, I was mistaken," I said as I walked away.

"Tell Clara it's over!" the recently awakened man shouted after me.

I spun in a circle outside the store. Nothing struck me as suspicious. I could leave without the cash, or take the risk and start my life off right as Amelia Keen. I strolled into the Western Union store, waited in line, collected my money, and walked outside. I returned to the Buick and drove ten miles, looking in the rearview mirror more than the road in front of me. I pulled the car onto the shoulder, collected all of my recently purchased possessions, and walked half a mile, with my luggage in tow, to another used car lot. I bought a half-decent, decade-old Toyota Camry for $4,950 cash. Technically, Tanya Pitts bought it for Amelia Keen, since Amelia didn't yet have a driver's license. I put my possessions in the trunk and drove off the lot, not stopping for the next four hours.

Driving seventy after night fell, I felt this internal shift, almost as if my DNA were restructuring itself. I could feel Tanya Pitts-Dubois's death. She was where she had always been, was always supposed to be. I was now Amelia Keen.

October 22, 2005
To: Ryan
From: Jo

I know I'm breaking an unspoken rule by writing to you, but no one has to know unless you tell them. You've kept some secrets pretty well. I'm hoping you can keep this one. Maybe you're surprised to hear from me. I'm surprised

I'm writing. I haven't quite gotten the hang of this new life. Some days I honestly think about coming home and accepting my fate. I can't tell that to anyone here, so I'm telling you. You're the only person who really knows me. Knows what I've done and what I haven't done. I think that's why I'm so surprised by what you did. But I'm not writing to punish you. I'm writing because I'm lonely.

I miss home, I miss Edie, although I don't miss the look she gave me the last time I saw her. When I'm feeling generous, I miss my mother. I miss you, mostly. I miss you all of the time even though the rational part of my brain tells me I should hate you. There were many different ways I imagined our future playing out. In some variations you ended up with someone else. It never occurred to me that I might not see you again. But that's the truth, isn't it? One day you'll have gray hair or no hair, but I'll only remember the boy. Do you ever think about those things?

I don't want to talk about what happened. I guess I just want to know how everyone is doing. How their lives are turning out. You can call it curiosity, nostalgia, homesickness, or just plain sickness. I miss knowing people. I don't know anyone anymore. And no one knows me.

Please break the rules and write back. I just want to hear about what I'm missing. Maybe you'll tell me there's nothing to miss. Maybe I got out of that town before it turned into a junkyard.

I think that's all.

Jo

November 2, 2005
To: Jo
From: Ryan

Your e-mail practically gave me a heart attack. But it also got my attention. That was the point, wasn't it? You knew I was going to write back, but you also know that this is a bad idea for so many reasons. I had hoped that maybe you'd found a place that suited you. I even had a notion that maybe you were happier there than here. I suppose I just wanted to ease my conscience. I'm sorry about how things turned out. I know that you'll never understand what I did. Sometimes I don't understand it. But if you asked me to make that choice again today, I'd do it the same way.

I still love you and I still miss you. When I let myself think about you. I don't let myself do that too often. A few months ago, I started pretending that you had died. There's an unmarked grave behind St. Gabriel's Church. I pretend it's yours. I pick flowers from that meadow behind the high school and I pay my respects. It sounds sick, I know. But you were there and then you were gone and I had to grieve in some way. I really did think I'd never hear from you again.

If you think it'll help keep your head straight, I'll tell you about home. But, remember, you need to keep your head straight.

I don't socialize as much as I used to, so this is all I know: Nelly is engaged to Brad Fox. That enormous mole on his forehead is now gone. They're demolishing that run-down apartment building on Green Street and building upscale condos. The gentrification of Bilman has begun. Edie is back in town. She decided to take a year off before college. The girl-most-likely-to-succeed is working full-time at her father's hardware store. I saw Jason Lyons once over the summer. He asks too many questions. If you ever think of contacting anyone, please don't. We're all hanging from a ledge right now.

I know you want to hear about your mother. She's the same. Not any worse, if that makes you feel better. I think she's seeing a guy. He's better than the last one from the looks of him. I haven't seen her with any bruises lately. That's the kind of stuff you want to know, right?

It's probably not safe, you using my regular e-mail and all. You never know when people are watching you. Use this address instead, if you must.

Be careful out there.

R

P.S. You're not missing anything.

November 14, 2005
To: Ryan
From: Jo

Liar. But thanks. I guess that's the kind of stuff I want to hear about. Although I kind of expected more to have happened since I left. To me it feels like an eternity. You didn't tell me much about yourself. I suppose that was deliberate. I looked you up. You stayed. Why would you stay there? You could have been anyone.

Please stop visiting that grave. I'm not in it.

J

December 25, 2005
To: Ryan
From: Jo
Re: Merry Christmas

I guess it's getting easier to forget about me. I hope you're having a happy holiday season. I'm alone in a cheap motel in the Midwest watching the Disney parade and eating chocolate pudding from a tin can.

Here's the one good thing that's come from all of this. I don't love you anymore.

Jo

AMELIA KEEN

3

I told myself I was just window-shopping for a home; I didn't have to commit to any one place. But at some point I found myself following the signs for Austin, Texas, and when I landed there it felt right. I checked in to a cheap motel the first night, took a walk, got lost on the other side of the river. I asked a middle-aged woman sitting on a bus bench, engrossed in a novel, for directions. She pointed me to Congress Street and told me to cross the bridge and keep going.

A few blocks later, I saw a gathering of people. Some families, a few couples, most of them with the unmistakable shine of tourists—clothes too bright, shoes too flat, and sunglasses too attached to ropes. They were all leaning over the rails of the bridge; there was a vague hum of anticipation. Like a sheep, I followed, stepping into a gap along the railing. I waited, not knowing what I was waiting for. Then as the last light began to creep away, thousands, maybe hundreds of thousands, of bats emerged from under the bridge, swarming into a beautiful black cloud in the sky. One group was making figure eights as other flocks began to depart in waves. I stayed until every last bat was gone and Congress Bridge was dark.

On my way back to the hotel, a neon sign beckoned me: MAY'S WELL. I don't know why it called to me. Maybe because I thought someone named May owned the place and it seemed wise for a single woman in new terrain to patronize an establishment run by a female.

I opened the heavy mahogany door; it looked like it came from a barn. It had a satisfying weight to it, as if you had to commit to entering this bar. Inside it was cool and dim and the air smelled like spirits, not spilled beer and cheap nuts cemented into the floor. A pretty woman stood behind the counter. She wore a tank top and a skirt just above the knee and white sneakers. I clocked a few other patrons who may have been a few sheets to the wind but seemed harmless enough. By the front door there was a local circular. I picked it up and strode over to the bar.

I sat two chairs away from a man in a suit. Not a nice suit, but what looked like the man's only suit. It was wrinkled and dusty. He'd finished it off with a white shirt, a skinny black tie from the eighties, and scuffed brown wingtips. I could feel his eyes on me when I sat down, but then I saw him turn back to his drink. My military jacket was doing its job, I thought.

"What'll it be?" the woman behind the bar asked.

What does Amelia Keen drink? Tanya drank beer or bourbon. That wouldn't do.

"Gin and tonic, please."

"Any gin preference?"

In time I ought to cultivate a preference, I thought. But I hadn't done so yet.

"Surprise me," I said.

"You don't want the well," she said, as if sizing me up.

"No," I said. What's the point in starting at the bottom? You always have time to land there.

"Bombay?"

"Sure."

She had a heavy pour, which would be nice if I liked gin, but the drink was too strong and tasted like it might have some medicinal properties. I drank it, though, trying to convince my taste buds to transform.

"Blue, can I get another?" Bad Suit asked, pointing at his empty shot glass.

I'm guessing he called her "Blue" because she had astonishing ice-blue eyes. They were unadorned by cosmetics, as if she were trying to hide them. Unsuccessfully. In fact, her only nod at vanity was a mild cherry stain on her lips. She wore her thick blond hair in a severe braid down her back. In an occupation where tips can be directly linked to your physical attributes, Blue seemed decidedly resistant to pulling in some extra cash.

The overhead television had the news on mute, which was interrupted by a commercial for some kind of fancy car.

"If I was a millionaire, that's the first thing I would buy," Bad Suit said to Blue, maybe to me, maybe to no one in particular.

" 'If I *were* a millionaire,' " Blue said. "You need to use the subjunctive when you're speaking of hypothetical situations."

"Why are you always telling me how to talk?" Bad Suit asked.

"I'm simply encouraging respect for the English language," Blue said.

"I respect the hell out of it," Bad Suit said. "But if you're so keen on doling out lesson plans all day long, why don't you become a schoolteacher?"

"I'll think about it," Blue said, with a sharp edge in her voice.

I opened the circular and began looking at job listings. I wasn't qualified for anything. I didn't even understand some of the criteria. What the hell was Quark? I knew how to use a computer, sort of. I took typing in high school. I got a C-plus, and I doubted my skills had improved since then. I didn't have much cash left after buying the Toyota, just under two grand. Apartment, furniture, new clothes, food. How long until the money ran out?

Bad Suit eventually turned to me, hoping for less educational conversation, I guess. "You new in town?" he said.

"Yes," I said.

"Where you from? Pardon me. Where do you hail from?"

"Oklahoma."

"I got people there. Whereabouts?"

"Norman."

"What did you do there?"

"Nothing much."

"What brings you to Austin?" Bad Suit asked.

"Dennis, you ask too many questions," Blue said.

"I'm making conversation," Dennis said.

"Maybe this lady does not want to converse. Did that ever occur to you?"

"No. In fact, it did not. My apologies," Dennis said with a polite nod. "I had a rough day and I was merely seeking friendly conversation."

"You can talk to me, Dennis."

"You don't like to talk, Blue. Everybody knows that."

"But I listen," she said.

Blue lifted two shot glasses from behind the bar and plucked a bottle of high-shelf bourbon. She poured two shots and slid one in front of Dennis.

Dennis's and Blue's glasses met in the middle.

Dennis said, "To Margaret Rose Todd, may that old bag rest in peace."

"Don't talk about your mother like that," Blue said. She poured Dennis one more shot.

"Do you have a mom?" Dennis asked Blue.

"Doesn't everyone?"

"What was her name?"

Blue sighed, poured herself another drink, took a sip, and said, "Janet."

I would have bet every last penny I had to my fake name that Blue was lying. A stupid lie, it seemed to me. But watching a bad liar made me a little queasy, like maybe it would rub off on me. I needed my skills of deception to be sharper than ever. I finished my antiseptic drink, left a few bills on the bar, and told Blue and Dennis to have a good night.

"Come back anytime," Blue said. "No one will bother you here."

Becoming Amelia Keen was a pain in the ass. She needed a place to live, a job, and a Texas driver's license, which required slicing through so much bureaucratic red tape I was just about ready to move into the Texas backwoods and live off the land. I opened a bank account with my passport and fifteen hundred in cash. I tried to find an apartment, but without a job, references, or agreeing to a credit report, which struck me as a risky move, I was out of luck.

I found a boardinghouse run by a woman named Ruth. She wore a housecoat from morning until night, her large breasts dangling beneath the flimsy fabric without any sense of modesty. The room was one hundred square feet and one hundred dollars a week. I shared a single restroom with three men. Two of them were filthy pigs, but, blessedly, the third, Marcus, had an intense cleaning disorder. He also had a pronounced tic, which involved a guttural note at the end of every sentence he spoke. This made his company, which was otherwise pleasant, agitating for someone on high alert.

One of the hurdles between me and a Texas driver's license was a lease agreement. When I asked Ruth for a formal rental contract, she looked at me as if I'd requested she serenade me to sleep with a violin concerto. I suggested, if she agreed to sign the paperwork, that I would pay her five hundred dollars and sign another document that essentially voided the aforementioned contract. I had a feeling she'd say yes, as long as I drew up all the paperwork.

I went to the library that afternoon, logged on to the computer, and printed out form leases. While I had access to the Internet, I decided to check the local news in Waterloo, see how wanted a woman I really was. I typed in the website for the local rag and was met face-to-face with a grainy photo of the old me standing behind the bar. I hadn't been accused of murder just yet. I was merely a "person of interest." The article suggested the timing of my disappearance was suspicious. A perfectly sound assessment. Blake Shaw, who ran the *Waterloo Watch* and wrote just about every piece in it, resisted the urge to sensationalize the story and accuse me outright of murder. He might have had a soft spot for me. I'd never refused him service even when he could barely hold himself up on his bar stool. I just asked for his keys and poured the next drink. But it was only a matter of time before Blake and everyone else turned on me.

I filled in the lease forms, drew up the nullification agreement, and returned to my temporary home. Ruth accepted my bribe and signed the paperwork. The only hitch in my plan was that I needed a vehicle registered in Texas to take the driver's test. My Toyota had been purchased under my old name and still had temporary Oklahoma plates.

Marcus had a car. I think he liked me because I didn't

leave tiny hairs in the sink. At least I think I caught him nodding hello once or twice. I decided I'd play nice with him for a while. Always said hello with a smile, which isn't as easy as it sounds. I offered to get him more coffee in the kitchen, and I was extra careful about cleaning up in the bathroom and publicly shaming Rufus and Tom, my hall-mates, for their slovenly ways. But at night, I couldn't join in their card games and group television consumption. It was heartbreaking to see three impoverished middle-aged men, living on the fringe, seeking out the only company that would have them.

There was just one other woman in the house, besides Ruth. She had a basement room with her own bathroom. If you ever caught her eye, you'd know what a person who was irretrievably gone looked like. If I believed in spirits and souls, I would say she was an empty vessel.

At night I'd eat alone in a diner or a vegetarian restaurant, which Austin seemed to have in shocking numbers. I learned that seitan wasn't my thing. Actually, I learned that not eating meat wasn't my thing. After dinner I'd try to find a bar where I felt invisible. For a few nights I frequented a dive by the University of Texas campus called the Hole in the Wall. I liked watching the students try to meld with the regulars, ordering whiskey that was too strong for their new taste buds. And yet they'd always order shots, like they were taking their medicine. I liked that funny grimace they'd make when the elixir cleared their throat. I don't remember ever making that face. It always felt nice and warm to me.

As the evening wore on, their voices would rise as if an outside source were controlling the volume on a stereo. The more foolish they looked, the more envious I became. What a luxury it seemed to have four years to try to figure out who you are.

On the third night I was at the Hole, a regular who resembled a young Roy Orbison, with that same mop of black hair and tinted glasses—an accessory that I find decidedly untrustworthy—tried to strike up a conversation after he'd lost a game of pool.

"Haven't I seen you here before?" Young Roy asked. He said it like it was a normal question, not an old line, but still. He should have known better.

"I don't know what you've seen or not seen."

"You're a smart one, aren't you?"

"Not particularly."

"You new around here?"

"Yes."

"Where are you from?"

"I'm from a lot of places," I said. Tell the truth when possible. The lies add up and you'll never keep track.

"Maybe I know one of them."

"Maybe you do."

"I'm just being friendly."

"Maybe someone else here would be more receptive to your friendliness."

"I can take a hint," Young Roy said, sweeping up his pint and strolling back to the pool table.

Out of the corner of my eye I saw a man watching our exchange. He didn't even bother to avert his gaze when he saw me notice him. To the naked eye, he looked far more normal than Young Roy. He was maybe in his early thirties, wearing a starched white shirt and black trousers and steel-rimmed glasses, his suit jacket hung over the back of his chair. His shirt was so crisp it looked like he had just picked it up from the cleaners and slipped it on before he walked through the doors of the Hole. The day was almost done. Everyone in the bar had a pattern of creases drawn on their clothes, but this man was like an Etch A Sketch shook clean. There was even something blank and unreadable about his face. He looked like a cruel accountant.

I forgot to be invisible for a moment and just stared at him, mouth agape. He didn't look away; he didn't smile; he simply regarded me for a moment and then returned his gaze to the newspaper sitting in front of him. Maybe he was just a guy who liked to watch people. It's a harmless enough pastime, but not one that sits well with me.

I left a few bills on the bar and returned to my one-hundred-square-foot bedroom and slept in dream-filled fits for the next eight hours. Asleep, I was once again Tanya Pitts-Dubois. Frank was snoring next to me. In my dream I smothered him with a pillow, just to stop the noise. I woke with an aching guilt, eased only slightly when I remembered what really happened.

* * *

Three days after I landed at Castle Ruth, I went to the DMV and took the written test. I squeaked by with 72 percent. I went to the library every day and searched employment websites for anything that I might be qualified to do, which I discovered wasn't much. Those seven years I was married to Frank I'd squandered on keeping house and drinking away my free nights, when I could have done something to prepare myself for this day.

Five days after I began my extra-niceness campaign with Marcus, I asked if I could borrow his car for the driver's exam. Marcus informed me that his car was registered in Arkansas and he was currently uninsured, which meant that I had been smiling and serving the man coffee for no good reason at all.

A few days later, I returned to May's Well, remembering Blue's promise that I could be left alone. Blue was behind the bar again. Two old men in well-seasoned flannel shirts sat with a lone bar stool dividing them, but clearly they were drinking together.

I sat down at the other end of the bar, where I could still listen in on the old guys but couldn't smell them so much.

"You again," Blue said.

"Yes."

"Gin and tonic?"

Fuck, she remembered.

"Make it vodka."

"Preference?"

"Surprise me," I said.

"May I see some ID?" Blue said with the tone of an

apology. "I hear the cops are cracking down."

I took out my passport and flipped it open. Blue gently tugged it out of my grip and struck a flashlight on it. She studied it a little too carefully, if you ask me. As if sensing my discomfort, she spoke.

"I don't get too many passports in here," she said.

"I lost my license," I said.

"I've done that."

She closed the passport and slid it in front of me. I shoved it back in my bag. Blue served me a vodka tonic.

"Cheers," she said.

I picked up the local rag and began reading job listings. Anything that I might be qualified to do would likely plummet me to depths of despair I hadn't known in years. I hated my old life, but it still resembled a life. I was unconvinced I'd ever be able to duplicate that status. I shoved the paper into my bag and read the etchings on the bar and listened to the old men talk about how the president was on a mission to steal their guns and their human rights.

"Another?" said Blue.

"Why not?"

As Blue mixed my drink, I heard the heavy whine of hinges and saw her clock a new customer. She slid my drink in front of me. I was about to pay, but she patted the bar.

"It gets easier," she said.

"What does?"

"Starting fresh."

She said it like she knew more than she should. I felt like

bolting, but that would have looked all wrong and I needed to blend. I was about to say something when I saw Blue scowl at the corner of the bar. The new customer had parked himself at a table and opened a newspaper. When she locked eyes with him, he waved her over.

"I suppose the professor thinks we have table service," Blue said.

The man was wearing a dark brown cable-knit sweater with a shawl collar over a button-down shirt. I suppose there was something academic in the overall effect, even though his forehead was on the brink of Neanderthal.

Blue took his order. I heard her mention that if he needed anything else, he could always walk ten paces over to the bar. She did, however, deliver his Budweiser to his table; the Professor nodded an acknowledgment without looking up from his newspaper.

I was thinking about leaving when Blue came over to me and whispered so softly, "Where did you get it?"

"Where'd I get what?" I said.

"That lovely passport of yours," she whispered.

"From the passport department," I said, which I realize sounded stupid the moment I said it. Truth be told, I had never left the country, never applied for a legitimate passport, so I had no idea how it was done. Seemed like a woman my age—what was it again? Twenty-eight?—ought to know these things.

Blue smiled from only the left side of her face. I drained the rest of my drink.

"I should be on my way," I said.

"I know it's fake," Blue said.

"I don't know what you're talking about."

"How long have you been Amelia Keen?"

I felt ice-cold and overheated at once. I had been Amelia Keen less than two weeks and could feel myself on the brink of losing her. I guess Blue saw the look of dead fear in my eyes. She softened a bit.

"I don't want to give you any trouble," she said. "I simply want to know where you acquired such a fine piece of forgery."

This wasn't the kind of discussion one wants to have in a public place. I took inventory of each customer; no one was watching us, but still.

"Not here," I said.

"I close in an hour," said Blue. "Why don't you have another drink while you wait?"

The old guys departed before last call. The solo dart player gulped one more beer as he clobbered himself in another game. The Professor sipped his Budweiser like a lady. It took him almost ninety minutes to finish one beer. He left a twenty on his table and departed without a word. Blue locked the door after all of the customers left, finished cleaning up behind the bar, and then said, like we were old friends, "Hungry? Let's grab a burger while you tell me all of your dark secrets."

I wasn't planning on telling Blue anything, but I had

to tell her something because she knew my new name and I needed to keep it safe. We left through the back door, which she secured with a dead bolt and a padlock. The alley smelled like urine and motor oil. One floodlight was the only illumination besides the crescent moon.

"My car is around the corner," Blue said, crunching the gravel as she strolled toward the street.

A black Lincoln Town Car was parked ten yards in front of us. As we passed the car, the door opened and the Professor slid out of the driver's seat, barely making a sound.

"Amelia?" he said.

My throat felt like fingers were tightening around it.

"Sorry. You got the wrong girl," I said, surprised I could get the words out.

The back door of the sedan swung open and another man crawled out of the car. Looked like he'd been sitting for a while; his limbs worked out the kinks slowly, like a spider. The floodlight gave me a quick look at his face before he slipped into the shadows again. I'd seen him before. I remembered that crisp white shirt and the steel frames of his glasses. It was the cruel accountant from the bar the other night. The Accountant swept his gaze across Blue, sizing her up.

"Miss," he said to Blue, holding the back door for her, "why don't you take a seat?"

"This looks like a personal matter that's got nothing to do with me. How about I just head on home, like every other day," Blue said. "Nothing happened here. At least nothing that I could remember."

I had a feeling Blue was telling the truth. She could walk away without calling the cops or giving the matter a second thought.

"We'll give you a ride home. It's not safe for a lady to be out alone this time of night," said the Accountant.

The Professor pulled a gun from the small of his back and gently guided Blue into the backseat.

"Where were we, Amelia?" said the Accountant.

"Like I said, you got the wrong girl."

"Maybe you're right. Is it Tanya, then?"

"Who are you?"

"Never mind that. Tell me something, Tanya. Did you kill Frank, or was it an accident?"

4

The Professor and the Accountant seemed bent on taking me and Blue for a drive. Even with a gun trained on me and under direct orders, I found myself looking for a way out. The Professor opened the front passenger door and told me to get inside. When I didn't move, he pressed the muzzle of the gun into my rib cage. This left me conflicted between two impossible options.

"I really don't want to get in the car," I said, trying to sound calm and reasonable. "Maybe we can just discuss this here."

"Sweetheart, get in the car," said the Professor.

"Why don't I take the backseat and Blue can have shotgun. Wouldn't you prefer that, Blue?"

"Actually, I'd prefer driving myself home," Blue said. "My car is just around the corner and this looks like a private matter."

"Get in the car," the Professor repeated.

"The trunk," I said. "You should put me in the trunk."

The Professor turned to the Accountant and said, "There's something wrong with this one."

"It's safer for you if I'm in the trunk," I said. It really was. I was speaking to him logically, but he just figured I had an angle he hadn't calculated yet.

The Accountant nodded some unspoken motivation to the Professor, who moved the gun up to that soft spot under my jaw. It seemed more real then; the balance of fear shifted, like a seesaw.

"Have you changed your mind yet?"

"I think I have." I got into the car, put on the seat belt, and tried to do those deep-breathing exercises Carol once taught me.

The Professor slipped the gun into the small of his back, circled the car, and got into the driver's seat. The Accountant, sitting in the backseat, rested his weapon on his thigh, but the barrel was aimed at my side. If he pulled the trigger, the bullet would likely go right through my arm and pierce my heart.

We pulled out of the alley onto a dark side street. My head burned hot, like I had a fever.

"Where are we going?" Blue said.

"Nowhere in particular," said the Accountant. "We just need to have a quick chat with Tanya here."

"That's not my name," I said.

"Whatever your name is," said the Accountant.

"I'm Amelia Keen. I was born November third, nineteen eighty-six, in Tacoma, Washington. My parents were George Arthur Keen and Marianne Louise Keen."

The Professor, despite the Accountant's claim, looked like he had a destination in mind. He turned onto Bee

Cave Road and then Barton Creek Boulevard, while the Accountant continued what might have sounded like a friendly interrogation to an outside observer who didn't see the gun trained on me.

"And how are you liking Austin?" the Accountant asked.

"I like it fine."

"You plan on staying?"

"I don't know."

"Are you going to become a problem?"

"Who's asking?" I said.

It was hard to concentrate on what the Accountant was saying with the car jerking sideways as the Professor wove through traffic. He had a lead foot, either gunning the engine or hitting the brakes. I began to feel nauseated and dizzy. A bead of sweat trickled down my forehead.

"I am," said the Accountant.

"Who is really asking?"

I could barely get the words out. It felt like I was breathing in a vacuum.

"Are you going to become a problem, Tanya, Amelia?"

"No," I said, but I knew my answer didn't matter.

The Professor drove at the same warp speed and the Accountant's gun remained at its casual but deadly angle.

"Can you pull over?" I said. My heart was beating holes in my chest. I felt like I might die of something unknown if I couldn't get out of the car. I almost wished the Accountant would put a bullet in me.

We started driving through a park or greenbelt or

something. The Professor was speeding, going maybe eighty miles an hour in a forty-mile zone. When I looked at the driver, he'd changed. It wasn't the Professor anymore. It was *him*. And all I could think was that this drive had to end. Before I completed that thought, I swung my legs counterclockwise and bashed the Professor's head against the window. Then I pulled on the emergency brake and kicked him again. The car careened off the road, down an embankment, and into woods. The Accountant, trying to brace himself, fired his weapon through the roof. The car tumbled once and landed back on its wheels, angled sideways along the rise of the hill.

The Professor was out cold, his head resting against the window. He looked peaceful, like he was taking a short nap.

"Get his gun," Blue shouted.

I reached out in the darkness and found the Professor's gun behind his back. Blue wrestled in the backseat with the Accountant.

"Shoot him," she said.

I didn't. I just froze, watching Blue try to wrest the gun from the Accountant. It fired through the front windshield, turning the window into a glass spiderweb.

"Shoot him," she said again.

At first I couldn't get the trigger to work, but then I remembered Frank's Uncle Tom showing me how to use his revolver. I pulled the safety and shot the Accountant in the leg.

While he wailed in pain, Blue seized the Accountant's gun and fired one shot through his head and one through his heart. Then she fired two shots through the back of the driver's seat. The Professor made a hiccup sound after the second hit.

That's not how I would have played it. I just wanted out of the car. Maybe they planned to kill us; maybe they didn't. But killing them truly was not on my agenda. This might have been a temporary fix, but I had a feeling it was going to dig me so deep into a hole I might never find my way out.

"You there?" Blue asked.

"Yes," I said.

Blue turned on the dome light and looked over at the Accountant. Her face was cold and hard. She felt for a pulse, even though I'd never seen anyone that dead. She then reached around to the front seat and checked the Professor's pulse.

"Dead," she said.

Then she looked at me for a moment, the gun still cradled in her palm. She had the expression of someone making a hard decision. I could have sworn that it was determining whether I should live or die. I thought about the gun in my hand and wondered if I could use it. I felt a cold sweat trickle down my back. As I was trying to figure out how far I would go to stay alive, Blue clicked the safety, wiped the gun with her sleeve, and dropped it on the Accountant's lap. I finally caught my breath again.

Blue slipped off the plaid shirt she was wearing over her tank top and started wiping down the door handle. She used the shirt to unlatch the back door. She had to throw her shoulder into getting it open, since we were on a slope. She opened the passenger door for me and tossed me her shirt.

"Wipe down anything you might have touched," she said. "And put the gun back where you found it."

Blue seemed a little too clearheaded for my liking, but at least she had a plan.

I followed Blue's lead, wiped the gun for prints, and stuffed it in the Professor's coat pocket. I had no idea where I had laid my hands, so I buffed down everyplace my arms could reach. I heard a car in the distance.

"Kill the lights," Blue said.

I fumbled to find the switch. The car passed on the road above the embankment just as the lights went dead.

"We have to get out of here," I said.

"What we have to do is keep our heads straight. One fingerprint and the police can put you at the crime scene. Assuming you're in the system." Blue said the last bit as a deliberate jab. I wasn't in the system, but it was safe to assume my fingerprints were on file somewhere.

I finished wiping down the front seat as thoroughly as I could manage. Then we crawled up the embankment to the road. It was as good as any place for our detour. At this hour the street was so dark you couldn't even see the toppled town car unless you were looking hard for it.

"What do we do now?" I asked.

"Walk," she said. "I don't live far from here."

I wasn't sure it was wise tagging along with someone of Blue's nature, but I didn't see another choice at that moment. We walked for more than an hour, until Blue stopped in front of a long driveway on an unlit street. Up a twisty walkway flanked by neglected topiaries was a mansion-size Tudor-style house. From the road it looked a bit haunted.

"You live here?" I said. The accommodations seemed tony for a bartender.

"An old lady lives in the house. I have the place in back."

One single light glowed from the upstairs bedroom in the big house. We walked along a stone footpath on the side of the property to a guesthouse behind the kidney-shaped pool. The guesthouse didn't match the house. It looked like an afterthought. Blue used her key and opened the door.

Inside was the sparest home I'd ever seen. It was nice, but like an extended stay hotel room with a cheap kitchenette. The bedroom had a queen bed and a dresser. The small living room had a couch, a coffee table, and a television. There was nothing else, nothing personal to give life to the space. The coldness of her accommodations unsettled me. I'm not sure what I expected. Maybe a painting or a family photo or some kind of personal knickknack to let me know that the woman I'd just killed two men with was part of this world.

Blue got a bottle of bourbon from the kitchen and poured us each a shot. As I felt the slow burn down my throat, I finally woke up. Blue took her shot and poured another, sipping it this time.

She gave me a few minutes to gather myself before she started in.

"You have a few enemies, don't you?"

"Guess so."

"Considering I just committed a double murder for you, I think an explanation is due."

I'd never had to explain before. Until I called him and asked for a new me, I hadn't uttered Roland Oliver's name in nine years, not even to curse him. But I didn't see any way of getting out of this, and since Blue had pulled the trigger, I figured we were now in the trenches together. She hadn't killed me just yet; in fact, she was the only reason I was still alive. I hadn't trusted a soul in ten years. Maybe it was time. I made the decision like the flip of a coin. I told Blue, I told her everything. I told her things I never told Frank, Carol, or Dr. Mike. Until the day I met Blue I could have won a gold medal in keeping secrets. I had fought so hard to forget my past, forget who I once was, that as I said my story, it felt like fiction.

When I was done, that slicing pain across my back, like an invisible scar, seemed to ease. It had been so long since I'd spoken the truth, it sounded like a lie. I had a hell of a story to tell, but Blue seemed to take it in stride.

"We all have something," she said when I was done. "I'm starving. Do you want a grilled cheese sandwich?"

Blue devoured two sandwiches in less than fifteen minutes. She seemed wildly unfazed by my predicament and the two kills that had happened just a few hours before. When her appetite was sated, Blue asked a few practical questions.

"Do you think Mr. Oliver will send someone else after you?"

"Probably, when he figures out his friends are dead."

"You should lay low for a while. Where are you currently hiding out?"

"In a rooming house near the capitol."

"Let's get your things," she said. "You can stay here."

"The old lady won't mind?"

"The old lady's senses aren't what they used to be. If she sees two of us, she'll merely think she's seeing double."

Blue always had lots of plans, I noticed. It seemed like a trait I ought to adopt, considering my predicament, which I had to come to accept was permanent.

It was just after five a.m. when we left the guesthouse and strolled down the driveway. A shiny blue 1980s Cadillac Fleetwood in impeccable condition was parked next to the big house.

"We'll take the old lady's car," said Blue. "Get your things first, then pick up my car from May's."

"Do you mind if I drive?" I said.

Blue pondered the request for a moment. "That sounds like a good idea. I wouldn't want a repeat performance."

She tossed me the keys and we got into the well-preserved vehicle. The sedan felt like a ship leaving port as I backed out of the driveway.

In the quiet of the early morning, my mind got noisy. I replayed recent events, like watching a movie in fast-forward.

"It's funny how you were fine bashing a man's face in with your boots but couldn't muster a clean shot to the head or the heart," Blue said.

"It was not my intention to kill anyone."

"What was your intention?"

"To stop the car. That's all."

I still felt adrenaline pumping and the pain in my back returned. But it all seemed to pass through Blue.

"It didn't bother you, killing them?" I said.

"Not one bit. It shouldn't have bothered you, either."

We found ourselves cruising down the road where it all went down. We passed the crash site, which was as still as ice. You couldn't even see the car from the road. But dawn was breaking and it was just a matter of minutes before it would become a scene of flashing lights, flares, ambulances, and yellow tape.

"Wake. Up. Amelia," Blue said as I stared into the distance, trying to draw an image of the crash into my imagination. A hardness in her delivery gave me the chills. I did wake up a bit.

"I'm awake," I said.

"You can't just start a fight. You have to finish it. No matter what it takes."

My departure from Castle Ruth didn't cause much of a stir in the house. Marcus shook my hand and erupted in that noise he makes. It sounded almost like good-bye. I tried to look calm and collected as I gathered my things under Ruth's watch, but I could feel this all-over shiver, a constant vibration of nerves that I had a hard time believing no one else could see.

"You in some kind of trouble?" Ruth asked.

"No trouble," I said. "I just found a place to stay, long-term."

"Don't fool yourself," she said. "It's all temporary."

I stuck my one suitcase in my Toyota and drove back to the old lady's house, parking a few doors down and dragging my suitcase up the twisty driveway. I dropped my bags in the guesthouse, then took Blue in the Cadillac back to the side street near the bar, where she picked up her black VW Jetta. We convened back at the house at noon.

"I need to check in with the old lady. Make sure she's got enough food and the cats are fed. Make yourself at home," Blue said as we entered her home.

"Who is she to you?" I asked.

"Family, in a way. She and my aunt Greta were something to each other once, although they never told you what."

Blue strode over to the big house. I walked through Blue's modest quarters, looking for signs of habitation. I opened a closet to find old housecoats and dresses from decades past. Probably the old woman's or Greta's. I found one drawer loaded with china figurines of ballet dancers, orchestra players, and zoo animals. Another drawer contained two antique dolls, one blond and one brunette. Under the bed was a suitcase filled with clothes. Modern ones. Blue was prepped to run at a moment's notice. I could learn a few things from her.

I checked the window and saw Blue's silhouette in the main house. I looked inside the bathroom. At least she had a few luxuries she couldn't live without. Perched on the ledge of the shower were a fragrant body wash and shampoo and conditioner that looked pricey; at least, the bottles had this foreign design that you never see in a drugstore.

I roamed into the bedroom while I still had time and opened the nightstand, the place where most people hide their secrets. Inside I found a battered old teddy bear and a gun. When Blue came back, I was lying on the couch, pretending that her entrance had woken me. Blue clocked the entire apartment and looked me in the eye.

"You saw the gun, didn't you?" she said.

"Yes," I said. No point in denying it.

"I have a husband. Although I regard him as more of an ex-husband," she said as if that were the common explanation for owning a firearm.

"Is he a violent man?" I asked.

Then I realized the answer was obvious. I'd never noticed it before, but Blue had a slice above her brow, and her left eye drooped slightly, almost like a reflection in a carnival mirror. Nerve damage. I'd seen it once before, at Frank's bar. I never got her name; she was passing through town with a man. She had that haunted look you see in some women. In Blue it was different, though; whatever happened to her didn't exactly seem to have stolen anything from her, except maybe a conscience. She was like a person turned upside down.

"He's no more violent than I am," Blue said. "Then

again, it wasn't always that way."

"Who are you?" I asked. It was a reasonable question. I'd already told her everything about myself, but all I knew was that people called her Blue, and she poured drinks at May's Well, and she was putting as much ground as possible between herself and her ex.

"My first name was Debra Maze," Blue said. "Then I got married and became Debra Reed. I was a third-grade teacher for a few years until I stopped being presentable in front of the children. Then I had to run, and my cousin who looks maybe like my sister let me have her old driver's license. I'm Carla Wright for now, and as long as I don't apply for credit or anything official, I can probably hang on to this name for a little while. But my past will catch up to me eventually, just like yours did."

"How long did you stay with him?"

"Seven years."

"How long have you been gone?"

"Six months," Blue said. "When I saw your fake passport, which is as fine a forgery as I've ever seen, I figured you might be connected. It never occurred to me that your predicament could be further south than my own."

"Sorry to get you tangled in my mess."

"No apology necessary. Who knows, one day you might get tangled in mine. Then we'd be even." She opened a cupboard overstuffed with towels and bedding and withdrew a blanket and pillows. "You need to sleep," she said, "as do I. Everything looks so much simpler after a bit of shut-eye."

Then she walked into her bedroom and shut the door.

I found her bourbon and took a slug, slipped off my shoes, and put the blanket over my head, blocking the midday sun, which seemed to shine directly on the couch. I could feel that exhaustion where every part of your body seems to be sinking into itself, but I couldn't quiet my mind. On a loop I replayed the car accident in jump cuts. Each clip began with that queasy feeling in my gut, sitting there, powerless. Someone else's hands gripping the wheel, foot to the floor, knuckles white, tendons bucking under the skin.

In the dream, I know what I have to do because I didn't do it before. I've replayed this again and again in my head. Only *he's* driving, and I can see that look on his face. I remember the moment when he decided what he was going to do. That hard line set in his jaw. Knowing that the time was long past for stopping it, knowing that I should have seen it coming, knowing that I knew what he was going to do before he did. Ten years ago and it felt like tomorrow, like it could happen again and again.

I do what I should have done the first time. I swing my legs over the wheel and I kick him in the face. He loses control of the car and we jump the guardrail, landing in the frigid lake. We're slowly submerging. I know what to do. I unbuckle my seat belt and roll down the window before we go under. I look at him; he's out cold. I have enough breath to pull him out of the car, but he looks so peaceful behind the wheel. I leave him behind. I look in the backseat and see the other passenger. For a second I wonder whether I should leave him too. Then I feel the blast of cold water as it spills into the car. I jolt awake.

Blue is sitting in a chair, watching me.

"Nightmare?"

"No. A dream."

A dream I have again and again, a simple fantasy of what I should have done. And then I would be free.

June 10, 2008
To: Ryan
From: Jo

I'm married. Got a new name. It's better than the last one. I won't tell you what it is. Plausible deniability. You won't be lying if you don't know. Should I still be looking over my shoulder or have people forgotten about me?

My husband, I'll call him Lou, if I ever need to call him anything. Lou's all right. When I was a girl I dreamed of better than all right. For a while you were my better-than-all-right. Look how that turned out. Anyway, I couldn't tell anyone else from home. You're all I've got. You and Lou.

So what's happened since I last heard from you?

Jo

June 21, 2008
To: Jo
From: Ryan

Congratulations, I guess. I just had eight bourbons at

the Sundowners to celebrate. Celebrate might be the wrong word for it. Who is he? What is he? Do you love him?

Here's to a long and prosperous marriage to a man who has no idea who you really are. I'd give you advice, but according to my parents, the secret to staying together is never being in the same room.

Shit, you got married. I think I'm going to need to do more celebrating.

R

August 30, 2008
To: Ryan
From: Jo

If I didn't know you better, I'd say you were jealous.

No, Ryan, I don't love him. But getting married seemed wise, or more precisely, getting a new name seemed wise. Besides, I didn't get just a husband, I got a husband and a job. Lou owns a bar. I serve drinks. Not exactly the career path I had in mind for myself, but it's better than cleaning houses, which is what I was doing for the first year I was out on my own. We were married by Otis, the local mechanic. He's a minister with the Church of Auto Parts. I didn't even know such a thing existed. He cleaned under his fingernails for the ceremony. I was touched. When Otis said, "'Til death do you part," the first thing I thought was that I hoped longevity didn't run in Lou's family. If we last five years, I'd be surprised. But at least I got a new name out of it.

This is my life now. But it's not my only life. When I close my eyes, sometimes I enter into a different world, my alternate universe. That night never happened. Or if it did, we weren't involved. We did all of the things we said we were going to do. I even have a clear picture of the cheap one-bedroom apartment we're sharing. It's a third-floor walk-up. We sit on the fire escape on hot summer nights and drink beer and look at the stars. Come to think of it, we could be there right now.

But that isn't real. So tell me what is. What have I missed?

Jo

October 5, 2008
To: Jo
From: Ryan

I don't know if we should do this anymore. It wasn't part of the original plan. The point of all of this was for you to have a chance at a real life. Stop thinking about what might have been. Maybe you haven't given Lou a chance. Let's quit this for a while. You haven't missed a thing. Go live your life, Jo. Please.

R

November 5, 2008
To: Ryan
From: Jo

You can't keep telling me to disappear. I've done what

I've been told. I've disappeared enough. In the meantime, I'd like to continue this arrangement. Don't disappoint me and I won't disappoint you.

Jo

5

It took a few days for the facts to sink in. Being Amelia Keen wasn't going to work for me anymore. I thought about phoning an old friend who owed me a debt that can't be quantified, but it seemed risky making any contact after I'd exterminated Mr. Oliver's colleagues. I wasn't sure what side my old friend was on. I had to accept the fact that I was on my own and needed a new name to inhabit. I was going to miss Amelia Keen; I'd had high hopes for her. I still wasn't sure what to do about the car registration. It was a danger having a vehicle in Tanya's name, but Amelia was also a liability.

For two weeks, from the end of March until the beginning of April, I laid low in Blue's home, earning my keep by cleaning house and buying groceries with my dwindling savings. I read the news to keep abreast of the investigation into the mysterious car crash. The detectives on the case believed two unknown assailants were in the vehicle with the victims. The identities of the two men had yet to be discerned, and no one had come forward to claim the bodies. I was convinced the police were holding out on the press. I figured it was just a matter of time before the SWAT team raided Blue's and my home. Each rustle of leaves outside or an engine purring down the road fed my paranoia. I would start to drink early just to calm my nerves, to stop the constant vibration of the world around me.

At night I watched the main house. There were always exactly two lights on, one upstairs and one downstairs, and always the jittery glow of a television hidden behind opaque curtains. The television seemed to be on all night long, but the upstairs light flicked off like clockwork at ten fifteen p.m. Blue would always check on the old woman after her shift at the bar, killing the downstairs light on her way out. The old lady—I eventually learned that her name was Myrna— was housebound: arthritis, glaucoma, dementia. Only a few times did I see Myrna's shadow shuffling through the house. She only traveled from one room to the other. Blue said that even when she was young, she kept to herself. Left the house with the rarity of an eclipse—only when Blue's Aunt Greta threatened to leave her if she didn't get out and about. I wasn't to bother Myrna. She didn't take well to new people, I was told. I could relate. I didn't take well to people in general.

I had only been at the house two weeks, but it seemed like months had passed. I felt as if I were tumbling at high speed toward the bottom of a ravine. I started to read the obituaries every morning because they brought me some comfort, reminding me that I wasn't the only one whose time was running out. More people die young than you'd think.

That was when it occurred to me that I might be able to find the next person to inhabit at the local mortuary. Every day I scoured the obits for a likely candidate. At first my criteria were pretty simple: I needed a woman who had died prematurely and lived alone. I told Blue about my plan, and she wanted in on the action. We decided to join forces on the hunt, and whoever looked the most like the deceased could call dibs.

We donned black dresses and conservative makeup and drove to the mortuary listed in the paper. We took Blue's car, but she always let me drive. Our first funeral was for Joan Clayton. She was only two years older than me when she died of ovarian cancer. There was a large photo of her next to the open coffin at Marker & Family Funeral Home. In the photo she was still in full bloom. It had probably been taken several years ago. Her cheeks were peach plump; the emaciated body in the coffin looked like a cheap impostor.

"How tall do you think she was?" Blue whispered in my ear. All business.

"I don't know. But she doesn't look anything like you or me. Before or after," I said. "This won't work."

A mourner approached. He looked like he might be Joan's father.

"I don't believe we've met," the maybe father said.

"So sorry for your loss," Blue said.

"Did you know my Joan?"

"Indeed, I did," said Blue.

"From school?"

"Yes. From school."

"I thought I met all of Joan's school friends."

"We were more acquaintances," said Blue. "But I wanted to pay my respects."

"Grover Cleveland or Van Buren?" the father asked.

"Cleveland," Blue guessed, losing her conviction.

"When did you leave Houston?" he asked.

"A few years ago," Blue said, realizing she had to quickly shut down the conversation.

"Did you know Jacob?"

"No. I'm afraid we never met. I'll leave you to your family," said Blue, slowly backing away. "And I am so sorry for your loss."

Blue turned around and began walking down the aisle and out the door. I was right behind her.

"That was close," I said on the way home.

"As long as we don't go back to the same funeral home twice, there shouldn't be a problem."

The next funeral was Laura Cartwright's. She was twenty-eight when she committed suicide. She was just two years younger than me. According to the obituary she left behind a mother, a father, and a husband. No children. She only had about twenty or so mourners at Hammel & Sons funeral home. There was a picture of Laura next to the coffin. She was blond and blue-eyed, like Blue, but so plump—obese, really—that her features were hard to distinguish.

Blue and I regarded the plus-sized woman in the coffin.

"No bullet wound, and her neck looks fine. Probably pills," said Blue.

"I guess."

"I could be her in no time," said Blue, "if I started off my day with half a dozen doughnuts."

"You'd need to devour an entire doughnut factory," I said. A man approached and stood next to us.

"Were you friends?" he asked.

"Yes," Blue said. "Although I hadn't seen her in years. Were you close?"

"You could say that," the man said. "We were married."

"My condolences," I said.

"Thank you. I should have seen it coming. But she acted like everything was fine."

When the man spoke, I felt a sick shiver up my spine. Something wasn't right.

"She wasn't depressed?" I asked.

"I didn't think so," Mr. Cartwright said. "But she must have been. We were trying to have a baby. It wasn't working out."

"She looks so unblemished. Pills?" I said.

Blue squeezed my elbow in warning, but Mr. Cartwright seemed warmed by my interest.

"She put antifreeze in her lemonade."

"Oh my. That *is* terrible. She was so young. How did you meet?" I said.

"At a bar. She was the prettiest woman in there. Put on a few pounds since then," he said dryly.

"How long were you married?" I asked.

Blue pinched my arm again. Harder.

"Five years. What's your name again?"

"Jane Green," I said. No point in getting Amelia Keen mixed up in this.

"And how did you know Laura?"

"Elementary school."

"And you haven't seen her since?"

"No. I just saw the obituary and thought I'd pay my respects."

"I'm sure she would have appreciated that."

"It was a pleasure meeting you," I said. "I never got a name."

"Lester. Lester Cartwright. Did you know Laura's friend Kelly Block? I think she went to elementary school with Laura, too."

"Name doesn't ring a bell. But it was a long time ago. Excuse me, I need to use the ladies' room."

Blue followed me into the bathroom and we waited until the mourners were seated and Lester was delivering the eulogy before we made our exit. He wasn't exactly silver-tongued.

"Laura went too soon," Lester said. "But she's in a better place now."

"I truly loathe that saying," Blue muttered under her breath as we shoved our combined weight against the fat wooden doors.

Once we were in the parking lot, Blue questioned my interview technique.

"We should probably keep a lower profile than that,

especially if I decide to become Laura Cartwright. I think she's an excellent option. Now I just need to figure out how to go about it. I could probably call the parents up and just get them to give me her social security number. But it would be quite a bit easier if I had access to her driver's license and other identification."

"How would you get that?" I said.

"Well, they're hardly going to bury her with her wallet. It's got to be around somewhere. I think we should follow the husband home and then break into their house when he's away."

"You can't be serious," I said.

"Have you got a better idea?"

I didn't. I pulled the VW around the corner and parked behind an old maple tree. The fresh leaves had just opened like the palm of a hand.

All these years, while I've done nothing significant with my life, I've acquired one perfect skill. I know when a man is lying to me. I know a black heart when I see one.

"He killed her," I said.

"What? The husband?"

"Yes."

"How do you know?" said Blue.

"His wife is dead less than a week and he's commenting on her weight. That's not normal."

"Normal or not, it isn't proof."

"Nobody takes antifreeze when they want to off themselves. So many better ways to go about it," I said.

"Should we leave an anonymous tip for the cops?" Blue said.

"Not if you think she's a viable candidate. Be easier if her death goes unnoticed," I said.

"Doesn't really matter how she died, does it?" Blue said.

"Guess not."

"I think I'd like to try on Laura Cartwright. See if she fits."

We waited until the mourners departed and followed the husband in his red GMC Sierra. He drove several miles to a suburb in some place called Fairview and parked his car in front of a white clapboard house. The lawn was brown and patchy and there was old furniture on the porch. We kept vigil in Blue's car for the next hour. When Lester departed, he looked up and down the block as if he were checking to see if he was being tailed. He drove off in his truck and Blue got out of the car.

"Text my mobile if you see anyone coming," Blue said.

"What are you going to do?"

"Break in and see if I can find her wallet."

I slumped in the driver's seat of the car and waited for Blue. My nerves felt like rockets firing under my skin. Every sound from wind chimes to the rustling of leaves sent a jolt through me.

Blue was in the house for thirty minutes before I sent her a text.

Get out. This isn't safe.

Blue texted back. *Still looking.*

Cars drifted past. I couldn't tell if they could see me or not, but one or two might remember an unfamiliar Jetta parked in the neighborhood. A middle-aged woman in a housecoat was watering her lawn and she looked right at me.

The red truck returned and pulled into the driveway. I texted Blue again.

He's back. Get out.

Blue didn't reply. Lester hoisted a case of beer and a bag of groceries from the flatbed. He walked up the front steps, unlocked the door, and went inside. Blue didn't return to the car.

Where are you? He's in the house.

Ten minutes later, Blue slipped out of the bathroom window and casually walked to the car.

"Let's go," she said.

I started the engine and drove slowly out of the neighborhood and onto the highway.

"What happened in there?" I asked.

"I couldn't find her paperwork," said Blue, deflated. "But even if I did, I'm not sure this plan would pan out. I could never get a job with her social security number, since the husband probably filed for some kind of death benefit, and without a bribable contact at the DMV, I'd be using a license with a picture that barely resembled me. No matter how many doughnuts I ate."

"There has to be a way," I said.

"I'm sure there is," said Blue. "We just haven't figured it out yet."

6

I never quite knew what to make of Blue. I never trusted her and yet I owed her an immeasurable debt because my quality of life improved greatly under her roof. She worked nights, so I got out of her hair during the day; I couldn't yet risk being kicked to the curb. Blue never told me her life story. She was an ex-schoolteacher with a bad husband named Jack. Whenever I inquired about the rest of her history, she was cagey and vague. I asked her once what her childhood was like. *I did what kids did. Played and stuff.* I inquired about her family. *I had some*, she said. I don't remember sleeping well during those days with Blue. It always seemed possible that I could wake up with a gun trained on my head.

Blue wasn't, however, my primary cause of concern. I still had Mr. Oliver to contend with. I tried to imagine what his next step would be. Where would one begin looking for a single woman who matched the description of all kinds of single women in Austin? Sometimes being unremarkable is a good thing.

The Austin library circuit became my second home. Since I couldn't risk becoming too familiar, I never paid a repeat visit to the same branch in a week. I mixed it up as much as I could. Yarborough, Twin Oaks, North Village, Carver, and Faulk Central; I got to the computer banks before the children escaped from school. If I didn't beat the afternoon rush, I'd roam the stacks and peruse travel books, pretending my imaginary new life was just an ambitious vacation.

I checked up on the investigation into the death of my recently departed husband. The coroner's report claimed that Frank died from blunt force trauma to the head. In the papers, they never mentioned that blunt force could happen from the cranium tumbling toward a static object like the edge of a stair. I remained a person of interest, mostly because I disappeared right after he died. My whereabouts were still unknown. If I had stayed, maybe all of this could've blown over and I'd have the house, a name, and a life without Frank. I thought about going back, but now that I had angered Mr. Oliver and painted myself as a black widow to my old neighbors, I couldn't see my return playing out as smoothly as I'd want.

I turned back to the obituaries to get my mind off the living. I found a promising corpse named Charlotte Clark. A name I could get used to. She was survived by only her sister and a niece and nephew. I jotted down the information for the funeral and headed back to Blue's place.

* * *

When I opened the door, Blue was sitting on the couch, watching the news. Her foot pounded the rug like a jackhammer. She clicked off the remote and got to her feet.

"Good. You're home. I've been waiting hours for you."

Blue always managed to look cool as an iceberg, but now she was jittery, charged, like someone had given her a shot of adrenaline. Something in her manner set me on edge, more than usual.

"Everything all right?"

"It will be, eventually. But now we have to go."

"Where?"

"I'll tell you in the car," Blue said.

She walked out of the front door expecting me to follow, so I did. When we reached her car, she tossed me the keys.

"I assume you want to drive," she said.

We got into the car without any more words and I backed out of the snaky driveway.

The sky turned dark; Blue's taciturn directions laid a track on top of the rush hour traffic. *Turn right, turn left, left up ahead, right.*

"Take 290 East for about thirty miles and then take 21," she said.

"You plan on telling me where we're going?"

"We're going on a nature excursion," Blue said.

"At night?"

"Yes."

"Wouldn't we be able to see the nature better during the day?"

"Fewer tourists at night."

Blue didn't seem like she was in the mood for conversation and I wasn't in the spirit of inquisition. No one said another word until she told me to turn right onto FM 60. Traffic quieted and I began to see signs for a state park. The absence of lights and conversation sent my head to the wrong place.

"You're not planning on killing me—are you, Blue?"

Blue took a deep breath. I tried to read its meaning, but nothing came. She opened the glove compartment and pulled out her gun and I swerved the car into opposing traffic. It felt like all of the blood in my veins had to turned to ice. A truck blasted its horn; I steadied our vehicle and tried to quiet the pounding in my chest.

"You need to calm down," said Blue. She released the cylinder on the revolver and tipped the bullets into the palm of her hand. "Take them," she said. "Then you can stop thinking whatever nonsense you're thinking."

She dropped the bullets into my hand and closed my fingers around them. I slipped my hand into my jacket pocket, counting as my fingers released each slug. One. Two. Three. Four. Five . . .

"Slow down when you see the sign for Park Road 57. That's where we're headed," Blue said.

"I'm not exactly in the mood for a camping trip."

"We'll keep it brief."

I pulled off the road at Lake Somerville State Park. The

ranger station was closed. A chain blocked the entrance, secured only by a hook slipped into an eye. Blue unhooked it. We drove up a dirt driveway and parked in an empty lot. Blue plucked a flashlight from the backseat, got out of the car, and strolled up a short trail leading to the campsites. I followed the bright beam of her light. The only sounds were gravel crunching under our feet and the steady chirp of crickets. The fire pits looked like they hadn't seen a glow in months.

Blue walked back to the car. I followed her. She passed me the flashlight and opened the trunk.

"Keep your cool. Can you do that for me, Amelia?"

Blue didn't wait for an answer. She opened the trunk. Inside was a large, bulky blanket. I stepped closer and saw that it was a large, bulky blanket with shoes. Looked like size-twelve work boots, to be precise. I let the light drift along the body until I got to the head, where I saw a giant blot of blood. Resting on top of the body was a shovel.

"Did you kill someone, Blue?"

I realize now that was a foolish question.

"Indeed, I did." She said it as if I'd asked her if she'd picked up milk at the store.

"Who?"

"Amelia, allow me to introduce you to my husband, Jack Reed. I wish you could have met under better circumstances."

As Blue and I lugged Jack's body as deep into the woods as our feet could carry him, I gleaned the following information: Jack found Blue; he tried to kill her;

she killed him instead. She made it sound as simple as counting to three.

I asked Blue how Jack found her. He learned she had an aunt, found a few letters from before Greta died, with the address for her house printed clear as day on the envelope. He drove straight to Austin, to the last known address of one Greta Miles. He sat on the house for less than a day and spotted his wife. Soon after I left for the library, he knocked on her door. But Blue had seen him traipsing up the driveway. Got her gun, invited him in. When he pulled a knife, she pulled her gun and marched him over to her car. She figured it wouldn't be so easy getting a body into the trunk, and she didn't want to bother cleaning up the mess in her house, so she laid a tarp and asked Jack to get in the trunk. He obliged. She shot him then and there. That was why there was so much blood.

"If someone put a tarp inside a trunk and told me to get inside, I'm not sure I'd go without a fight," I said. "It'd be like climbing into my own grave."

"If you put a gun to someone's head, they'll do just about anything you ask, including climbing into their own grave," said Blue.

"You make a good point," I said.

The woods smelled like pine and oak and that damn pureness only nature can offer. Jack smelled like the taste of a nine-volt battery.

Blue took the first turn at digging the grave. When her breath got raspy and I could see sweat trickling down her brow in the cold of night, I took over, even though I didn't exactly see how burying her husband was any responsibility of mine. For the record, it did occur to me that I was becoming an accessory after the fact, but considering I had already been an accessory to a double homicide, one more charge felt like a drop in the bucket. At this point, it almost seemed wise to go home and face the music for the crimes I didn't commit.

The dirt was soft at first. Then it got hard, and we had to throw our weight into the chore.

"How deep should this be?" I said.

"At the cemetery, it's six feet, I think. For our purposes, four should do," said Blue.

I got the feeling maybe Blue had done this before. Or thought about it considerably.

It took us two hours to get the hole just right. Blue rolled her husband over into the grave. The blanket came off, his blasted face now exposed. I looked away and tried to keep my stomach from turning over.

"My apologies," Blue said.

She shifted the blanket to cover his head and began shoveling the dirt over the body. When she was done, a small mound rested over the shallow grave.

"That doesn't look right," Blue said.

She gathered rocks and moss and studied the earth adjacent to the grave and tried to make Jack's final resting place resemble the surrounding landscape. It still resembled a fresh grave, but less than before.

Blue took a moment to regard her work. Maybe she was paying some kind of respect to the dead.

"Good-bye, Jack," she said. "Sorry how things worked out. But you only have yourself to blame."

That was the shortest funeral service I'd ever attended. Even I took the time to drink a hand of whiskey as I said good-bye to Frank. Then again, I didn't kill Frank. If you kill someone, I'm not sure a eulogy is in order. Or maybe it's even more in order.

Blue picked up the shovel and returned to the car. I followed, holding the flashlight.

The first part of the drive home was quiet. I'd like to think that Blue was feeling an itch of guilt and trying to find a way to scratch it.

"How do you feel?" I asked. I didn't ask to make conversation or slice the tension. I asked because I honestly couldn't read Blue at all. She didn't look scared or relieved or guilty or sad. Her eyes seemed to drift in thought, pensive in an academic manner. Her face was in complete repose, not a worry wrinkle in sight, not a single tear at the start of a slide. I didn't know the man and I didn't kill the man, but I'm fairly certain I felt more of an ache of guilt for my part in the ordeal than Blue did for her far more ample role.

"I feel free," Blue said plainly.

"Huh," I said.

In my experience when you leave a dead body in your wake, you are decidedly less free.

"I don't have to run anymore," Blue said.

"Not from Jack. But maybe now you have to run from the law."

"He wouldn't have told anyone he was coming for me. I should be long dead by now, according to any plan of my dearly departed. Jack was the kind of person who would run off without telling anyone, just plain disappear. Or get himself in a mess with someone who would disappear him."

"Is it that simple?" I said.

"Of course not. I still have to clean the blood out of the trunk of the car," Blue said. "That could take *hours*."

July 20, 2009
To: Ryan
From: Jo

I'll admit you people have done a hell of a job keeping me secret. But, in general, you have to assume that you don't have any secrets anymore. Even from me. If you're bored and still living in the past, like I am, it's easy to trawl those websites and follow comment after comment until you find a truly intriguing thread. You were in a mental hospital, weren't you? That's why you haven't written in over six months.

Why hide that? I was almost relieved when I figured it out. Not that I want you unwell, but knowing that maybe sometimes you can't live with yourself makes me feel a little bit better. You don't have to tell me what it was like, none of the cuckoo's nest details. But you don't have to keep it a secret, either.

I'd probably have ended up there too, if my life weren't such a high-wire act. Vigilance keeps you sharp, like an animal. There isn't much time for melancholy.

So, when you were in the nuthouse, did you get to the bottom of all of your troubles?

Jo

August 14, 2009
To: Jo
From: Ryan

I didn't tell anyone anything when I was in there. That's what you really want to know, right? I hardly said a word the whole time, which might be why they kept me so long. Some days I wanted to talk. It's not like they could tell anyone. But I knew it might ease my conscience and I didn't want that. You don't want that for me either.

September 3, 2009
To: Ryan
From: Jo

You don't know me anymore, Ryan. You don't know what I want for you.

It's unnatural to keep this kind of secret. It surfaces in other ways. Frank sent me to a priest last year, thought maybe I needed clerical intervention. I had these nightmares that scared the hell out of him. More importantly, they were interrupting his precious sleep. So

I went to the priest, who suggested that guilt was causing my sleep disturbances. I think he figured I was stepping out on my husband, maybe stealing from the till to go on shopping sprees. I could tell that he thought my crimes were trivial. I found his tone insulting and so I confessed. Not to my exact crime, but one that rang a bell.

I went into one of those booths you see in gangster films, with the mesh screen that divides you. I could still recognize Father Paul, but I pretended like we hadn't just spoken for an hour.

And so I made a false confession. I was young, I told him, and in love. But the boy I was in love with had spurned me. I drank, I drank to the point of complete oblivion. I got in my car and drove. I must have blacked out, I told the priest. Because the next thing I remember, I was in a hospital. They told me I was in a car accident, an accident that had killed a girl, the girl who had stolen my boy. The priest asked if I had been punished for my crime. I said I had. Wouldn't you agree? He told me to do ten Hail Marys and twenty Our Fathers. I found the prayers on the Internet and did as I was told. The nightmares ceased for a few weeks and then returned. Maybe that was a coincidence.

You could give it a try. Might give you a few weeks of rest from your soul.

Jo

* * *

September 30, 2009
To: Jo
From: Ryan

Who is Frank? Do you mean Lou, your husband? I suppose if that's not his real name it might be easy to forget. Or maybe you slipped and told me his real name. How is Frank?

Don't answer that, I don't want to know about your new life. Sometimes I try to imagine that alternate universe of yours, where we turn out like we thought we might. But in my version something always goes wrong. Let's face it, we were fucked from the start.

I have some news for you. Maybe you'll think it's good news. Your mother got clean. Went into a ninety-day rehab program. She's only been out a few months, but she looks different. Maybe not like when you were little, the way you described her when your father was still alive, when you still had the store, but better than she's been since I've known her.

R

October 3, 2009
To: Ryan
From: Jo

Who paid for my mother's rehab? I know her insurance didn't cover any ninety-day program. Is she still with that man you told me about? The one whose primary virtue was that he didn't beat her?

I don't even know why I care.
J

October 23, 2009
To: Jo
From: Ryan
   I haven't seen that guy around. You know who paid.
Why do you even ask?
   R

November 11, 2009
To: Ryan
From: Jo
   You're right, I knew he paid. Has he been paying for
other things? What is my mother to him?

November 13, 2009
To: Jo
From: Ryan
   I don't know. I don't ask.

November 15, 2009
To: Ryan
From: Jo
   You don't question anything. You just sit quietly and
do as you're told.

7

Blue made it seem so easy, this life we led, like an endless game of hide-and-seek. She went on with her days, not worrying for a moment about the past catching up with her. I have no doubt that Jack was a bad man and maybe he did get what he deserved. I've met my share of bad men in my day; sometimes I think I wouldn't mind killing one or two of them, but if I did, I would feel it afterward. It would have meant something. I'm not saying I wouldn't take the opportunity if it arose, but I couldn't keep humming in the shower in the carefree way that Blue's voice looped the jingle she'd just heard on the television.

A few days after it was all over, my nerves had finally settled down to a slow vibration, like a piano wire after the last note of a song. I checked my finances and decided that I couldn't dip any further into my paltry savings. I was down to just over seven hundred dollars and I didn't pretend that I could remain a guest of Blue's without contributing anything to the household.

When I'd first struck out on my own, ten years ago, the

only work I could get was manual labor, specifically janitorial or maid services. I wouldn't have minded a construction job. My old friend Edie Parsons's parents had a hardware store. We used to hang out there some afternoons. Mr. Parsons taught us a few things. I knew how to wield a hammer and I wasn't inept with a table saw. I'd refinished the hardwood floors in my childhood home after I got a few too many splinters on my feet and it was clear my mother wasn't going to do anything about it. But I discovered, after a few failed attempts, that men don't hire women for construction jobs. They'll tell you you're not qualified, but what they're really thinking is that you can't pull your weight. Literally.

Once I met Frank and those cleaning days were long gone, I promised myself they'd never return. But you make all kinds of promises to yourself in life, and most of them you don't keep. I printed flyers at the library offering my domestic services with my phone number fringed on the bottom. I waited only a few days before the first call came in.

His name was Kyle. A confirmed bachelor, from the looks of things. He rented a one-bedroom apartment near the capitol building. It has been my experience that men of little means who like a clean home will clean it themselves. They like it done just so. The rest hire maids to keep their apartments from turning into giant petri dishes. As it turned out, Kyle's last housekeeper had quit. He said it was family trouble, but I could tell from the odor that hit me when I walked in the door that she just didn't have the stomach for it.

Kyle hired me on the spot and left for work. He was one

of those closet slobs. Looked put together and just fine on the outside. Handsome, maybe even a heartbreaker judging from the collection of used condoms under the bed. I wore thick yellow gloves and a surgical mask. While I had done this job before, and it kept me afloat, I can't say that I ever took to it. Every time I left a home spic-and-span, I didn't feel the satisfaction of a job well done. Instead, I felt like the filth I had touched had somehow transferred onto me. No matter how many showers I took, the invisible layer of scum would remain.

The next call came from the daughter of an old woman who was near the end. I would have to clean around Mrs. Smythe and her oxygen tank and her humidifier and her day nurse, who, as far as I was concerned, didn't seem to do much of anything other than watch television, deliver a rainbow of pills three times a day, and tell Mrs. Smythe to quiet down so as not to disturb her programs. The television always blasted at a notch above the rattle of Mrs. Smythe's respirator. It was one of those old houses where every corner was etched with ancient grime. The grout in the bathroom held mold with a history unto itself, impossible to return to its original whitish hue. I vacuumed around the day nurse, who stayed put on the couch. I couldn't do much about the overall odor in the air. That came straight from the old lady, and after three weeks of working there, I got the feeling that sponge baths were as rare as a rainstorm in the Sahara. I even offered to do it myself one time after I got a whiff so nauseating I had to choke back bile. The nurse returned my offer with a chilling stare.

I had some funny idea that I might find one good house in my mix, one place I could visit that restored my belief that the world wasn't composed of filth and sin.

When I'd return to Blue's place, I'd take a half-hour shower and then slide onto the couch, turn on the television, and try to pretend that none of this was my life. But every morning I'd wake up and realize that this was it and maybe it wasn't ever going to get any better.

One night Blue tried to cheer me up with a home-cooked meal, the kind people who have lives and families eat. She made pasta carbonara and salad and we drank two not-bad bottles of wine that Blue had nicked from May's Well. After dinner, we ate strawberries with cream and Blue picked up the newspaper and began studying the obituaries.

"They don't usually mention unidentified bodies in the obits," I said.

"Oh, I'm not looking for Jack," Blue said.

"Just ghoulish curiosity?"

"Amelia-slash-Tanya, you still need a new identity, unless you want to spend the rest of your days living as a maid with no name. I honestly think you'd be happier as a bank robber."

"Perhaps," I said.

"Well, if you're open to it, I've noticed the security at the Fairview Savings and Loan is lacking . . ."

I honestly couldn't tell if she was serious or not. I poured myself a drink and let the question hang in the air. *Maybe*, I thought. Was there really any reason for me to remain a law-abiding citizen?

Blue returned her attention to the obits. "There's a promising corpse at Morgan and Sons mortuary. Allison Wade. Car accident. The funeral is tomorrow at eleven."

A storm came through that night and decided to stay awhile. The next morning, outside the funeral home, all you could see was a knot of blackness, like a murder of crows. Umbrellas shaded mourners from a torrential downpour. Blue and I rushed from the parking lot to the awning, our feet dipping in puddles along the way and soaked by the time we were indoors.

Inside it smelled like damp wool. Throngs of mourners mingled and cried, and my eyes caught the shimmer of light on metal. Men in uniform, police uniforms, everywhere. Had to be about twenty cops in the room.

"What's going on here, Blue?"

Blue looked surprised herself, and maybe a little agitated. "There seems to be a large police presence here," she said.

"You don't say."

A man in a sergeant's uniform was sitting in the back pew. He tried to look stoic and strong, but as each mourner approached him with their treacly comforts, his resolve seemed to weaken.

I walked back to the exit, swiped a black umbrella that I could not claim ownership of, and stepped outside, opening the umbrella under the persistent downpour. Blue followed my lead.

"We hardly got a look at her," Blue said.

"Even if I found my doppelgänger, I don't plan on impersonating the dead wife of a police officer. I understand that risks are involved in my particular predicament, but this is about as sane-minded as rewiring your house without turning off the circuit breaker."

We left, defeated. The drive home was that kind of noisy quiet where all you can hear is that brutal voice inside your head telling you there's no way out. Before computers and mammoth databases and the NSA, I could have picked a name, moved to a new town, and run with it. But now it felt like every time I wanted to try on an identity coat, it began to unravel the moment I slipped my arm into the sleeve.

Back at Blue's place, I climbed onto the couch, covered my head with a blanket, and tried to sleep away my worries. Blue retired to her room and stayed mute. Sometime in the early hours of the morning, I heard sounds emanating from Blue's room. Rustling, creaking, shuffling. She wasn't even bothering to be quiet. I checked the clock: 2:48 a.m. The light in her room was on and her door was slightly ajar.

I padded over to the light and peeked inside. Blue was packing a suitcase. Not so much with clothes, but papers and books. She set a large wool coat on top of everything.

"Blue, what's going on?"

"Good, you're up," Blue said. "Would you please make us a pot of coffee?"

Since there was no chance I was going to return to the land of unconsciousness, I figured I'd rather deal with my Blue inquisition caffeinated. I brewed a pot of coffee, waiting patiently for the drip to near its end; poured two cups of bitter brew; and returned to Blue's bedroom.

I passed her a mug, waited a moment for some of the caffeine to hit her gut, and then asked the obvious question.

"You going somewhere, Blue?"

"No," Blue said. "You are."

It had only been a matter of time before I wore out my welcome. I wasn't surprised, although I couldn't account for Blue's packing a suitcase that was neither mine nor contained my belongings.

"I can pack on my own," I said. "And I don't have any need for your—whatever all those papers are."

"I don't think you understand, Tanya-slash-Amelia," Blue said.

"Feel free to enlighten me."

"I found you a new identity," Blue said.

"Who?"

"You're going to become me. Debra Maze."

It took a few ticks of the long hand for the words to register. Once they did, it took a few more ticks for them to register again.

"I think it's possible I misunderstood you," I said.

"You did not," said Blue.

"I believe your plan has a few holes in it."

"Probably, but nothing that some creative spackling can't fix."

"Answer this, then. If I'm you, who are you going to be?"

"I'm going to be Amelia Keen."

"Have you conveniently forgotten about the two men who recently tried to kill Amelia Keen?"

"I have not," said Blue. "However, those men and whoever sent them seem to know what you look like. So, I don't think they've got anything particularly against the name Amelia Keen. I think they don't like the person who has been inhabiting that name, and the name before that. If they manage to track me down, they'll find *me*, not you. Once I have the identity, I could get married, take my new husband's last name, mix up my social security numbers—I hear that's a good trick to stay off the grid—and the next thing you know, Amelia Keen is gone. I'm now Amelia Lightfoot."

"Lightfoot?"

"In my fantasy I've met a beautiful Native American man and we live on a reservation. But I could be just as happy and invisible with a man named Jones or Smith."

"Blue, I appreciate all that you've done for me, but your identity comes with about as much baggage as mine."

"I'm offering you a life. A real way out. What was your plan?" Blue said. "To leech off of me forever?"

Her voice was calm and even, but the threat was clear. I did this or I was out. I tried to figure what Blue's angle was, what my identity could do for her, but in my desperate state my mind fumbled over possible outcomes. All I knew was that my run as Amelia Keen, my hiding out with Debra Maze, was done. Still, I had to ask the obvious question.

"What do you get out of this, Blue?"

"I get to leave the past behind."

"Isn't your past buried in a nature preserve?"

Blue traveled into the kitchen and poured herself another mug of coffee. Then she grabbed the whiskey and added a shot. She took a sip, closed her eyes, and leaned against the wall. It looked like she was taking a standing catnap. Then she opened her eyes and her expression humbled some.

"I don't think anyone is looking for Debra Maze. But with Jack missing and me missing, one can hypothesize as to what his extended family might do. When they do come hunting for me and they find you, they'll know they've hit a dead end. Besides, there is surely more than one Debra Maze in this universe. My maiden name should serve you well for a while. But you'll want to change it as soon as you can. I wouldn't bother with a legal name change. You need someone to vouch for you. I recommend getting married. He doesn't have to be the love of your life, just a guy you get hitched to for a few months with a name you can swap out. Then do that social security number trick. Even if someone tracks you down, they'll figure they were mistaken. We can help each other. You don't want to be Amelia anymore, and I don't want to be Debra."

"Have you really thought this through?" I said. It was my final attempt to talk her down.

Blue strode into the bedroom and lugged a pile of books and papers out of the suitcase. She slid a certificate out of a plastic sheath and passed it to me.

"You could have a real life and a real job as me," she said. "That's my teaching credential. I taught grade school for seven years. I have lesson plans in here for grades two through five. Do you like children?"

"I don't know. I think so."

"At that age, they're pure, they're good. Well, every once in a while you'll find a bad seed. But mostly they're better than the rest of us. And I can say with certainty that being in a classroom is better than working in a factory, cleaning houses, or being a day laborer. When you go home at night, you won't think about your dead husband or any of those other demons you have. The chorus of untamed children will shove away all the voices in your head."

Blue was shoving away the voices in my head that were telling me that this plan had as many holes as a Wiffle ball. Thing is, I liked the idea, as inconceivable as it was. I couldn't see going on as I had been, living without a name, without a home, finding jobs I couldn't report to the IRS. I wanted a real life; that was all I ever wanted.

I don't remember saying anything to Blue. Maybe I nodded my head once or twice. She interpreted whatever gesture I made as acquiescence.

"I'll go out for supplies," she said.

An hour later, I was sitting on the edge of the bathtub while Blue painted my hair with bleach. My scalp burned and my eyes watered from the pungent chemical. An hour later, we washed out the bleach and Blue dried my hair. It was the color of straw, one of those obvious dye jobs you see on women all across the country. They're usually trapped behind a cash register that's trapped behind ballistic glass. I didn't look like Blue; I looked like one of them. Washed out and haunted.

"Don't worry," Blue said. "I'm not done."

She removed a box of Nice'n Easy golden blond from her plastic bag, mixed the color and developer together. Then she began striping my scalp with the creamy blend, which made my head feel like it was in a refrigerator. While we waited for my color to set, Blue unboxed her own disguise. Medium brown. She regarded herself in the mirror with a meaty pause.

"It's time I see how the other half lives," Blue said as she passed me the bottle. "Will you do the honors?"

Forty-five minutes later, Blue was a brunette and I was a blonde. I watched Blue remove colored contact lenses from a case and blot them over her cold, beautiful eyes. When she was done, she turned to me and said, "Well?"

What do you say to a woman who has lost her looks in just under an hour? I tried to picture her as an outsider would, but it didn't help matters. She'd rendered herself plain with her disguise as Amelia Keen, and I couldn't help but feel a twinge of guilt.

"I don't think even Jack could recognize you," I said.

Blue applied red lipstick, which took a chunk out of the overall plain effect, but it was hardly the transformation that

Blue was hoping for. She tried to hide her disappointment when she passed me a small plastic container.

"Your turn," Blue said. "Those brown eyes have got to go."

I unscrewed the cap and saw an ice-blue contact lens staring back at me.

"What are you doing with blue contact lenses?" I said.

"Oh, I have an entire set, including green and purple."

"Purple?"

"I tried them once. It was disturbing."

The first time I tried to stick those cruel craters into my eyes, my body revolted in convulsions, then tears. Blue served me a shot of whiskey and told me to take a couple deep breaths. I steeled myself for the task, yet again, and managed to shove those blue lies over my bloodshot golden browns. I looked in the mirror and saw someone else. It wasn't Blue, but it also wasn't me anymore. It felt deeply wrong, almost as wrong as I felt digging Jack's grave. Changing your hair color is like putting on makeup. It's a cheat, but a fair one. Altering your DNA, turning brown eyes to blue, is a deceit, and one you'd be reminded of every time you looked in the mirror.

Blue made up my face like her driver's license photo, which had been taken when she still lacquered on war paint as if she were on a high-stakes hunt for a husband. Sharp black eyeliner, gray eye shadow, crimson lips, and rose blush.

Blue stepped back and regarded her painting. She sighed with deep satisfaction.

"Almost done," Blue said, rifling through her bag. "We

just have a few practical matters to sort out. Here's Debra Maze's birth certificate and social. You'll need that for a driver's license. Now go get the pink slip for your Toyota. Tanya Dubois needs to sell Amelia Keen her car. It was risky for you to change the title before, but I think we're safe now."

"And what am I supposed to drive, your VW Crime Scene?"

"That's a good point. I'll get rid of that car. You take the old lady's Cadillac."

"It's not the best car for blending in, Blue."

"But it's a beauty, isn't it? I wish I could keep it for myself, but practically speaking you need to take the car because it's mine. Myrna signed it over to me a few months ago during a lucid moment. The title is in your new name, so it's your car."

"What does it get, like fifteen miles to the gallon?"

"Twenty on highways," Blue said. "Why are you harping on minor details and such? Trade it in when you get settled. It's in mint condition. It'll get you where you need to go. And I'll throw in a little cash just to cover the fuel."

We retrieved the pink slips for both vehicles, swapped names, swapped cars, and Blue gave me five hundred in cash. The paperwork was complete. It was time to say good-bye.

We walked outside to the car and Blue retrieved the gun she'd used on Jack. She put it in the glove compartment of the Cadillac.

"What's that for?" I said.

"It's a parting gift," Blue said.

"I don't need a gun."

"Take it," she said. "It's a dangerous world out there, Debra Maze."

As I drove away, the realization came into full relief. I had just taken over the identity of a felon, with the murder weapon sitting right in my glove compartment.

March 22, 2010
To: Jo
From: Ryan

Jo,

I've probably written this twenty times, scrapped it, and started over again. It shouldn't be this hard. At least it shouldn't be harder than anything else that has transpired between us.

I'm engaged. There, I did it.

You don't know her. She's not connected to anyone from our past. I'm trying to anticipate the questions you might have. It's a game I'm playing. How well do I know you? Let's see how I do.

I met her on a vacation last year in Hawaii. I didn't tell you about that, I know. It didn't seem right, me on a tropical island and you wherever you are—I'm betting on Wisconsin. I was miserable the entire time. Drunk by the swimming pool, starting each day with coffee and bourbon. I fell asleep under the blazing sun. She walked over to me, drizzled sunscreen on my chest in the shape of a happy face. When I woke up, she said, "You're turning into a lobster. But now you're a happy lobster," and walked away.

She's a schoolteacher in Idaho, but she's moving out here. I know it would be better for me to go to her, but I feel like I have to stay, to stand guard and make sure that people do what they're supposed to do.

She's blond and, yes, she's pretty. Not beautiful, just easy on the eyes. She has rosy cheeks and gray eyes and perpetually chapped lips that she's always gnawing on. I know you want to know other things, but those are the questions you wouldn't ask. You would think it was undignified, so even though I can imagine your voice posing inquiries, I don't think I'll answer them.

Aside from being a schoolteacher, she's a churchgoer, knitter, baker, and charitably minded. I can see your face right now, as you're reading this. She's not you. Don't be offended by that. I couldn't be with anyone who reminded me of you because I'm already reminded of you more than I can manage.

Here's all that matters: She's sweet and kind and I feel like I can trust her. And she seems to be able to live with the fact that I'm a bit of a shell. When she sees my mind wandering, she doesn't ask me what I'm thinking. I've found that's the single most important trait I could ask for in a woman.

There, I told you.

I'm starting to wonder about continuing this thing we have. Isn't it time we played the cards we were dealt?

Yours,

R

* * *

April 29, 2010
To: Ryan
From: Jo

Fuck. Well, congratulations. I've just celebrated with five shots of bourbon. Whenever I need to drink myself into oblivion, I'm always kinda grateful that I married a barkeep.

Your wife sounds perfect. So, Carnac the Magnificent, here are some very basic questions of mine that you failed to answer. What is the name of your betrothed? And, do you love her? But I have so many more questions than that. What gives you the right to get married, to try to be happy, after what you've done? Shouldn't there be a penance of some kind? Three people died that day, not two. My only consolation, the thing that eases my envy— that word seems so small for what this is. The only thing that gives me comfort is knowing that you're not you. That She, whatever her name is, will never know you like I did, the old you, the you that was kind and sweet and had a bigger heart than anyone I ever knew. I used to think you were better than everyone. Now I could pick a dozen souls out on the street that surely surpass you in integrity.

Yes, I'm being cruel. But every day you don't tell the truth, you are being even crueler.

Jo

* * *

June 20, 2010
To: Jo
From: Ryan
    I don't know what I'm supposed to say. I did what I had to, but I'm still sorry. I will be sorry every day for the rest of my days. I gave up living for six years because of you. It's a long life. Don't we all deserve just a bit of comfort? To answer your question, yes, I love her. It's a different kind of love. If she broke my heart, I'd stay the same. Do you know what I mean? Not like the last time.
    R

July 2, 2010
To: Ryan
From: Jo
    I didn't break your heart. You broke mine. Now twice.
    Good luck with your life. I wish you the best. I really do. I think maybe I'll leave you alone for a while. You're right, it is a long life and this is not how I want to live it.
    Good-bye.
    Jo

DEBRA MAZE

8

It was only as I sailed out of Austin in that gas-guzzling American classic that more doubts and questions compounded in my brain. Looking at my reflection in the rearview mirror, I still wondered whether a new life was possible. Could I really pull off being Ms. Debra Maze? Or was this just some long con that Blue had figured from the moment she laid eyes on my foolish soul at May's Well?

The Cadillac handled like a boat on the calm seas. After a few hours of sailing away from that sorry mess of Tanya Dubois and Amelia Keen, my memory of other failed attempts to start anew faded just enough for my sense of hope to come back to life. I gazed at myself once again and tried to believe it was possible. I was going to be whoever the hell I wanted to be.

Before I departed, when my brain was still a jumbled mess of suspicion and fear, Blue gave me the lowdown on acquiring a teaching position with her credentials.

"By the way," she said all casually, "if you get a job, they're going to want your fingerprints."

"I can't be fingerprinted, Blue. You know that," I said.

"But *my* prints are still clean," she said, sliding an official-looking card out of an envelope.

Black fingerprints, swirls in various forms, dotted the cards.

"I've done some preliminary research. I think it would be unwise to teach in Ohio, where I taught. But in Wyoming, they just mail the fingerprint cards to you. If you get a job, then they'll instruct you where to go to get printed officially. You're bound to find someplace where they're lax with the rules. Maybe you can deliver these prints straight to the principal, or maybe when you're being printed at the police station you can swap out the card at some point. I gave you five cards. You have five chances to beat the system."

"And if that doesn't work?"

"I'd try one of those private Christian schools. They don't have the same appreciation for government protocol as public schools. Any other questions?"

"Yeah. These cards are for Wyoming. Will they transfer to any state?"

"No, sweetheart," Blue said. I can't remember when she stopped calling me Amelia or Tanya, but it felt sudden and deliberate.

"So, the only way this plan works out is if I go to Wyoming. I don't have a choice of destinations?"

That was the one thing about being on the run that appealed to me, leaving town and just randomly choosing a new home off of a map.

"I think that's the best place to beat the system. Besides, Jackson is nice this time of year," said Blue.

"How do you know?"

"I went there on my honeymoon," she said.

It sounded like Blue had thought this through, but she had the gift of conviction, a salesman's heart.

There wasn't one direct artery from Austin, Texas, to Jackson, Wyoming. Every few hours I had to consult my map to make sure I was headed in the right direction. I got a late start my first day on the road. I drove until my eyes betrayed me and I began to see flashing red lights in my rearview mirror. I found a rest stop and slept until dawn. I drove another full day, under a bright sun passing through the untamed mountains of Colorado. I stopped for gas every few hours, worked the kinks out of my back and legs, and kept going until I reached Casper, Wyoming. I checked the temperature gauge the entire ride, certain that my antique vehicle would overheat in the mountains. The old lady must have treated her Cadillac with great kindness over the years. It was as reliable a ride as anything else I've driven, but not easy to handle on mountain roads. By the time I got to Casper, I decided I could use a proper bed for the night. I found a cheap motel called the Friendly Ghost Inn. I picked up a bag of pretzels and a soda for supper from the corner shop and retired to my room. I took a shower and stared at my new self in the mirror. The image staring back at me was so startling it was like waking up again. I couldn't sleep just then, so I decided to test the waters of my new identity.

I left my stale motel room and walked down the main road until I found a bar that looked like the kind of place you could get lost in. It was one of those sports bars with a cheap menu and expensive TVs. It was called Sidelines. I figured the patrons would be too interested in the games to bother with me. But I also figured since it was a notch above a dive, there was at least a chance I'd get ID'd, and I could take mine out for a spin.

An older gentleman was behind the bar. He had the kind of nose that let you know he'd sampled a fair share of his product in his day. A knot of high-volume men gathered in the back, playing pool and clocking the baseball game that was broadcast from the corner of the room.

I sat down at the bar next to a woman who looked like she'd forgotten her own name a few hours ago. I always had a policy when I worked at Frank's bar to tuck a woman in a cab long before she reached the point of no return.

"Welcome, darling, can I see some ID?"

I slipped Blue's Ohio driver's license out of my wallet and slid it across the bar. I felt my heart beat strong inside my chest, but then the old man slid it right back and said, "You're far from home."

I took a breath to settle my nerves and said, "Road trip."

"What can I get you?"

There was that decision again. Did I change my habits to adapt to my new person or were these details ultimately trivial? Fuck it. There was time enough to figure out who Debra Maze was. Right now, *I* needed a whiskey.

"Whiskey, neat."

"Well okay?"

"Sure," I said. I was pinching pennies these days.

"Name's Hal," the bartender said as he served my drink. "Holler if you need anything." Then he winked. It looked sinister, but I believe his intent was friendly. A wink is a difficult gesture to master and yet practiced by volumes of men who lack the panache to pull it off.

The lady a few bar stools away rested her head on the splintered wood and began to snore. I heard a man in the corner give some kind of doglike yelp after he failed to make his shot.

Then some other male voice shouted, "Blondie, come here and bring me some luck."

Another man said, "Leave the woman be."

Yet another voice in the low register said, "A woman like that should not be sitting alone."

I took inventory of the bar to see whom the men might be speaking of. Other than a short phase in junior high school, after my mother gave me a brutal perm, I'd never been unsightly. I've heard myself described as pretty, handsome, easy on the eyes. But the only two men who ever thought I was truly beautiful were my daddy and Ryan; I don't believe I heard it after they were gone, even from Frank when he was courting me in that mild manner in which he courted. Only one other woman was in the bar besides me and the sleeping one. I couldn't comment on her looks; she was wearing a cumbersome neck brace, which is hardly an accessory that invites flirtation.

I'd never gotten the chance to turn Amelia Keen into a real person. She was still just a little bit more than a shell when I shed that disguise. And here I was again, trying on a new disguise that felt about as natural as that powdered orange juice I used to drink as a child.

One man unhitched himself from the knot of pool players and approached the bar. He was tall and lean and a bit weather-beaten, like an actor in an old western. His long-sleeved shirt retreated to his elbows, revealing the trail of a tribal tattoo that probably snaked up his entire torso, like overgrown ivy.

Hal was serving another customer, so the man reached over the bar, took a bottle of whiskey—better than the stuff I was drinking—and poured himself a shot. He let the bottle hover over my cordial glass.

"Can I buy you another?" Tribal Tattoo said.

"Looks like you're stealing another," I said.

"Hal knows I'm good for it."

"But I don't know what you're good for," I said.

"That's because you've known me for less than a minute. I need at least two for a deep, personal connection." The man refilled my drink and dropped a twenty on the bar. "This seat taken?"

"No," I said. Because the seat wasn't taken, not because I wanted to encourage the man. I've never quite figured out a way to answer that question honestly and gain the desired result (man not sitting down). This time, it didn't make any difference; Tribal Tattoo sat down before I had time to respond.

He shoved his shirtsleeve above his elbow and lifted his glass to toast. "Bottoms up," he said.

I clinked his glass because the last time I didn't clink a strange man's glass, he called me a bitch and things got out of hand. Sometimes it's easier to be agreeable, as long as the demands are reasonable. I'm generally willing to clink glasses with anyone, but I draw the line in other places.

"I hope you don't think I'm being forward, but you have the most . . . striking blue eyes I've ever seen."

"Thank you," I said, keeping my gaze on the bar.

Men are so easily drawn to fake things.

"I'm sure you hear that all the time."

"Nope," I said. "That would be the first."

Tribal Tattoo thought I was being droll and laughed. "You're not going to make this easy on me, are you?"

I took a sip of my whiskey and said, "Thanks for the drink."

One of the guys playing pool shouted, "Hey, Your Majesty, you're up."

"Next game," His Majesty said.

I offered a quizzical gaze and waited for an explanation.

"Name's King," he said, with a note of tedium. "King Domenic Lowell. Just call me Domenic."

He extended his hand; I shook it. He had a warm firm grip, but nothing showy.

"That's quite a name to live up to."

"Tell me about it," he said. "Now, what's your name?"

This used to be the easiest question under the sun. Now it was like a riddle trapped in a lockbox. I'd given the bartender my Debra ID, but I still wasn't certain this one would stick and I had to wonder whether it was wise tossing around a name that might be fraught with complications. That said, if you take too long to answer the question, it's going to sound like a lie even if it's the truth.

"Debra."

It was the first time I'd said it as my own. It felt like a jacket that was a few sizes too small.

"A fine name," Domenic said. "But it doesn't do you justice."

Some fraction of my being enjoyed the flattery. The rest felt a danger as palpable as playing a drunken game of William Tell. What was it about blondness that jumbled men's brains? Half the blondes out there are chemically induced, and yet the result is exactly the same. How could I hide in plain sight if eyes were always trained on me? I would have to figure out a way to remedy this situation. But for now, in this bar, I accepted Domenic's flattery, because it had been so long since I'd been truly flattered and there was something about him beyond his square jaw and deep brown eyes. He seemed like the kind of man who had nothing to prove. I hadn't met one of those in ages. Sometimes I wondered if I ever had.

"It's my name, nonetheless," I said.

"You new in town?"

"I'm just passing through," I said.

"Where are you headed, Debra?"

"Jackson, probably. Not sure yet." No point in conjuring yet another lie.

"What brings you to our fine state of Wyoming?"

"A job."

"What kind of job?"

"Teacher," I said. I have to admit it felt nice offering up a solid profession, even if it wasn't real yet.

"What grade?"

"You ask a lot of questions."

"How else are we going to get to know each other?"

"Is that what we're doing?"

"Yes. I already know you better than I did when I first walked over."

I guess I was staring at Domenic's tattoo because eye contact seemed unwise. He rolled up his sleeve a little more so I could get a better look. It was more elaborate than I thought.

"That must have hurt like hell," I said. It's always best to steer the conversation away from yourself.

"You've been inked, I take it."

"You inferred. I'm not sure I implied," I said. Then it occurred to me that that was the kind of thing Blue might say.

"Well, have you?"

"Yes," I said. I wondered whether it was wise to point

out any identifying marks. I also wondered if a time would ever come when answering questions about myself wouldn't require laborious internal calculations.

"Where? Someplace decent or indecent?" he asked.

"Decent enough."

"May I see?"

I nodded my head and finished my drink. Hal approached and asked if I wanted another. Domenic pointed to the top-shelf bourbon and ordered us both another round of drinks that were too costly for my new income bracket.

"Is it on your shoulder?"

"No."

"Wrist?"

I lifted up my leg and rested it on Domenic's thigh.

"Ankle," I said, pulling up my jeans, revealing three tiny Chinese symbols in red. It felt odd drawing attention to something I always tried to forget. Sometimes when I lived with Frank, I put a Band-Aid over it and pretended I had a cut.

"That's pretty," said Domenic, but I could tell that he was disappointed. What a cliché. Then again, he had a tribal tattoo, so who was he to judge? "What does it mean?" he asked.

"It means nothing," I said.

Domenic took in my response and then seemed to chew on it a bit. After a while, it had formed some kind of sense in his head.

"I think I understand you," Domenic said. "But tell me the story."

An old high school friend, Walt Burden, went out on the

town one night and came upon a small group of Chinese tourists, one of whom struck a chord of desire in him so deep, he never dated a white girl again. When the tourist rebuffed his advances, he told her about how he wanted to get a tattoo of the Chinese symbol meaning "peace." *Because no one had ever done that before.* He asked her to translate. The tourist girl wasn't giving him the time of day, but she did agree to draw the symbol for his tattoo on a napkin after his repeated pleas and an agreement that he would depart as soon as she did.

My friend Arthur Chang caught a glimpse of it in math class, and I could see him laughing to himself. I slipped Arthur a note: "What's so funny?" He said that Walt had no idea what words he had branded himself with, and then he told me.

Six months later, after a successful swim meet, my best friend, Melinda, insisted that we celebrate by getting tattoos to mark the occasion. We marched into a tattoo parlor with our respective designs. She got a dolphin—which she had decided two days earlier was her spirit animal. She wanted me to get a dolphin, too, but I didn't much like the idea of matching tattoos or spirit animals. I was distinctly aware that I was marking myself with a regrettable rite of passage, and I let it be just that. I had a photo of Walt's tattoo and asked the artist to duplicate it in miniature on the inside of my ankle.

I'm not sure why I wanted that tattoo more than a dolphin or a frog or Chinese symbols that meant something that was supposed to remind you to do things that come naturally, like breathing. But now it seems so apt that I chose these particular symbols, which literally mean "this means nothing." Although when Melinda asked me what those symbols meant, I told her they meant "swim."

I told Domenic the abbreviated version, minus the lie to Melinda; he smiled and nodded.

"That's a fine tattoo story. Better than most," he said.

"Thank you," I said, flattered.

It felt nice to speak the truth for once. I couldn't remember the last time I'd told a real story about myself to someone other than Blue. "Now, what's your excuse? You going to tell me you're two percent Cherokee or something?"

Domenic roared with laughter. It was a real, solid belly laugh. "Nah, nothing like that."

"So then, why are you branded like every other man I meet?"

"Because the Forty-Niners lost the Super Bowl."

"I can't see how far that ink travels—"

"I'd be happy to show you," Domenic said.

"—but that's a lot of time sitting in a chair in minor agony because you lost a bet."

Domenic finished his drink and said, "I'm a man of my word."

I believed him. As you might imagine, men hadn't been on the top of my list for a very long time. I knew they weren't all bad, but I had come across a few who were so rotten that they tainted the rest of the pool. But as far as men went, Domenic seemed all right to me, as all right as a man you've known less than an hour can seem.

Hal stepped behind the bar again.

"Is His Majesty giving you any trouble?" he said. It was just something to say. He didn't mean it.

"Not just yet," I said. "But I'll let you know."

Domenic looked me straight in the eye. His eyes conveyed desire and curiosity, but there wasn't that ugliness you sometimes see when a man is trying to decide how much he can take from you. I tried not to avert my gaze, but that's all I'd been doing for the last three months. It was a tough habit to shake.

"Can I buy you a burger?" Domenic said.

"Huh?" I said. I had expected a question of a different variety.

"I'm starving. There's a diner down the road. They get a lot of things wrong, but for some reason their burgers are special. I wouldn't touch their meatloaf, and the chicken fried steak should be a health code violation." He was just rattling on, waiting for me to answer.

"Yes," I said.

Domenic's brand-new Ford F-150 was parked right outside the bar. He opened the passenger door, just like a gentleman. My heart started pumping as if I were on speed. It felt like the air had thinned and the only thing I could do to calm my nerves was walk away.

Domenic slammed the door and followed after me.

"Sure, we can walk," he said. "It's only two miles up this road."

9

Domenic was right about the burgers, but I didn't care much for the ambiance. The bright lights of the diner were hardly flattering, and I didn't yet know how those blue contact lenses looked under the flickering glow of fluorescents. Every once in a while I caught Domenic giving me a sidelong glance, suspicious like. But I didn't know the guy, so maybe that was how he looked at people.

We were both hungry and ate in silence. When Domenic finished the last bite, he put his napkin on his plate and shoved it to the middle of the table. The waitress came by and asked if we needed anything else. Domenic complimented the chef and winked. On him it worked. The waitress dropped the check in front of the man. Domenic took it right away. I legitimately reached for my wallet, but he waved me off.

After the bill was dispensed with, Domenic leaned back in the booth, sated and lazy limbed. He smiled, a satisfied customer. "Debra, tell me something about yourself."

Now, that's a hell of a question. Not one I was inclined to answer too ambitiously.

"These lights are giving me a headache," I said.

"Then let's get out from under them."

It was easy in the bar and then the diner. There was a point to our companionship. Out on the street, I felt unmoored. There were things I wanted, things I missed, that my brain fought strongly against. I felt heat on the back of my neck. Few men had stirred such a response. The last time I felt it was with my chiropractor, but it hadn't been nearly as strong as it was at that moment on the desolate sidewalk. It reminded me of high school crushes, the hot flash of desire that could make a task as simple as tying your shoelaces impossible. I remember Ryan passing by the window in English class. He looked at me and smiled. I returned my gaze to *The Great Gatsby* and read the same line over and over and over again. I still remember the line:

It takes two to make an accident.
It takes two to make an accident.
It takes two to make an accident.

When it came down to it, it took three.

Domenic and I were walking in the same direction, but it wasn't toward my hotel or the bar or any destination I was aware of. I thought I should take my leave, but he took my hand instead and led me across the street. It had been so long since another person had touched me, I was stunned by how warm he felt.

"Are we going somewhere?"

"That's up to you," Domenic said.

I had changed direction enough in my life. Sometimes it was easier to follow the path that was paved for me. We walked in silence for a while, until Domenic stopped in front of a red door that adorned a Craftsman-style house. The moonlight cast enough of a glow on the home for me to see that it was painted blue with white trim, and looked old-fashioned, innocent, and well cared for.

"I live here," Domenic said.

"Nice place," I said.

"That's just the outside," he said. "I can either walk you back to the bar or wherever you're staying, or you could come in for a cup of tea."

"A cup of tea?"

"I have other things to drink too."

"I see."

He waited patiently for an answer. I was wary on principle. Men have done me wrong more than one too many times, but they aren't all bad, and Domenic seemed a step above anyone I had met in a while. Mind you, I hadn't known him that long and my instincts had once failed me so deeply I've still never quite forgiven them. But his hand felt so warm, and I was tired of being alone, always alone.

"I'll have some tea," I said.

The inside of the house was like the outside, in that cared-for manner. The wide-plank wood floors looked smooth and shiny. The furniture, a mismatch of new and old, neither in fashion, was still well considered and polished to the bone. A few family photos were hung on the walls next to several thoughtfully framed amateurish paintings of flowers, all signed by an artist named Mary.

Domenic saw me looking at one of the paintings, a bowl of daisies. "I got a good deal on those," he said.

"They're nice," I said politely. They weren't not nice.

"My mother," he said.

This made me like him more and less. He seemed harmless, for a complete stranger, maybe a little too harmless. While my mind was tumbling through dangerous scenarios, Domenic kissed me. He put one hand behind my neck and the other wrapped around my waist, and I felt human again. My needs were simple at that moment, not attached to a map with plots and schemes and an assortment of names.

His lips felt familiar. It wasn't one of those fumbling first kisses where you're all distracted by the details. Domenic pulled away and led me into the bedroom. I felt tingly and warm and expectant and safe, sensations that I thought might be lost to me forever.

And then I saw the gun and the badge on the dresser and I felt like I had just given blood, most of it. I must have visibly paled, because when Domenic turned to kiss me again, he took a step back.

"Are you all right, Debra?"

"Gun," was all I could sputter out with my heart jackhammering inside me.

"I'm sorry," Domenic said, opening the drawer and putting it inside. "It's okay, I'm a sheriff."

"You didn't mention that in the bar," I said.

"You didn't ask."

"Don't most off-duty cops carry their weapon?"

"Some do, but everyone in town knows who I am, and it always seemed pessimistic to take my gun when I'm just having a drink with friends."

I tried to breathe enough to catch my breath, but I was chasing oxygen like a marathoner.

"What's going on, Debra? Do you have something against cops?"

I sure did. But I didn't mention it. "I'm just not feeling very well. I think I better go."

"I'll walk you back."

"Not necessary," I said.

"It's late," he said.

I went to the front door and turned the knob. It was locked. The panic inside me was like an overflowing river. I fumbled with the lock. Domenic took my hands away and gave the knob a flick. He opened the door and gave me a wide berth. Until I stepped onto his porch in the cold night air, it was like I had been underwater in a swimming pool, having a breath-holding contest. I instantly felt better. Domenic noticed the look of relief on my face. He looked hurt.

He followed me back to the motel, I think just to make sure I returned safe. I stopped at the main lobby. I didn't want him to know what room I was in.

"Thank you," I said. "For, uh—the burger and the company."

"What just happened?"

"Nothing. I suddenly realized I shouldn't be alone with a stranger."

"Okay," Domenic said. "But let's say you pass through town again, we wouldn't be strangers then, would we?"

"I guess not," I said.

He reached into his wallet and handed me his card. "If you ever need anything, my mobile number is on there."

"Thanks," I said.

"Be careful out there," he said. "The world is full of all kinds of people."

"I figured that out a long time ago," I said.

May 11, 2011
To: Ryan
From: Jo

> *Did you think I wouldn't find out? I'm the only secret anyone seems able to keep these days. Everything else is out there. One hour at the library computer, checking on old friends, and I find it. Photos of Logan and Edie on a romantic vacation in Big Sur. They look so happy. How did you let that happen?*
>
> *I don't care what you have to do, what you have to tell her. Stop it.*
>
> *Jo*

* * *

June 10, 2011
To: Jo
From: Ryan

I tried. I tried before it started. I tried to stop it when I saw him look at her at the Sundowners that first time she came home after she quit college. Since I went to the hospital, people don't listen to me like they used to. I'm the crazy one. Logan's the strong, successful, responsible brother.

If it makes you feel any better, I think he's changed. Not that he's different inside, but he doesn't let that other part of him out as much. He might be good to her. I know that's not what you want to hear, but that's all I've got.

You seem to think that you can use me as a proxy. This isn't a game of chess where you can call out the moves and I'll just be the hand.

When someone is gone, and you're as good as dead here, you can't alter the course of events. If/when he does something wrong, I'll try to intervene.

June 15, 2011
To: Ryan
From: Jo

I take it married life is treating you well. I get it, you don't want to interrupt the status quo. Oh, and congratulations on your baby.

You always had a bit of a cowardly streak. I thought you'd grow out of it, not settle into it like a comfortable chair.

*I haven't asked you for anything. Fix the problem.
End them. If anything happens to Edie, it's on you. And
I won't stay quiet this time.*

    Jo

10

My first outing as Debra Maze was a reminder that my life was like a game of Jenga: if one piece was out of place, my entire world could collapse. The next day, I shoved my close call with the police out of my mind and drove the final leg of my journey.

By the time I landed in Jackson, Wyoming, I was just about dead broke. I drove on my last tank of gas to half a dozen motels and tried to strike up a deal—a warm room for services rendered. I had promised myself I would steer clear of the sanitation industry, but it was the middle of May, the school year was almost over, and I needed some time to secure my identity as Debra Maze. I didn't see myself managing all of that while bedding down in my Cadillac. I made a deal with the owner of the Moose Lodge, just off Flat Creek Drive. I even managed to get a small stipend to supplement my temporary living situation.

There was one thing I knew for sure: if this plan was going to work, I needed to figure out how to look less like Blue and more like me. Every time I passed my reflection in the mirror, I saw deceit. If I couldn't buy the lie, there was no way I could expect anyone else to.

Blue had once told me that the best way to hide in plain sight was to get fat. So I purchased three six-packs of mini-doughnuts, the kind I devoured for breakfast in junior high until my swim coach suggested I use my calories for something more nutritious.

I left my honey-blond dye job intact and touched up my roots whenever they made an entrance. For a month I maintained a strict doughnut, pizza, French fry, and beer diet, eating until I wanted to puke every night. I gained twenty pounds in three weeks. Looking at my bloated red complexion in the mirror, I felt like I could cry. My sudden fleshiness trumped the blondness that once drew stares. I became more and more invisible with each pound I gained. Once I'd packed on more than twenty-five pounds, I went to the Wyoming DMV and applied for a driver's license, using Debra Maze's social security card and birth certificate as identification. Once again, I barely passed the written exam. I returned a few days later for the road test. I fared better on that, although it didn't bode well that I failed to answer when the examiner called my new name.

When the paperwork was complete, the clerk pointed me in the direction of the line for photos. I retreated to the bathroom, plucked out those blue contact lenses, and lined up for my picture. The photographer didn't pay much attention to my paperwork. He told me to smile; I didn't. Then I was instructed to wait two to four weeks.

It took two and a half weeks for my license to arrive. Cleaning other people's filth and waiting to be discovered as a fraud, then a murderer, then who knows what else, turned each twenty-four hours into a slow-motion vigil on the long hand of a clock. When the envelope arrived at my PO box, I half expected to open it and find an arrest warrant. But there I was: Debra Maze, five foot five, one hundred and fifty pounds. Blue eyes, blond hair. Only my eyes in the photo were brown.

It took another month to finish my transition into being a Debra Maze I could live with. I dyed my hair brown— I'd spent enough years of my life bleaching my roots every month and I left those blue contacts in their case. I still hoped that, one day, someone might look into my eyes and see who I really was. That couldn't happen if my eyes were as phony as a porcelain doll's.

I quit my sumo wrestler's diet right after my first visit to the DMV. I shed twenty pounds fast, but the last five took some work. The motel had a blinking neon sign for a swimming pool. It was indoors, overheated, and the smell of chlorine wafted through the dank air and stuck in your throat. Three freestyle strokes, turn and kick, and another three strokes and you'd already completed one lap. After eleven p.m., the pool was closed to motel guests, but I had the key. It took me twenty minutes to swim one hundred laps.

I remembered being fourteen and swimming in the Waki Reservoir, thinking it was all mine because nobody knew it quite like I did. Doing abbreviated laps in that confined turquoise cement space wasn't remotely liberating or exhilarating. It was a reminder of what my life had become, like sitting in a trash compactor as it's closing in. When I was young, I thought anything was possible. The world seemed so large and available. Mine for the taking. I wished I had taken more when I had the chance.

Summer in Jackson was bright and warm and the mountains glittered. After work I'd stroll around the town under the hot sun, trying to erase the memories of all of the rooms I'd just cleaned. Some days, I'd go to a bar or a café and pretend I was just another tourist.

I barely socked away any money that summer, but I got by. I splurged on a proper haircut for once. The stylist colored my locks sandy blond and cut sharp bangs and gave the ends an even sweep just above my shoulders. When I looked in the mirror, I didn't resemble any version of Blue, but I didn't see Tanya Pitts or Amelia Keen, either. I saw someone completely new. She would go by the name of Debra Maze, but I knew I'd never really feel at home with that appellation.

I returned to the DMV, claiming that I'd lost my driver's license. Filled out the forms with one minor change. I checked the box for brown eyes instead of blue. It was nice to have one less lie to keep under my hat. Two weeks later, when my new ID arrived, I completed my transformation.

Now I was ready to make the leap from motel sanitation into the educational field. But when August and the beginning of the school year finally arrived, I was foiled immediately. I would have to undergo a constitutional exam and had to produce proof of state-accredited testing. I had Ohio paperwork, not Wyoming. Blue had made it sound so easy; she had only looked into the fingerprint challenge and hadn't considered the credential issue. My generous spirit chalked her error up to oversight. But in the back of my mind I wondered if it was deliberate.

Even lowering my expectations and applying for a substitute or teacher's assistant position was out of range in the real world. So I widened my net and found a small private school in a town called—I kid you not—Recluse, Wyoming. The school was bankrolled by the estate of John Allen Campbell, Recluse's most distinguished citizen. In a town where there's no industry or nothing happens, the tiny schoolhouse was hard up for a third-and-fourth-grade teacher. I e-mailed Blue's revised résumé and it only took a few days before I got a call for an interview.

A heat wave was just getting started that day. I wore a modest sundress and practical shoes, the kind I figured a teacher dealing with watercolors might wear. I hit the road early to make a good impression. The Cadillac felt like a sauna even as I was pumping air into the car; I watched the thermostat rise precariously. I took a few breaks to let the engine cool down.

I still arrived an hour before my appointment time, steaming off the highway into a town that seemed to be surviving in a chokehold, one tight squeeze away from becoming a ghost town. I found a gas station with an attendant and mentioned my car's difficulties. Gil, the mechanic, gave me a strong reprimand for not checking fluid levels. He made a good point. Once the Cadillac was rehydrated, Gil pointed me in the direction of John Allen Campbell Primary School.

I found Principal Walt Collins sitting behind a desk in a room not much larger than a storage closet. It looked like it might have been the maid's quarters one day a long time ago, when someone of means might have lived in this forgotten town. Hell, maybe it was his family's home. Principal Collins was long past the age of retirement and I had to wonder if he was holding on to this job because no one else would have it.

I had spent so much time bracing myself over the past six months that it was hard to notice when something was going right. I should have known when I walked through the front door that Collins was desperate and ready to hire anyone. You can never see anything clearly when you're running. That nervous buzz in your brain deafens the sounds of the outside world. But people believe what they want to believe. I was a pretty young woman applying for a job Mr. Collins needed to fill. All he saw was an honest, out-of-work educator, looking for a simple life in a small town.

"What brought you to the teaching profession, Miss Maze?"

"When I was young, I hated school." The truth when possible.

"You wanted to figure out how to reach children who had the same resistance to education as you did?" Principal Collins said.

"Yes, exactly."

"I see you worked for five years at an elementary school in Akron, Ohio."

"Yes."

"And you got your teaching credential from Cleveland State University?"

"Go Vikings," I said. Then I regretted it.

"Are you a football fan?"

"Not so much."

"I see you didn't list any references on your résumé. Was there a problem at your former school?"

"I'm afraid I have to bring up something delicate. I hope it doesn't leave this room, whether you decide to employ me or not. I had a husband back in Akron. He was not— he is not—a good man. When I left, I didn't provide any forwarding information. I have lived off of savings and have avoided using credit cards and anything else that could lead him to my current location." Always go with the partial truth when you can.

"Was he a violent man?" Principal Collins asked, adjusting his forehead to properly convey sympathy. He was playing a part just as much as I was.

I nodded my head, as if saying it aloud was too painful.

"I see," Principal Collins said, making a few minute adjustments to his forehead again.

"My husband can be very persuasive. I'm afraid that if anyone is called for a reference, they might inform him where that call originated. I lasted five years at that school. That's got to count for something."

"I'm sorry you had to go through that."

"It's in the past," I said. "Where I hope it will stay."

The conversation needed shifting. It was time to play the only card I had. I fished through my backpack and pulled out my fingerprint card. I slid it across the table to Principal Collins.

"I believe you need this for the background check."

"It seems you've come prepared," Collins said.

"Just dotting the i's."

Collins stared down at the card as if he wasn't quite sure what to do with it.

"We can't pay you much," he said.

"I understand."

"And there isn't much for a young woman to do with herself around here. You can see that, right?"

"I've never had grand ambitions," I said.

When I said that, I suddenly realized how many ambitions I had lost along the way. It was one of the biggest lies I had ever told.

"You're hired. You can start Monday."

I gave him the broad smile and flitter of excitement that I knew he needed to feel comfortable sealing the deal. It felt like pure theater. The better I got at the performance, the more I despised the show. But I got what I needed: a decent job, money, a new life.

"You have a place to live?" Collins asked.

"I'll start looking right away."

"Until you find something permanent, or even if you don't, we've got a little apartment in the basement. One hundred and fifty a month."

I took it sight unseen. I would need to be saving my pennies. Considering all that had transpired since Frank tumbled down the stairs, it was a great day. And yet, I would have given anything to be me again, whoever she was.

11

"Wake up. Wake up, Andrew."

Andrew raised his head from the desk and rubbed sleep out of his eyes.

"Good morning," Andrew said. He always said that when I woke him up.

"Do you need a cup of coffee?" I asked.

"No, I'm good," Andrew said.

"My mom lets me drink coffee," Abby said.

"My mom lets me have a sip of her beer sometimes," Cody said.

A chorus of beverage-consumption confessions followed, and order had to be restored.

"You can all discuss your drinking habits at recess. Back to our lesson."

I directed my quiet attention to Maggie. She was the alpha girl in my class of eighteen third and fourth graders. "Maggie, can you tell me the capital of Georgia?" I deliberately gave her an easy one to boost her ego.

"Atlanta."

"Very good. Who knows the capital of Oklahoma?"

Martin shouted, "Oklahoma City!" before he was called on.

"Martin, thank you for volunteering for our road trip game."

This was my twist on a geography lesson. Behind me were regional road maps of the US pieced together like a bad puzzle. I'd requested one huge national road map for my class, but since most curriculums don't care about highway arteries, I was denied. We were missing most of North and South Dakota, part of Michigan, and a small chunk of the Virginias.

"Martin, what is the capital of Idaho?"

"Boise."

"And what is the capital of Washington state?"

"Seattle?"

"I don't think so. Abby, do you know?"

Abby knew all of the capitals, plus the first ten presidents and the last three, and could multiply any two-digit number by a single-digit number. But she never raised her hand.

"Olympia," Abby said.

"Thank you," I said. "Now, Abby, let's say you're in Olympia, Washington, and you want to drive to Boise, Idaho. How would you get there?"

Abby timidly approached the map board and studied our collage, tracing her finger along the prominent blue lines.

"I'd take I-5 South, and then in Portland take 84 East or South. It goes both ways."

"Very good," I said. "Some highways run in clear

directions. North and south, east and west. Some take you in directions you'd never expect."

The bell rang for recess. I didn't make my class wait, like Miss June's combined first and second grade, for my go-ahead. The bell rang and they were free. I rolled my whiteboard in front of our map wall. My lesson plan wasn't exactly a secret, but I didn't put it on display. Once when Principal Collins asked me about my unorthodox teaching methods, I mentioned that the world today had become too dependent on GPS systems. Since no one in Recluse was too dependent on GPS systems, I could tell he didn't buy my argument—especially for eight- to ten-year-olds. So I told him I thought it encouraged problem solving. Privately, I wanted these children in this middle-of-nowhere town to look outside of it and start imagining all of the places they could go. And I wanted to learn a few things myself, if I was going to spend all day in a classroom.

Not that I didn't learn new things, or have my memory refreshed. I certainly never had the entire line of US presidents memorized before I took this job. I crammed all night for the next day's class, trying to create character associations with each commander in chief. But I still got stumped. The assignment was for students to bring in two biographical sketches of different presidents. They were encouraged to avoid the overexposed ones—Washington, Jefferson, Lincoln, either Roosevelt. Each student would stand in front of the classroom and read his or her sketch. Then the class would guess which president fit the bill.

"My president was born in Virginia in 1784. He was a member of the Whig party, a general in the army, and he died in office," said Andrew. He was the presidential expert in the class. He didn't simply have the names memorized, he could provide a general biography and occasionally some amusing trivia.

"Class, which president is Andrew talking about?" I said, improvising. I didn't have a clue who Andrew was talking about.

Presidential names bounced around the room without any guess becoming the dominating choice. Normally when I ran into gaps in my own education, I would simply say, "Class, what's the answer?" and I could rely on the general consensus being correct.

"Grover Cleveland!"

"James Buchanan!"

"Ulysses S. Grant!"

The way Andrew blandly regarded his classmates let me know that, so far, no one had hit the nail on the head. I decided to cut through the noise.

"Andrew," I said. "Congratulations. You've stumped the class. Why don't you tell everyone which president you chose?"

"Zachary Taylor, the twelfth president of the United States."

"Right. Zachary Taylor. Who's next?"

Some days the classroom felt as precarious as being on the road with Blue. One false move, one fact misstated, a child tattles to the parent, the parent starts to ask questions, one bad answer, more questions. If anyone really looked at me, they'd realize I was a fraud.

Trotting out my new identification still felt like walking under a row of icicles, so I was grateful to circumvent the perilous apartment hunt, but living inside a schoolhouse was hardly without its own drawbacks. My standard of living had plummeted in recent months, but when you start to look at things in a more permanent light, you start to question your standards. The schoolhouse apartment would have been advertised in the newspaper as a studio with a bathroom and kitchenette. It was furnished with a double bed and a wardrobe. The mattress on the bed was probably produced in the sixties or seventies. It had a deep end and a shallow end. No matter how much I tried to sleep in the shallow end, I found myself floating into the deep. I've slept comfortably on floors before and I considered it as an option, but something about the look of that well-traveled carpet discouraged me. The only thing to recommend the place was that it had a private entrance off the parking lot. The other door, secured by only a hook latch, led up a narrow staircase to the schoolhouse.

In a small town and an even smaller school, I knew to be friendly but to keep a healthy distance from my coworkers. There were only four of them, besides Principal Collins, so it wasn't all that difficult. There were June, Cora, Collette (whose real name was Jane; *Collette* sounded more Continental), and Joe, the only man. Joe had left Recluse ten years ago and made a solemn promise to himself never to return. Then his mom got sick, and then his dad, and he broke his own word, like so many of us do. My gut told me that Collette had an unrequited crush on Joe, so I did my best to pretend the man was invisible, since I was the only other woman of childbearing age on staff.

A new woman in a town where nothing happens is caviar bait. Collette's questions came like automatic-weapon fire. I tried to keep my answers short. Where do you hail from? *Ohio.* Ever been married? *Once.* What brings you to Recluse? *Recluse would take me.* If I shifted the conversation back to Collette, she could launch into some long-winded discussion about her sister's no-good boyfriend or her big plans to move to Jackson and buy one of those houses she once saw in a home décor magazine. People of modest means, she said, think they're unattainable because all they see is the price tag, but if you build one yourself, hell, all you need is some unclaimed land, lumber, a hammer, and some nails. At least that was Collette's line of thinking. She never did mention having a talent for carpentry.

As skilled as I was at returning Collette's volley of questions, I found Cora and June to be slightly more aggressive opponents. I don't think either had an agenda beyond curiosity and coloring in those dull gray patches in the day, but I chose to keep my distance. The staff had a spin-wheel chart designating recess and lunchtime yard duty. I cited fresh air as my excuse and marked myself down for all Monday through Friday lunch shifts. Most of the teachers, when given the opportunity, were happy for a reprieve from any student contact. I was left to my own devices for a while, enjoyed the peace when I got it, and broke up a few fights, bandaged a few knees, and tended to a few tears. Well, more than a few. My own recollection of my elementary school days was foggy at best. I remembered jungle gyms and accidents, alphabets and punishments, but I didn't remember the ceaseless weeping.

I never quite got the hang of how to comfort someone trapped in a salt mine of tears. I learned young that my mother would pay more attention to me if I didn't give in to emotion. Once I sliced open my knee when I crashed my bike and landed on a piece of glass. I didn't bother sopping up the blood. I walked home letting the crimson waterfall slide down my leg. I composed myself as I stepped on the porch and knocked on the door.

"I think I cut myself," I said so calmly even I stopped feeling the pain. It was the most attentive my mother ever was in my life.

With my class, I bribed the tears away. I kept candy in my purse, and anyone who could stanch the flow of waterworks got a Band-Aid and a packet of corn syrup worms or dinosaurs or bears, depending on their zoological preference. I got the feeling my colleagues didn't approve of my candy comforts.

Just a week into my tenure, Cora Lane decided I needed some company during my recess and lunch breaks. Cora was somewhere between fifty-five and seventy. Her big brown eyes had a youthful sparkle and her voice had a clear, even tone, missing any of the crackles of age. But her skin had a road map of creases that could have been from age, hardship, or a long, unrepentant love affair with the sun. She took a seat next to mine, after swiping the bench clean of dust, bird shit, and the drippings from a strawberry yogurt.

"Lovely day, isn't it," Cora said.

"Yes."

"My favorite time of year."

It was bright and sunny, the way most people like. I wouldn't have minded a bit of wind or rain or a chill in the air. The end of summer conjures images of one's childhood more than any other season. But all I said was yes. Two weather comments is the standard before following up with personal inquiries.

"How are you enjoying yourself here?" Cora asked.

"Very much."

"Why are you here?"

It's like a bull's-eye. The first question might miss the target completely, but then they start landing on the red outer rim and finally they just start aiming at the sweet spot in the middle. The only thing you can do is change the target.

"Excuse me?"

"You're young, you're pretty, you've got a lot of life left to live. Why would you move to a town that's already dead?"

Cora was more blunt than I thought she was capable of being. Something about the way her sun-battered forehead awaited a response made me want to give her an answer. Not an honest one, but one that would at least make her feel like she had been taken into confidence and trusted. In another life, I would have trusted her. Maybe we would have even been friends. The real kind.

"I have an ex-husband. He's looking for me. I figure the fewer people I know, the less likely it is that he'll find me."

"Did he . . . ?" Cora asked, letting the sentence hang with obvious implication.

"Yes."

"Oh, dear. I'm so sorry."

"Don't be. I'm free now. And I think I can be happy here."

This time, I didn't quite believe that statement.

The nights were quiet, too quiet. The school emptied out; the staff returned to their respective homes. Garth, the janitor, performed his cursory floor mopping and toilet scrubbing. When he left, it was quiet as a cave. I killed the hours by roaming the halls, exploring the study boards in other classrooms, and visiting the "computer lab." Once a linen closet, it now contained a decade-old IBM computer with an extremely sluggish Internet connection. It could take three hours just to read half a dozen news stories. But I had nothing but time to kill, and a few stories needed my attention.

Frank's death, according to the latest reports, remained

suspicious. I continued to be a person of interest. My whereabouts, I'm pleased to say, were still unknown. Although there were some Tanya Dubois sightings in some places I wouldn't have minded visiting. I'd always wanted to go to New York City.

The next news report I came upon was a bit more disheartening. A male body, thirty to forty years of age, had been found in Lake Somerville State Park. Some campers discovered it. More specifically, their hunting dog had a meltdown at the grave site. The campers—overly curious, if you ask me—thought something about the terrain was odd and started digging until they disinterred the body. Then they called the police. According to the papers, the police had no leads, and dental records were useless due to the location of the gunshot wound. A phone number at the end of the article asked for anyone with information to contact the authorities.

I'll admit I was surprised. I thought Jack would stay put and I'd never have to think of him again. In the scheme of things, I was due for a cosmic oversight. That said, without identifying the body, drumming up suspects could be challenging. I had to hope that Jack Reed would remain John Doe forever.

I also looked into those two thugs that Mr. Oliver sent after me. The police were convinced it was related to organized crime since they were shot execution-style. I wondered if Blue considered that at the time, or whether she was just firing on adrenaline. I doubted that I'd ever know.

For the first few weeks at John Allen Campbell Primary, I

probably checked my old selves half a dozen times. The news was always the same, and I realized that the itchy paranoia that accompanied looking back wasn't doing me any good. If I really was going to try to have a life for myself, I needed to be Debra Maze and no one else. I had learned some time ago that it isn't healthy to revisit the past.

Once I staked my claim on the lunch benches, Cora joined me intermittently. Whenever I saw her coming, I'd start compiling a list of questions to keep the conversation spinning in the right direction. Cora was a nice woman but not the most fascinating one. Still, I relied on her as an ally. I was good at thinking my own thoughts while mumbling encouraging conversation prompters—*yes*, *uh-huh*, *you don't say*—to make her think that her audience hadn't lost interest. I couldn't tell you much about her, even now, but when something important cropped up in conversation, I always managed to wake up and latch on to it.

Only a year ago, a second-grade teacher, young—maybe my age, maybe a little older, said Cora—had died. Fell off a ladder while changing a lightbulb in her garage. Hit her head. Cora offered all the information I needed. Widowed, hence the solo lightbulb change. Dead parents. One sister. Her name was Emma Lark.

That night I strolled into the admissions office, opened the unlocked file cabinet, and found all the paperwork I could on Emma. There were photocopies of her driver's license, birth certificate, and social security card. I made copies, returned the second generation to the file, and shoved mine into the inside pocket of my suitcase.

Emma Lark sounded like a gift that was long overdue. A woman, almost my age, dying in a town that didn't even have its own cemetery. Emma Lark was certainly a name one could live with. It was at the very least a solid spare. If I'd learned anything in the past six months, it was that one name was never enough.

February 9, 2012
To: Ryan
From: Jo

I'm having an affair. I suppose I should feel guilty, but that particular emotion was recalibrated a long time ago. I don't think it will ever operate normally. After six years of having sex with only him, it was like an electric charge. I feel alive, almost. It's definitely not love, but it's something more real than anything I've known since I became someone else.

He's a chiropractor. I've had back problems since the accident. No doctor has ever been able to provide a diagnosis. X-rays, MRIs, all show nothing and yet the pain persists. Sometimes I think of it as my conscience. But Dr. Mike sees it or feels it like a shaman. He knew I was in a car accident the first time he laid his hands on me. That's the closest I'll get these days to being understood. I don't know why I'm telling you all this. Maybe I just need to confess.

It feels like the world is moving forward, lives are being lived, and I'm stuck in this place in a half-life that will never be anything more.

I see you didn't fix the problem I told you to fix. You just keep breaking my heart.

Jo

March 10, 2012
To: Jo
From: Ryan
We're all in a half-life. It's not just you.

12

I had been at Campbell Primary just a month when the walls of John Allen's childhood home started feeling less like a safe haven and more like a prison. During the days I was kept alive by an assault of questions, tantrums, tattles, and shrieks that I'm fairly certain were doing permanent damage to my eardrums. At night I roamed the musty old house like a ghost.

Rainy days fucked with my equilibrium just as they did for the children. We had all grown weary of the close confines of the classroom walls. Children weren't meant to be shuttered in a large house all day long. As expansive as the old Campbell home was for a single family, try teaching a class of eight-, nine-, and ten-year-olds in an antique bedroom, still dripping in gold leaf wallpaper and thick velvet curtains. Instead of individual desks, the students sat along old dining tables, probably pilfered from other nearby houses that had come to ruin. We had to position all of the lefties at the ends of the tables to avoid the jostling and jousting of elbows.

During inclement weather we corralled the students into the old living room, which had been refurbished into an auditorium of sorts. Just picture any living room, and then add a few slabs of plywood hammered together and propped up on some legs and a bright velvet curtain in front of it. Three dozen folding chairs provided all of the seating required.

I watched Melissa, my all-too-earnest third grader, play the most dismal game of hide-and-seek I had ever witnessed. All of my other students seemed to have a solid grasp of the concept. Nolan hid in plain sight, tucked in the curtain crevice, his maroon sweatshirt serving as camouflage. Tiny Lola managed to wedge herself under a warren of chairs, tucked under a pile of rain slickers. Andrea locked herself in the dressing room (which was just a closet), and ginger-haired Martin fell asleep under a tarp. Melissa, an only child as I later learned, crouched at the base of the stage and giggled, discovered within seconds by Andrew, who showed obvious disappointment with the ease of detection.

I killed the rest of my lunch hour walking Melissa through the auditorium and pointing out superior hiding places—under the collection of knapsacks, in the janitor's closet, the crawl space under the stage (although I couldn't vouch for its structural integrity), the women's restroom (only if you stand on the toilet and leave the stall door unlocked), and under her winter coat, if she placed it just right over one of the auditorium seats. When I was certain that Melissa had reached her saturation point on our lesson plan, I leaned down, looked her in the eye, and tried to bring it home.

"Hide-and-seek may be just a game, but it's a game you ought to know how to play."

Some days, standing in front of the chalkboard, seeing all that innocence reflected back at me, I tried to tell myself that this was something that resembled a life. If it was going to stick, however, I had to get out from inside the walls of John Allen Campbell Primary School. My life was prison enough; I had to at least fool myself into the assumption that I was a free woman. It took a few weeks before I ventured out; I was pinching pennies until my first paycheck arrived. As soon as I had the check in my hands I drove two towns over to the local savings and loan and cashed the check. I put seven hundred dollars in an envelope and stowed it between the ancient mattress and the box spring. My money wouldn't earn any interest under my bed, but at least I wouldn't have to contend with ATM limits if I was ever on the run again.

Recluse, like every other town on the brink of extinction, looked like a bunch of shoe boxes glued together with windows painted on. It had a small grocery store that carried a lot of canned goods and wilted vegetables, a diner, and two bars. The teachers sometimes would get drinks at this place called the Homestead after work. I always declined their invitation. It was risky enough spending six or so hours a day in the vicinity of the exact same folk. I certainly wasn't going to join in an activity known for loosening lips and weakening resolve. So I found another watering hole on the edge of town, the other edge. Just over a mile from the schoolhouse.

When you walk into a bar for the first time, you can be anyone; you set the tone for every visit after that. I was Ms. Maze all day long, with sticky fingers and high-pitched voices clamoring for my attention. At the Lantern, I would finally receive the quiet that the days denied me.

I sat down at the bar and ordered a draft beer. I'd already given up imparting sophisticated tastes to Debra Maze. Besides, a beer sounded perfect after a breathtakingly bad lesson plan on grammar. Yes, a horse is a noun; a fork is a noun; a tire is a noun, and yet when I tried to explain how *strength*, *courage*, and *stubbornness* were also nouns, I could almost sense a mutiny.

"Haven't seen you around," the bartender said. It wasn't a question.

"First time," I said, trying to plot the conversation in advance without knowing the sharp turns it might take.

"What the hell would bring you to Recluse?"

"That's a good question," I said.

Some people are satisfied to let their questions dangle like a participle (we would not be having that lesson any time this year).

"My name's Sean, if you need anything."

I guess he was the kind of person who might let a question dangle.

I drank my beer and reread *From the Mixed-Up Files of Mrs. Basil E. Frankweiler*, the book I'd assigned to the class because

it was one I remembered so fondly from my childhood. In the
book a brother and sister run away from home and hide in the
Metropolitan Museum of Art. We didn't have any museums
in my hometown, but I did manage to break into the local
library when I was eleven and slept through the night. It
wasn't as exciting as I'd hoped it would be and I got in a hell
of a lot of trouble, but knowing that I could pull it off, slip
unnoticed between the stacks as Mrs. Cragmire swept the
library for patrons, gave me a certain sense of pride.

As I composed comprehension and discussion questions
for the class—*If you could break into any establishment in
Recluse, what would it be?*—I clocked the other patrons in
the bar, trying to get an angle on what would make someone
move to a town that had a two-to-one bar-to-diner ratio.
Apparently oblivion was much more important in Recluse
than sustenance.

Sean asked me if I wanted a refill. When he slid the pint
glass in front of my reading material, he seemed to come to
some conclusions about me.

"You must be the new teacher," Sean said.

I took inventory of Sean the second time he passed my way.
His age was hard to figure. He could have been forty-eight or
sixty-five. He was lean like a panther. His face was etched with
deep, perfectly symmetrical lines, lines that suggested he did
his fair share of smiling. His eyelids were hooded and tired,
hiding dark brown eyes. His hair needed a trimming; he kept
flicking it out of his eyes, like he was swatting a fly. He had all
of his teeth, which I couldn't say about too many other folks

in this establishment. He wore the uniform of the town: a plaid shirt, worn blue jeans, and work boots that looked like they'd seen more than the beer-stained floor of a saloon.

"That would be me," I said.

"I've heard about you," he said.

"What have you heard?"

"I heard you like road maps."

"You have a good source."

"I do," Sean said with a tiny smirk.

"I guess people talk in a town this size."

"My source is better than town gossip."

"Now you've got me curious," I said.

Maybe my voice had an edge to it. Maybe it didn't. I tried to hold my expression steady and open, but I didn't much like the idea of people talking about me and coming to conclusions.

"My grandson's in your class."

The tingling sensation in the back of my neck quieted.

"Is that so? Your grandson got a name?"

"Andrew."

"Andrew," I said.

With the connection drawn, I saw the resemblance, which is often the only time you spot it. They had the same red lips, and come to think of it, Andrew's eyes were kind of heavy for an eight-year-old.

"Has he made an impression?" Sean asked.

He had. Andrew's mother was always late to pick him up. Since I had nowhere to go, I always sat with him on the stoop. We'd sit and gossip about presidents. Well, Andrew did. Apparently Franklin Roosevelt wore dresses when he was a child; Abraham Lincoln was a licensed bartender; Grover Cleveland was a hangman; Andrew Johnson was a tailor. It's quite possible that Andrew—the child, not the president—had taught me more than I taught him. Not exactly a ringing endorsement for our educational system, but let's hope that unqualified teachers working under an assumed name are an anomaly.

I leaned in and whispered, "Tell you the truth, he's my favorite."

"He's my favorite too," said Sean. "You got him thinking about places other than Wyoming, places he might want to see. My daughter doesn't know anything but this town, so she can't advise him about the world beyond, but I'm hoping he gets out. I'm thinking you're giving him directions out of here. I hope he remembers them when the time comes."

"Me too."

A customer named Dave, covered in work dust, approached the bar. Sean poured his drink en route.

"You are a mind reader," Dave said.

"Cheers," said Sean.

No money exchanged hands, but a mild gesture communicated some kind of transaction. Dave returned to his table. Sean wiped the already shiny bar down with a rag. Either habit, or he was trying to stay close. He pretended to be working on a spot that was really a scrape that would only vanish with sandpaper.

"What are you really doing here?" Sean asked.

"Having a beer. Well, two beers, and to be perfectly honest, maybe three."

"No. Here. In Recluse."

"What is anyone doing anywhere? We all have to be someplace."

"Look around," said Sean. "Everyone in this bar was born here. Most had plans to leave at one time or another, but then at some point they got caught in a snare, and like an animal, lacked the cunning to undo the clamp."

"What was your snare?" I asked.

"This bar. I worked here a few years after I turned eighteen, was saving money to go to Alaska, where I heard real money could be had. Homer, the owner, had no kin and when he got lung cancer, he just left the whole thing to me."

"That was generous," I said.

Sean finally put down that rag, dropped two shot glasses on the table, and poured some decent stuff.

"Was it?" he said. "Because lately I've been thinking that Homer knew what he was doing. Way back in the day, when I'd talk about getting out, being free of Recluse, Homer liked to take a hammer to my dreams, knocking the legs out of my plans. I think he liked the idea of others facing his same sorry fate. Then he didn't feel as alone as he always had been. I think his *generous* gift was a curse, and he knew it. His final act as a dying man was to make sure that someone followed in his sorry footsteps."

"That's quite a sinister theory you've got there," I said.

Sean shrugged and slid the shot glass in front of me. He raised his.

"What are we drinking to?" I asked.

"To escape plans?"

"Whose?"

"Anyone with the guts," said Sean.

We clinked glasses. I downed my shot, put a few bills on the bar, and slid off the bar stool. Sean nodded so slightly it was almost imperceptible.

"Come back," he said.

"I'll think about it," I said.

But I knew I'd be back. I had no other place to go.

The next day Andrew and I were sitting on the stoop when Cora stepped outside and craned her neck to get a longer look down the road.

"Did you see that man?"

"What man?"

"There was this guy watching the school earlier. He was just standing outside the fence while the kids were at lunch. Then I just saw him again through my office window."

"Did he try talking to them?"

"No. He just stood there, like he was looking for someone."

"Maybe he's a relative of one of the kids or something."

"I know everyone's kin," said Cora.

"Really?"

"Yes," Cora said sadly. "It's that kind of town."

"I'll keep my eyes open," I said. "It's probably nothing."

Thing is, I knew it wasn't nothing. You know that stumbling walk you do after you've tripped? That's what my brain felt like.

"Have you ever been to the Metropolitan Museum of Art?" Andrew asked.

We'd been talking about our class assignment and Andrew had gotten quite fixated not just on the idea of breaking into a place and staying the night, but on art museums and places that only big cities had to offer. It's not that he hadn't been some places worth seeing—the Grand Tetons, cowboy museums—but he was taking note of a world out there beyond his imagination. Lying low all this time, I hadn't seen much of the world, either.

"I'm afraid I haven't," I said.

"Have you been to New York City?"

"No."

"Huh." He looked disappointed in me, as if some of my shine had worn off.

If he only knew.

Before Andrew could quiz me any further about my narrow worldview, his mother mercifully arrived.

Recluse offered a limited number of patterns for a life to take. I had only been there a month and I was beating a well-worn path. There were lessons all day, class cleanup in the afternoon. A few nights a week I stayed in my basement apartment, made noodles on a hot plate, and studied up for the next day's assignment. A few other nights a week, always at least one night on the weekend, I ventured into the Lantern. I had one or two drinks, on rare occasions three, but I knew better than to get blotto.

On a three-drink night, Sean invited me to Andrew's birthday party, the next weekend at Dead Horse Lake, another name that didn't exactly instill confidence. Sean was taking his grandson and a few family friends out fishing on a friend's boat. Maybe another kid from the class would come, but so far no one had accepted the invitation. On a one-drink night, I would have thought wiser of exposing myself to a full day of socializing, but I accepted the invitation.

The next weekend I boarded a boat, baited a fishing rod that Sean had brought just for me, sat under a cold cloudy sky, and waited for something to bite. Andrew whined about the chill in the air. He'd managed one companion. His name was Clark. He was one grade below, had a deviated septum and a pronounced lisp. It was easy to conclude that Andrew didn't much care for Clark, but he was better than nothing, which was an idea that I was all too well acquainted with. Also on board the *Royal Fortune*—the boat's owner had affection for pirate lore, I learned—was Andrew's perpetually tardy mother, Shawna, and her boyfriend, Cal, who as far as I could tell was under a strict word quota for the day. He answered questions with a minimalism that would have impressed a monk under a vow of silence. If a nod could suffice instead of a yes or no, Cal took that option. Sean had also invited a few of his fishing buddies, all amiable sun-baked men far more interested in the cooler of Bud Light than any bounty the lake had to offer.

The wind picked up at midday and the sky swirled gray and blue and dank. The cold air felt like impending rain. We weren't far from shore, so Sean suggested we wait it out despite the lurching of the boat and Andrew's determined pleas to return to land. No one caught anything and Clark was leaning over the railing, fighting to keep the contents of his stomach from spilling into the choppy waters.

I picked up a beer, uncapped it, and got tossed onto the deck at the bow, spilling the watery brew all over my shirt. I heard a howl and when I returned my gaze to where Clark had been buckling over the railing, he was gone.

My companions were staring into the blue abyss, panic pumping their blood but also freezing their feet in place. I quickly shucked my shoes and jacket and jumped overboard.

Diving into the frigid lake knocked the breath out of me. I surfaced in the choppy waters, gobbled air, and dove under, eyes searching in the murk. *There are no damn fish in this godforsaken lake*, I thought. There was also no sign of Clark.

I kicked to the surface again, to check for signs of him. On deck, they were all gesturing for me to swim toward the bow. I crawled against the current, dove under again, and caught a glimpse of Clark's orange windbreaker, the color choice a stroke of luck. I grasped a tiny purchase on his sleeve, pulling him into a vise grip until I could swing my other arm around him and lift him above the lapping waves. He gurgled and coughed, and I saw the lifesaver Sean had thrown overboard. I backstroked until I had my free arm looped around it.

Clark thrashed in my arms, still in a panic. I wasn't sure how we were going to get him on the boat. But Sean was quick on his feet and tossed me a rope. I tied it under Clark's arms and the crew hoisted him up along the gunwale. When he was safely on board, I dolphin-kicked over to the pontoon ladder and climbed back on deck.

Clark and I huddled under a blanket while Sean guided the motorboat back to dock at such a clip, he forgot to release the throttle and beached, which caused a sound that would have made the boat's owner cry dollar signs.

Andrew, Clark, and I drove in Sean's four-seater pickup back to Recluse. The heat was cranked so high, I could see drips of sweat spilling down Andrew's cheeks. He didn't say a word. He simply looked cautiously back and forth between me and Clark.

"You okay, young man?" Sean asked the sopping-wet boy.

Clark stuttered a bit before he spoke. "I-I-I don't feel like throwing up anymore."

We dropped the boy off first at his parents' house. It was a cabin so small and square you could hardly imagine it fitting more than a single room inside. I watched the exchange through the fogged-up window of the truck. They seemed to take matters in stride. The mother took him into the house to get him out of his clothes, and the father nodded earnestly and patted Sean on the shoulders in that no-hard-feelings kind of way. At some point Sean gestured toward our truck and the father saluted me, as a signal of thanks, I suppose.

Andrew climbed in the middle of the front seat next to me.

"I can't wait to tell everyone at school about this," he said.

I knew then that my days in Recluse were numbered. I just hadn't started the countdown yet.

13

I got the nickname Nemo because Andrew told the class I swam like a dolphin. Being landlocked, the kids had never heard of any of the Sea World stars, so they named me after the only famous fish they could think of. It beat Shamu. The local rag gave it all a small write-up. I generally avoided having my picture taken, but one of my colleagues managed to capture from a distance a grainy shot of me refereeing a game of dodgeball. Because the tiny paper was run by a retired newsman, not inclined toward modern technology, the article never made it online. I ran a series of searches on "Debra Maze" just to be sure. I found others, and I think I caught a reference to the real one—a missing person from Ohio. But I figured I was safe for a while.

I figured wrong.

Clark didn't warm to me as I had expected after I pulled him from the lake. I used to catch him giving me sidelong glances whenever he was in my vicinity. I could always feel a cactus resting softly on my neck when he looked my way. If I tried to meet his gaze, he'd avert his eyes. If I offered a greeting, warm and friendly, he returned it with a mumble and an almost imperceptible nod.

Andrew had noted Clark's unease and commented one afternoon while we kept our vigil on the stoop, awaiting his mother.

"I think some boys don't like to be saved by girls," Andrew said.

Even though we had just been discussing whether the Boston Tea Party resulted in a spell of overly caffeinated fish in Boston Harbor, the transition didn't shake me. I knew exactly what Andrew was talking about.

"Why do you bring that up?" I asked.

"Clark looks scared of you now or something," said Andrew.

"I noticed that too."

"Don't seem right, you saving his life and all. He should be grateful."

"You don't save a person for the gratitude."

"Have you done that before?" Andrew asked. "Saved a life?"

"I guess so," I said.

"What did you do?"

It had been a long time since I had spoken anything true about my past. I could have evaded the question, but it was easy to be yourself around a child. Besides, I felt like Andrew of all people deserved the truth.

"I pulled someone out of the water who might have drowned otherwise," I said.

"Did the person also fall off of a boat?"

"No, the person was trapped in a car after we drove off a bridge."

"Why did you drive off a bridge?"

"That's a really good question," I said as I realized I was saying too much.

"See, I knew you'd done it before," Andrew said.

"Just that once."

"Was it a boy or a girl that you saved?" Andrew asked.

"A boy."

"Was he grateful?"

I felt a lump in my throat. For a moment I wasn't sure I could hold back the tears. "No. He was not."

I could feel another question on the tip of Andrew's tongue, but then his mother pulled up in front of the schoolhouse and he gathered his books together.

"See you tomorrow, Ms. Maze."

"Tomorrow, Andrew."

I saw the man after Shawna's Pontiac was long gone. He was standing across the empty street watching me, or maybe he had been watching Andrew. When our eyes met, he should have walked away. Any man these days knows that loitering outside a schoolhouse is suspect, no matter what his intent. Instead he just stood there, letting me memorize his face for a sketch artist.

He looked perfectly ordinary, aside from that unwavering

gaze. He wore unflattering tan trousers and a button-down blue shirt with a wrinkled cardigan. He had on scuffed-up sneakers, perfect for making a quick and quiet escape. His cold brown eyes were stuck in a squint. We stared at each other across the asphalt divide. I stood up and walked down the steps, waiting for him to say something.

"Beautiful afternoon, isn't it, ma'am?" his said in a slow, lazy tone.

"Who are you?" I said.

I figured he'd run, but he didn't.

"I think the more pertinent question is, *who are you?*"

Then the ordinary-looking man nodded a good-bye and walked away.

I went to the Lantern for a drink to settle my nerves. I hadn't yet established a regular order at the bar, but Sean poured me a whiskey before I even sat down. As it turned out, that was what I was thirsty for. It went down so smooth, like gulping water after a scorching day in the sun. He poured me another. We had an unspoken exchange of head nods and eyebrow lifts. Sean thought I looked tired. I agreed. The constant vigilance of life as an impostor had begun to take its toll. Being a sentry even in sleep can only be sustained for so long.

The door to the bar whined open and shut. I felt the flash of daylight blink on and off. Wood-soled boots clopped slowly along the concrete floor, adding a beat to the John

Fogerty song playing in the background. The man in the boots took a seat one bar stool away from mine. Before he spoke, before I recognized the voice; before I saw the face I had seen before, I could feel it was him. I also knew he had come for me, even though he held his gaze on the shiny stable of booze that hung on the mirrored wall behind the bar. If he'd tried to catch my eye through the reflection, I wouldn't have seen it. I stared straight down at my drink and tried to make myself as small as possible.

Sean approached the new patron.

"What can I get you?"

"Two of whatever she's having," he said.

His voice scared me, even though I kind of liked the tenor of it. It was a deep and solid voice, missing some of that twang you often get in these rural parts. I remained mute with the foolish notion that I could somehow slip away unnoticed. Sean poured the man two whiskeys. I finished my drink and started a slow climb off the bar stool. Just when I thought I might be able to leave without any trouble, he slid the second whiskey in front of me.

"Have a drink with me, Debra."

This caught Sean's attention, since I had yet to arrive or leave the bar with another person or show the slightest interest in getting acquainted with anyone besides Sean and a mixed bag of students.

"This a friend of yours, Debra?"

"We didn't know each other for very long," he said. "But Debra here made an impression."

"She does that," Sean said.

He must have seemed more friendly than sinister to Sean. I've discovered that men don't always pick up on the dark subtext.

Sean extended his hand to the man and said, "Sean. Proprietor."

The man said, "Domenic. Customer."

"Pleasure meeting you. Now, how do you know our Debra?"

This time I had only Sean to blame for encouraging the conversation. From what I saw his pleasantries were a guise to feed his hungry curiosity about me.

"It's a long story," Domenic said.

"Well, I'll leave you two to catch up."

I finally looked Domenic in the eye, which must have been a shocker for him, and searched for his intentions. He didn't give anything away.

We were quite a pair.

Domenic scrutinized my new look with a shadow of amusement. Last time we met, I'd been blond and blue eyed, and didn't wear sundresses and sneakers that were covered in finger paint. Although I only noticed the finger paint when I looked down at my lap to avoid eye contact.

"You look different, Debra. What is it?"

"Haircut," I said.

"I like it. What else is different? You look more *natural* or something."

Run, was the message my whole body was telling me.

But I knew if I ran, I was chucking whatever life I had in the trash. A new life would be an unknown, and I had seen where the unknown could take me. I didn't like it all that much.

Domenic put his hand over mine. "Don't go," he said. "Have your drink."

I swallowed my whiskey, hoping it would settle me, but instead I felt like I'd stepped in quicksand. I tried to remind myself not to fight it.

"What are you doing here?" I said.

"Visiting," Domenic said. He motioned for Sean to pour two more drinks.

"What do you want?" I said, looking him straight on.

"That's a complicated question. One I doubt I could answer in just one day."

"Why are you here?"

"I have to say, you have the most beautiful b—brown?— eyes I have ever seen. Brown. Hmm, I have to admit I remember them differently. Still, they suit you."

This didn't look good. A cop tracking me to a new town where I'd made a transformation that looked far more like a disguise than a makeover. Hell, it was even possible he'd found out who I really was, or at least who I once was. I had no idea what Domenic knew or didn't know, and I was pretty sure at that moment that the game was up. So I finished my drink because, as far as I knew, you couldn't get whiskey behind bars—at least the kind made in a barrel, not a toilet.

"That's more like it," Domenic said.

A few more patrons fell into the bar—Glen, one of the mechanics at the local gas station, and his buddy George, the town electrician, although he got most of his work in Jackson. Both men had children at JAC Primary School.

"Miss Maze," Glen said, tipping an imaginary hat.

"Gentlemen," I said, nodding in return.

Domenic observed the exchange and smiled. He took the opportunity of new arrivals to take the seat right next to mine. This allowed us to converse in tones too quiet for even Sean to decipher when he'd lean on the bar, cleaning an imaginary spill.

"How's Recluse treating you?" Domenic said.

"Quite well, thank you. Recluse minds its own business. What more can you want from a town?"

"Maybe a movie theater," Domenic said.

"We have all of the essentials here," I said.

"That's enough for you?"

"What do you want?" I repeated, because we were going to get to that at some point and my insides were turning to rubble.

"I want to know what your secret is," Domenic whispered in my ear.

It sent chills down my spine. The good kind, I hate to admit.

"Maybe I've got more than one," I said.

"I *know* you've got more than one," he said.

"Is there any way I could convince you to just leave?" I said.

"Sure," said Domenic. "If you leave with me."

"It's a small town, in case you didn't notice. I have something of a reputation to uphold."

"Well, I wouldn't want to sully your reputation, Miss Maze. Why don't I meet you outside the schoolhouse in an hour."

"The schoolhouse?"

"That's where you live, right?"

There was that quicksand again, only I was starting to struggle and sink.

"Half hour," he said as he departed.

I should have cut myself off in the interim. A clear head—or at least a head as clear as mine had been two whiskeys ago—is generally wise when confronting an unknown human variable, but my nerves jangled like a set of janitor's keys. Sean must have noticed the vibration from my general direction.

"You okay?" he asked as he served me yet another dose of slow reaction time.

"I'm great."

"Ex-boyfriend?"

"What makes you say that?"

"Because you look like you're trying to stuff a bear in a gopher hole."

"That's an unusual analogy."

"I'm not sure anyone else can see it, if that makes you feel any better."

"A little," I said, tossing some bills on the bar.

"You leaving?"

"Well, it's a school night and I have exceeded my usual limit and tomorrow we have a long lesson on the Louisiana Purchase and I better get my numbers straight, because if there's one thing I've learned teaching kids this age, they like to know the cost of things. Even things that they'll never be able to buy, like one-third of the United States."

I slipped off the bar stool and already felt my legs were far less trustworthy than when I entered the Lantern.

"Be good," Sean said. He said it in a less casual way than I would have liked.

"Too late," I said.

I beat a semistraight path back to John Allen Campbell. As I neared the stone steps of the Victorian building, I began searching for Domenic. I circled the house and returned to the front. I sat on the stoop where I sat with Andrew almost every afternoon and waited a few minutes. Maybe Domenic was running late. I had a foolish but hopeful notion that he'd decided against whatever he had planned. Or perhaps, as an officer of the law, he had been called away on a crime in progress. He had to have more pressing civic matters than a cagey schoolteacher with a new hairdo.

After fifteen minutes passed, I got up, dusted myself off, and strolled around to the side entrance, which led into my humble abode. I put my key in the lock, but the door was already open.

My reading lamp was on and Domenic was reclining

on my bed, reading my battered paperback of *From the Mixed-Up Files of Mrs. Basil E. Frankweiler*.

Domenic barely looked up when I entered my home. "What took you so long?" he said.

"I stayed for another drink."

Domenic kept his eye on the paperback. "I remember this book," he said. "Damn, when you're a kid, you think you can do anything. Live in a museum, become president, break into a used car lot and take a Corvette for a spin, fly."

"You thought you could fly?"

"Briefly. I might have been under the influence at the time."

"That explains it," I said.

"But then you grow up and realize that you're bound by laws of nature and society. That could be quite limiting for some people, I would imagine." Domenic closed the book and returned it to my nightstand. "We should talk," he said.

July 30, 2013
To: Jo
From: Ryan

 There's something you should know and I didn't want you to hear about it from your routine cyber strolls down memory lane. You've been declared legally dead. Your mom took care of it just after the seventh anniversary of your disappearance.

 They're not looking for you anymore. I hope that helps you move on. People still talk about you, but no one believes they'll ever find you.

Maybe severing ties from your past will give you some peace. Maybe it's time for us to sever ties.

Always,
R

August 15, 2013
To: Ryan
From: Jo

I died seven years ago. I'm not interested in the official line. Out of curiosity, what do people say about me? How did I die?

September 1, 2013
To: Jo
From: Ryan

Do you really want to get into that? Remember, most of the rumors are being spread by people you went to high school with. You know the kind of lies people tell.

September 13, 2013
To: Ryan
From: Jo

Ryan, if there's one thing you know better than anyone, it's how to tell a lie. Spill the dirt. I want to hear all about it. I also want to hear all about your domestic bliss. I see the photos your wife posts for the world to see. You look much happier than your guilt-ridden e-mails would suggest. How about, for once, you just tell me the truth? However cruel it might be.

September 25, 2013
To: Jo
From: Ryan

Here you go. The current consensus, since you were never found, is that you drowned yourself in Moses Lake after you left the hospital. You tied something to your ankle and jumped. In some theories, it was an antique anchor, in others it was the base from the stop sign you stole during that scavenger hunt. Roger Bly (that confederate nut from US history class) thinks it's just a plain old bag of rocks. Edie thinks you finally took that trip to San Francisco and jumped off the Golden Gate Bridge. I heard a few more fanciful tales. You hitchhiked and were murdered on the road—just one of thousands of missing girls who die at the hands of an unknown assailant. And then there is Eunice, who has a very dark imagination, as you may recall. Eunice thinks your mother killed you out of shame and buried your body deep in the woods behind your house.

Have you heard enough?

November 11, 2013
To: Ryan
From: Jo

Do you remember what drowning feels like? You

only know about the first part. That vise grip on your chest. It hurts. Probably hurts more than what you felt. But then it eases up, and before you lose consciousness it doesn't hurt at all. It's kind of pleasant. That's why people say drowning isn't a bad way to go. Because the end is peaceful. I should have given you that peace. But how could I know that saving your life would ruin mine?

Drowning would be just fine with me. Let's pretend that's how I went. When you think of me, try to imagine me tied to a glorious antique anchor at the bottom of San Francisco Bay.

Since I'm dead, you won't be hearing from me again. Good-bye, Ryan.

Jo

14

"M ake yourself at home," I said, not pleasantly. Not unpleasantly.

"You left the key under the dead plant," Domenic said.

"That's not exactly an invitation inside."

"My point was that you don't seem the type."

"The type to leave keys under dead plants?" I said.

"The trusting type."

"I'm not."

"And yet you left the key to your living quarters in the second-most obvious hiding place."

"I don't have a doormat."

"Which made finding your key all the more easy."

"What do you want from me, Domenic?"

"I want to understand you."

"That might never happen."

"I'm willing to give it a shot," he said.

I still couldn't read him, and I had learned how to read men over the years, after reading a few of them so wrong it cost me everything. I noticed Domenic had left his shoes neatly at the door, abiding by an unspoken apartment rule. He had also refrained from rifling through my belongings, which would be the obvious next step for someone who wanted to understand me. I did appreciate those small tokens of courtesy, and I thought it best to try the hospitable approach.

"I'm hungry," I said. "I'm going to make a peanut butter and jelly sandwich. Do you want one?"

"I'm allergic to peanuts."

"Really?"

"Don't get any ideas."

"I wasn't," I said. "Can I get you something else?"

"I wouldn't say no to a jelly sandwich."

I made the jelly sandwich first. Domenic devoured it like a twelve-year-old boy after a Little League game. I turned my head, turned back, and it was gone.

"I think I've got some bologna in the refrigerator. Maybe you need something with more sustenance."

"I didn't expect you to be so hospitable," he said.

"I didn't expect you at all. How did you find me?"

"It wasn't easy. But you mentioned being in the educational profession. All of our public school teachers register with the police, but you weren't on that list. So, after the school year started, I just started calling around to private schools that don't generally follow protocol."

"That's a lot of work just to find a girl you had a burger with."

"Maybe," he said. "But I think it was probably worth the effort."

I made Domenic a sandwich of processed meat and cheese. We sat down at my card table and ate in silence. I had a bottle of decent bourbon that was a gift from Sean for saving the kid, so I broke that out. It wasn't like I ever had visitors.

Despite the looming threat of exposure, I enjoyed the company. In some ways it felt perfectly ordinary, and I had missed ordinary. Sure, I was lying to Domenic, had lied to him fro the start, but he knew I was a liar and at least that pretense had been lifted. You can't imagine how exhausting it is to spend your entire life in performance.

Domenic took the last bite of his bologna and American cheese sandwich, leaned back in my wobbly wooden chair, and sighed as if he'd just finished a Thanksgiving feast.

"I needed that. Thank you."

"You're welcome."

He was going to start talking soon and the spell of ease would be broken, but I tried to enjoy his simple company for just a moment longer. Domenic finished his bourbon and I poured him another. I fortified myself as last-minute adjuncts, amendments, and loophole fixes to my fake history swirled in my booze-soaked brain.

"What are you running from?" Domenic asked.

"Who says I'm running?"

"I do."

"Well, then, it must be true."

"Women change their hair, their clothes, the color they paint their lips, but they don't generally try to look like someone else completely."

"They do if they don't want anyone to find them." The truth when possible.

"Have you decided to get honest with me?" Domenic asked.

"I don't know."

"I think you're in trouble. I'd like to know if you're the cause of injury or the collateral damage."

"The second thing."

"Would you like to tell me the story?"

"Not really."

"Maybe later?" he said.

"You planning on staying?"

"How long does it take to drive from Cleveland to Chicago?" Domenic said.

I had no idea what he was getting at, but he was asking the right girl for directions.

"It's about five hours on I-90. Why? You thinking of taking a trip?"

"Now how long a drive is it from Cleveland to Akron?"

"I don't know. Two hours maybe." I wasn't particularly captivated by brief intrastate jaunts.

"Under an hour, even with traffic," Domenic said.

I had fucked up. I wasn't entirely sure how, but I could sense that Domenic had come to some conclusion about me. Not a good one. He got to his feet as if making to leave, but he was a bit wobbly. He'd had a few at the bar and we'd put a dent in my lifesaving bourbon.

"You're not Debra Maze," he said. "Debra Maze was from

Cleveland, Ohio. She went to school in Akron, Ohio. She would know how long it takes to get from Cleveland to Akron. She would have probably made that drive at least a couple dozen times in her life."

"What do you want?"

"I want to know who you *really* are."

"I'm not anyone anymore."

Domenic shrugged on his jacket and slipped on his shoes. I got up, took my key, locked the dead bolt, and blocked my door.

"What are you doing?" Domenic said as he moved closer to me. He stood just a few inches away from me. A head taller, so I had to look up, and yet, at that moment, I still hung on to some power. He didn't look as sure of himself; I could see it in his cautious gaze.

"You're drunk," I said. "It's my civic responsibility to keep you off the road."

"A civic-minded outlaw. Is that what you are?"

"I've been called worse," I said. "Still, can't let you on the road in your condition."

"Back away from the door. I promise I won't drive."

"There aren't any motels in Recluse. You know that, right?"

"I'll sleep in my car."

"You can sleep on the floor."

"My car is more comfortable."

"Then you can have the bed."

Domenic mulled over the offer for a little while, then made up his mind. He took off his coat and kicked off his shoes. Then he leaned close and whispered in my ear. He smelled like bourbon and man. That musky odor that can be nauseating or intoxicating, depending on the source.

"Are you scared of me?" he asked.

"No," I said. I meant it just then. Scared was not remotely what I was feeling.

Domenic put his hand behind my neck. His fingers were warm and strong, and he kissed me. It was like the last time, only more intimate since I kind of knew him now. He pulled away, confused, as if he were having a moral conundrum. Sometimes I had to remember that some people considered me genuinely bad, or at least a questionable character.

I pushed him onto the bed and straddled him. I kissed him, hoping that he could forget for just a little while who he thought I might be. I wondered how long we could pretend that we were a normal couple, fucking on a twin bed in the basement of a schoolhouse.

Our clothes came off so fast, I felt like I'd had a sixty-second spell of amnesia when I noticed that they were gone. Being with him seemed as natural as breathing. He was as familiar to me as just about any man I'd ever known. He almost made me forget the one I was always trying to forget.

When we were done, Domenic kissed me on the forehead and looked me in the eye, searching, but still sweet, suspiciously sweet.

"Please tell me you've never killed anyone," he said.

Talk about breaking the mood. I'm sure he saw the

flash of hurt, followed by anger, that swelled inside me. In retrospect, it was a fair question.

"I've never killed anyone," I said.

That was a point of pride with me. I'd never gone to college, never made anything of myself. But I'd never killed another human being, and considering the lives I'd lived so far, that was something.

Domenic could probably have slept through a train wreck right outside his window. I have an alarm clock that sounds like a foghorn in your ear. It was a self-serving gift from Principal Collins, after I was tardy for class a few times. If you lived for seven years on tavern hours, you'd likely feel as if you had permanent jet lag if you had to wake up at seven on the dot five days a week. In fact, sometimes I thought my circadian rhythms gave me away more than my unconventional take on the grammar school curriculum.

I showered and changed into a flowered sundress with a cardigan that I would wear on occasions when I felt strongly about playing my role. Domenic continued to snore quietly. I sat next to him on my bed and listened for a moment. It was a comforting sound, hearing another human at peace. I took Blue's gun from the nightstand, stuffed it in a paper bag, and shoved it in my purse. I left a glass of water on the nightstand and departed through the back door. I quickly dropped by my Cadillac to hide my weapon in the glove compartment. Then I walked up the steps of John Allen Campbell Primary School for another day in the trenches.

Long division killed the morning. I always got the most tedious lessons out of the way first thing. By the time the recess bell rang, my students looked like inmates on death row who'd just been given a reprieve. I sat on the bench—my usual post—my head hanging in exhaustion more than usual. I heard a whistle and looked up.

"Teach," Domenic said, beckoning me to the fence.

I walked over, trying to gauge his expression. It wasn't like last night had changed everything. He was a cop; I was on the run. He hadn't figured out all of the details, but he'd figured something out.

"Morning, sleepyhead," I said.

"Thanks for your hospitality."

"Is that what they call it these days?"

"Let me ask you a question," Domenic said. "Is that *your* Cadillac parked out back?"

"Yes," I said. It was registered under Debra Maze. Seemed a safe point to concede.

"That's a hell of a getaway car," he said.

"A gift from an old friend," I said.

"You plan on sticking around for a while?" Domenic asked.

Good question. One that I didn't have the answer to. I shrugged.

"If you ever feel like talking or confessing or . . . something else, you have my number," he said.

"That's mighty professional of you," I said.

Domenic wrapped his hands around the chain-link fence. His finger lightly grazed mine.

"I'll be seeing you, Debra."

I heard Margo wailing from the other end of the yard. She was in the middle of a soccer game and had taken to flopping after a long weekend of watching Premier League football on ESPN. Asphalt and flopping, however, are a rotten combination.

"I better go. There's a fake injury I must attend to."

"Don't do anything stupid," Domenic said.

"Like what?"

"Run."

15

"Who was that tall drink of water?" Cora asked as I returned to the lunch benches.

"Just an old friend," I said.

"From where?"

The bell rang. I had never been more grateful to return to class. The second lesson of the day involved making homemade thermometers with Mason jars, straws, Play-Doh, and rubbing alcohol. It wasn't as exciting as I had hoped since we had no heat source in the room to show the rise in temperature. Billy Peters was so impatient with his ho-hum product, he pulled out a lighter from his pocket and held it under the glass.

Lighters were generally frowned upon at the school, so I had to confiscate it. It was one of those ornate metal deals. The initials JP were inscribed on the back. I gave Billy a look that informed him I knew I was handling stolen goods. I gave him a follow-up look indicating that I wouldn't rat him out. I'm not a rat, which some people might consider an asset, but I'm fairly certain it is my fatal flaw.

* * *

I don't remember what time it was when I heard the knock at my side door. It was long past bedtime hours, I know that. The knock woke me from a deep sleep and set my heart pounding; I shot upright in bed gasping for air, disoriented by my still-unfamiliar surroundings.

Three more steady knocks took me from groggy to wide awake. I assumed that Domenic had returned, to finish our conversation or start something else. The side door had no peephole. I opened it as if I were expecting company. It wasn't the company I was expecting.

The ordinary-looking man was standing there. Same boring khakis and blue shirt that he wore when I saw him loitering outside the schoolyard. He was so dull in appearance, I wasn't scared, which was a mistake. I was alone in the schoolhouse for another seven hours. If I screamed, no one would hear me.

"Good evening, ma'am," he said.

"More like good morning," I said. "It's a bit late for a house call, don't you think?"

"I do apologize from dropping by at such an hour, but I just wanted to make sure I caught you by your lonesome. I had intended to call on you last night, but you were otherwise occupied."

"I don't think we've been officially introduced," I said.

The ordinary man extended his hand in a perfectly ordinary way, as if we were having a business meeting.

"Jack Reed, pleased to meet you," he said.

I thought for sure I'd buried Jack Reed in a state park a few months back. But that's not the kind of thing you say to someone upon first introduction.

I shook his hand and said, "What can I do for you, Mr. Reed?"

"You wouldn't by chance be Debra Maze, from Cleveland, Ohio?"

"Most people around here just call me Miss Maze."

"Well, Miss Maze, why don't you tell me where on this godforsaken planet my wife is?"

"I've never met you before. How would I know where your wife is?"

Jack took a few steps closer. He was breathing on me now. He smelled like Old Spice, sweat, and decay. It wasn't that good kind of man smell.

"Blue might have told you a few stories about me," Jack said. "Tell me the truth, have you heard any stories?"

His eyes were so dark I could barely see the pupils. He didn't seem so ordinary anymore. I could have played dumb a little longer, but I didn't see the point.

"Maybe a few," I said.

"Then I'll ask you again, ma'am. Where is my wife?"

"I. Don't. Know."

His hands clamped around my neck, squeezing slowly like a boa constrictor's embrace. It gave me ample time to think about what was happening to me, to feel each breath I was missing, to experience the slow fade into unconsciousness.

He released his grip right before I went dark. I gasped for air, like coming up from a deep dive. He backhanded me across the cheek before I'd had my fill of oxygen.

"Where is my wife?" he asked again.

Before I could answer, Jack kicked me in the gut. It made me wonder what particular character traits had attracted Blue to him in the first place.

"Are you a rich man?" I asked.

"What was that?" Jack said, clearly confused by the question. "You are not trying to extort money from me."

"God no," I said, still wheezing. "I'm just trying to figure out why Blue married you. Because you do not have a single quality that recommends you as a mate."

He kicked me again. "Don't be smart."

"I'm clearly not smart. Or I would have seen this coming."

"Where is my wife?"

I crawled against the corner of the room to get some distance, hoping to avoid another blow. My oxygen-deprived brain was scrambling for an exit route out of this hellish maze.

"We switched," I said. "She's my old me. I'm now her."

Jack's hands unclenched. I had finally given him the kind of information he could use.

"Keep talking."

"She's going by the name Amelia Keen. Born 1986, Tacoma, Washington. I think I have my old ID in my car. I will give you everything you need, including her social—although she might be staying off-grid, and she might have changed her last name to Lightfoot. I can't say for sure. We haven't been in contact since we parted ways in Austin."

Jack stepped back, giving me space to stand. He gallantly opened the door for me. I swiped my car keys from my desk and stepped outside. The cold air jolted me into another level of alertness. My car was parked only about twenty yards away, but it felt like a two-mile stroll.

I unlocked the passenger door, sat down in the seat, and opened the glove compartment. I reached inside, gripped the gun, and aimed it right at Jack's forehead.

"Step back," I said.

"Do you even know how to use that thing? I must say, it does not look natural in your hands," he said.

He didn't step back. I could see him thinking of ways out of this, and I didn't need him thinking, so I shot him in the shoulder. He stepped back then. More like a stagger. I got out of the passenger seat, circled the car, and took a page from Blue's playbook.

"Get in the trunk, Jack."

"Now I'll have to kill you," Jack said.

"That seems improbable right now since I'm the one holding the gun, but I can't fault you for having ambitions. Now could you please get inside the trunk before you bleed all over this parking lot? You're making a hell of a mess."

Jack staggered about, muttering expletives and searching for a way out of this nasty fix that, let's be frank, he had gotten himself into.

"Jack, I will shoot you somewhere less pleasant if you don't get in the trunk right now."

He thought about it and realized that there were places way worse to be shot than the shoulder. He got in the trunk. I shut the hood. I scanned the parking lot, just to be sure no one was watching. Then I got into my Cadillac and drove. I wasn't driving anywhere in particular. I needed time to think, to weigh my options, to decide what kind of person I was, what kind of person I had become, and what kind of person I was going to be.

I drove around for two hours. Jack started kicking during the final twenty minutes. I was worried he was going to disengage the taillight and I'd get pulled over by highway patrol. I've gotten pretty good at thinking on my feet, but explaining away a man with a bullet wound in the trunk of your car is an ambitious undertaking.

I came upon Bitter Creek Road and remembered it from our ill-fated fishing excursion. Dead Horse Lake would be quiet this time of night, so I followed the roads to the best of my recollection. The high beams on my car could barely pierce the darkness, but I eventually found the lake and pulled the car into the clearing. Jack's bucking in the trunk quieted as the car bounced on the uneven terrain. I put the car in reverse, backed as close as I could get to the water's edge, turned off the ignition, picked up my gun, circled the vehicle, and opened the trunk.

I shot Jack once in the head and once in the heart. I thought it would be more humane if he didn't have time to contemplate his demise, although he was probably contemplating it plenty during our two-hour road trip. I had looked at the situation from every angle during our rambling drive and come out of it with one simple fact: it was either Jack or me. If I didn't kill him right then, I'd be spending the rest of my life looking over my shoulder. It was not a decision I made lightly.

An old rowboat was on the shore. I dragged it up to the bumper of my car and hoisted Jack into the bed and dropped the gun in after him. With all of my might, I shoved, dragged, and pulled the rowboat back to the shoreline and set the boat into the water. I climbed inside the boat, my feet straddling the dead guy, and rowed us out to the middle of the lake. I was hot from exertion, but the night air still sent chills through me. Sweat turned icy on my back. I tossed the gun into the water.

My plan to dump Jack in the lake was a tad ill conceived. There was no way I could get Jack out of the rowboat without spilling into the water myself. I stood up, stepped onto the edge, and capsized the boat. Jack and I fell into the frigid lake in unison. I watched him slip under the water with his gun. It seemed like the two should be buried together. While I was treading water, saying a silent prayer for Jack, I lost track of the oars.

My brain felt foggy from the cold, and I was running out of time before hypothermia would set in. Rather than try to locate the oars and right the boat, I headed for shore. I swam head down, fighting the wind current, ignoring the shooting pain that sliced from the tips of my fingers down to my toes.

When I reached the shore I crawled to my car, removed the keys from the trunk, got inside, turned on the ignition, and powered up the heat as high as it had ever gone. I drove home in my soaking-wet pajamas.

Everything was quiet and still at JAC Primary. The headlights illuminated the bloodstains from Jack's wound, so I parked over them until I could figure out another plan. I raced inside and climbed into the shower and let it burn me back to life.

That was when I realized what I had done. In a way it was self-defense, and maybe it mattered that Jack Reed was a piece-of-shit human being, but I'd still killed a man. When you take another person's life, it changes you. It doesn't just change how you look at the world or how you see yourself. It alters you to your core, your DNA. All of the things I had once believed about myself, about my inherent decency—I didn't have the same foothold on them as I once had.

I got out of the shower when I realized that nothing would ever make me clean again. I drank the rest of the bourbon and tried to fall asleep.

As I drifted off, I had to wonder if this was part of Blue's plan all along. The gun, the identity swap, the burying of that poor man I thought was Jack. Did Blue know that Jack would find me? If this was all an elaborate plan, one part didn't make sense: how did she know I could kill him?

* * *

My drunken sleep was fueled by dreams, the likes of which would probably interest only me. That moment when I first woke I thought I was still in the original nightmare, not this new one. It wasn't until my bare feet touched the overworked carpet that I remembered what I had done.

I had worked hard at becoming Debra Maze, and I wasn't quite ready to give her up. Jack Reed was gone, and he wasn't coming back. As far as I could tell, there had been no witnesses. So I brushed my teeth, washed my face, dressed in a cheery blue sundress, checked under my fingernails for blood, and arrived fifteen minutes early for class.

Since I had been otherwise occupied the night before, I hadn't prepared a lesson plan. As my students filed in and I looked at all of their innocent faces, I knew I was no longer fit for this job. I felt like I was sullying their souls just being in the same room with them.

"Miss Maze. Miss Maze."

I don't know how many times Andrew said my name before I woke from my stupor.

"Yes?"

"Are you all right? You look sick or something."

"Everyone, take out your journals," I said. "I want you to write one page on what you want to be when you grow up, and then one page on what you want to be if that first thing doesn't work out, because sometimes things don't work out the way we'd like them to. Then another page on what you'd do if the first two things you'd like to be don't work out. Then two pages on the *one* thing you definitely don't want to be no matter what. It's really important not to let the bottom drop out of your life."

It was time for me to hang up my chalk and ruler, based on the distressed glances that came my way. The only student who didn't look at me as if I were wearing a straitjacket was Andrew. He got out his notebook and pen and made a big show of starting the assignment.

"Do you mind if I work my way backward?" Andrew asked. "Start with the thing I definitely don't want to do?"

"That's fine," I said.

The class got to work. I turned my back to my students and studied the road maps of the US, plotting the course to my next destination.

Class dismissed. I started packing. I would have to lose the car as soon as possible, which meant leaving most things behind. I counted the money I had earned from three paychecks. I couldn't stick around long enough for the fourth. After rent, food, and the Lantern, I had just over eighteen hundred dollars. Not much when you're on the run—beer and taxes certainly add up. I wrote a note to Principal Collins saying that I was making a last-minute trip to visit a sick family member. I would be back as soon as I could. No one would believe it, but I figured it would buy me a day or two.

I wanted to thank Collins for the opportunity he gave me, and I wanted to say good-bye to Cora, and I wanted to have one final drink at the Lantern and give Sean a hug. I wanted to tell him he was a good man and that if he really wanted to get out of Recluse, he still had time. I couldn't do any of those things. I knew just about everyone would be fine without a proper good-bye from me.

But Andrew was different. I couldn't take off without a word to him. I returned to the classroom, pulled the road maps from the board, neatly folded them one by one, and put them into an envelope. I had so many things I wanted to tell him, but I couldn't overstep my bounds. I just wrote on the envelope, *Dear Andrew, One day you might need these*, and I hoped he would.

I zipped up the suitcase, put it in the trunk of my car, and returned to the place I'd called home for almost two months to give it one final inspection. That was when I decided to wipe it for prints. I took the pillowcase off the bed and began polishing every shiny surface I laid my eyes on.

In retrospect, I should have just hit the road. It was possible to shine away all of my prints, but what was the point with my DNA all over the place?

There was a knock at the door. I put the money in my bag and searched the room for anything I might have to take with me. I sat quietly on the floor, next to the bed, and tried to wait out my uninvited guest, but the knocks continued.

"I know you're in there, Debra. Open up."

It was Domenic. I grabbed my purse and jacket and left my apartment through the school entrance, walking down the hallway to the kitchen where there was a servants' entrance off the pantry. I unlocked the door, slipped outside, and crouched down in the shrubbery. I could see Domenic's car parked next to mine, but he was no longer standing by the door to my apartment.

I crab-walked along the old house, trying to pinpoint his whereabouts. Maybe he had moved to the front of the school, anticipating my alternate escape. The servants' exit wasn't well-known. I had a clear shot to my Cadillac. If I got there in time I could probably get a head start, and he might never be able to catch me even with the V-8 engine in that truck of his.

I've made split-second decisions my whole life. I can't comment on the quality of any of them since I can't go back and see where the alternate route would have taken me. What I can say is that standing in the shrubbery of John Allen Campbell Primary School all night wasn't going to do me any good. So I made a run for it. I ran straight for my car. Got inside, gunned the engine, burned rubber as I backed out of the space and pulled out of the lot. I drove down Recluse to Greenborough, then pulled onto Moorcroft. When I saw the signs for the interstate I thought I was free, or free in the way I'd come to know freedom, which isn't exactly freedom at all.

Just as I'd caught up on my breath, I lost it again. My passenger leaned over the backseat and whispered in my ear, "Where are we headed, Debra?"

I swerved like a snake on meth over the double yellow line. Horns blared and high beams flashed in warning as I steadied the car and slammed on my brakes.

"Hardly seems like the right vehicle for a road trip. But it is a beauty. I'll give you that," said Domenic. "What kind of mileage does this thing get?"

"Not good," I said.

"Do you mind if I ask you where the blood came from?"

For a second I blanked and had no idea what he was talking about, which seemed like a bad sign.

"What blood?"

"I noticed a fair amount of blood under and near your Cadillac. Do you know anything about that?"

"I do not," I said.

"Why is the front seat all wet?"

I could feel Domenic's hands sliding down the seat along my back.

"I spilled coffee," I said.

"Over your shoulder?"

We ended up on a country road that I hadn't studied on any of my maps. I didn't know where it would take us, but we wouldn't be going far.

"I know you're not Debra, so who are you?"

"Nobody," I said.

"Who is Debra Maze?" Domenic asked.

"She's just a woman I met along the way."

"A woman who's been missing for over a year. It's a bit convenient, isn't it?"

"More inconvenient, if you think about it," I said.

Domenic sighed deeply. "What am I gonna do with you, teach?" he said. He said it the way a grown-up might say it to a delinquent teenager. But I knew he saw the situation as a bit more sinister.

"What am I going to do with you?" I said, although I had already decided.

We were traveling about fifty miles an hour. I was buckled up; Domenic wasn't. He was still leaning over that front seat, oblivious to all of the health risks involved in automobile travel. I slammed on the brakes and aimed the car at the cement guardrail. The front right fender of that classic beauty crumpled like an aluminum can.

Domenic went flying over the front seat and hit his head on the dashboard, then bounced back and wedged himself on the floor. His feet got caught in the steering wheel. He moaned, which I considered a good sign. I had hoped to keep his injuries minor. I'm not exactly a stunt driver, but I did my best. I shoved his feet out of the way, backed out of the wreckage, and pulled off the road about a mile away. I found a side street with solid tree cover and parked on the shoulder.

I got out of the car, opened the passenger door, helped Domenic onto a gravelly patch of dirt. Blood trickled down his forehead, but I figured if he got medical attention soon enough, he'd be just fine. I put an old blanket under his head and found his cell phone in his pocket. I dialed 911 with my knuckle and gave his coordinates and condition as best I could. I was about to leave when Domenic started muttering something. I leaned in and asked him what he needed.

"Thirsty," he said.

I found a bottle of water in the car and left it for him.

"I'm sorry about this, Domenic. Nothing personal. Survival makes you do things you never thought you were capable of."

"Don't leave."

"The ambulance should be here soon. Try to stay awake."

As I started to get up, Domenic grabbed my wrist in a vise grip. "Who are you? Who are you really?"

"I don't know anymore."

March 30, 2014
To: Jo
From: Ryan
    Where are you? Are you still alive?

July 19, 2014
To: Jo
From: Ryan
    I know you're on the run. I'll still check this e-mail on occasion, as long as I can. If you need something that I can give you, I'll try.
    I'm sorry.
    R

EMMA LARK

16

To my best calculations, I gave Domenic just over an hour to be found by paramedics and recover his senses enough to provide them with my license plate number or other identifying information. I figured that gave me two or so hours before I'd have to lose the car. I took Highway 16 West and drove for fifty minutes, barely cracking the speed limit. I watched enviously as other cars left me in the dust. Then I exited onto I-25 toward Casper, Wyoming. I had one hundred and ten miles, one hundred and ten minutes to contemplate my next destination. Since I didn't have a solid identity in my back pocket, I'd have to live off the grid; I also knew I should put as much distance as I could between myself, the body of the real Jack Reed, Domenic, and all of the people who had come to know me as Debra Maze.

I found the Greyhound station in Casper, drove a mile away, parked in a strip mall, and walked back to the bus depot. I went to the kiosk and bought a ticket to Denver, Colorado.

I boarded the bus at 1:05 a.m. I was awake for every single jostle, vibration, pothole, pit stop, toilet flush, and destination callout of the entire six-hour journey. At 10:00 a.m., I gazed bleary-eyed at the black-and-white departure board in the Denver Amtrak station. There are only two routes out of Denver. If you head west, your final destination is either Los Angeles or San Francisco; east, you end up in Chicago. I had a simple choice to make. East or west?

I had a strict policy against the West Coast, so the choice was simple. Unfortunately, the California Zephyr brought me into the vicinity of Wisconsin, Tanya Dubois's old stomping grounds. I'd have to tread carefully during my layover.

The Zephyr didn't depart for another four hours, which gave me ample time to find a fellow passenger with a credit card I could borrow. I had a few options—all women with their handbags on display. I chose the one with the nicest shoes. They were a strappy pump that dangled off of her heel as she napped on a bench. She didn't stir as I strolled past. Her purse was wide open; I could pluck the wallet right out. I took inventory of my surroundings and everyone was minding their business. I shrugged off my jacket and threw it over my right arm. I walked past the woman again, dropped my phone in front of her bench, and as I retrieved it, I plucked her wallet right out of her handbag. Once I was out of sight, I took her credit card and purchased a ticket to Chicago, splurging on a roomette. I needed the rest, and the fewer people who saw me while I still looked like the second Debra Maze, the better. My benefactress, Virginia White, also had $182 in her purse. I kept one credit card and the cash, but I didn't want to leave her stranded without any ID.

As I breezed back in her direction, I had planned to drop the wallet back in her bag. But she was already scavenging through her purse in a panic. I strolled to the other end of the train station and dropped her wallet on the ground. Maybe a good Samaritan would find it and return it to her.

During the four hours I had before I boarded the train, I found a thrift store, where I bought a small backpack and a change of clothes. Then I stopped in a drugstore, where I purchased water, energy bars, and a disposable cell phone.

I boarded the train without incident and slept for the first ten hours, waking here and there to guzzle water and reemerge into the nightmare that had become my life. When I had finally slept long enough to recover some from the last forty-eight hours, I woke to a hunger so incapacitating that the stroll down the train to the café car felt like a two-day journey through the desert. I wove through the narrow aisle like a drunk frat boy, steadying myself on the backs of the seats. When I finally arrived in the car and sat down at the bar, the menu appeared to be written in a foreign language.

The café car attendant—I think she said her name was Grace, or maybe I was just playing with names in my head—asked if I needed assistance. That was how in need of assistance I must have looked. It occurred to me that I probably shouldn't be behaving in any suspicious manner since people recall suspiciously behaving people better than normally behaving ones. I made a very strong mental note to start behaving normally.

"What's good?" I said.

"Everything," she said.

I admired her sense of pride in her product, but I had made so many complex, arduous, and life-altering decisions over the last two days that I needed to have one taken off my plate.

"Let me rephrase that," I said. "What would you have if you were sitting down for a meal?"

"A burger. I always order a burger," said Maybe Grace.

"I'll have a burger," I said.

The burger was adequate but not excellent. The speed with which I consumed it would only reinforce Maybe Grace's opinion of her favorite dish.

As she cleared my plate, she asked me where I was heading. Since I hadn't yet chosen a final destination, I said, "Chicago."

"Got family there?"

"Around there."

I bought a bag of potato chips, almonds, an apple, and water to hold me through the rest of the journey. Innocuous questions always lead to more personal ones, and I didn't have any answers at the moment. I returned to my roomette. There I sat by the picture window and watched the landscape dash by so fast I felt like I was in a perpetual state of just missing something important.

By the time we got to Nebraska, tedium had set in. Everything started to look the same, and I lost that nostalgic feeling I had for the landscape we'd left behind. I began checking my watch with a ticlike frequency as the first leg of my journey was coming to an end. Roomettes are a nice idea, but they're smaller than a prison cell and unless you're accustomed to that minimalist lifestyle, it gets old fast.

Detraining in Chicago gave me a fleeting sense of exultant freedom, until I came to the honest conclusion that I probably ought to get out of the Midwest with haste. If I hopped into a post office in Chicago, I'd likely find a grainy photocopy of my face thumbtacked to a bulletin board right next to the FBI's most wanted.

Chicago's Union Station was more populous than the entirety of Recluse, Wyoming. Fellow passengers, commuters, and lingerers jostled past me. I felt like I was in the middle of a swarm of bees, the movements so alarmed my quieted senses. It had been a long time since I'd experienced the bustle of city life. I have to admit, I'd longed for it. I missed being invisible in a room full of people, getting lost in a crowd.

Just as that hopeful vision cropped up, I stamped it down. Big cities require pricey apartments, which require well-paying legitimate jobs, and both of those require references and work history and, far more importantly, a goddamn ID, which I was currently lacking.

I contemplated the departure board. The one clear decision I had already made was that I should put more miles between myself and the Midwest. It was only a two-and-a-half-hour drive to Waterloo, Wisconsin, most of that along I-94 if I remembered correctly.

Virginia White's cash bought me a ticket on the Lake

Shore Limited to Albany, New York. The train didn't depart for another six hours, so I stuffed my bag in a locker, bought a couple of local newspapers, and hoped I wouldn't find a police sketch of myself inside those pages. I found a poorly lit and poorly populated bar that wasn't blasting sports on the television, and sat down four bar stools away from the other solo customer.

"What'll it be?" the bartender asked.

I ordered a beer, opened the newspaper, and realized the light was all wrong for reading. Still, if you're a woman sitting alone in a bar, it's always best to look occupied, even if you're faking it. Most men think they're doing you a favor, keeping you company, curing you of the shame of being alone in public.

It didn't take long for a fellow traveler to take a seat next to mine. I tensed my shoulders and raised the newspaper in a defensive posture. Some men would have read my body language for what it was—an indisputable DO NOT DISTURB sign. But some men can only read their internal weather report and have no concept that another human might not want the same things they want.

Out of the corner of my eye, I saw that he was in a wrinkled shirt, his tie at half mast, and his collar frayed and yellow, the way a man's collar gets when there's no woman around to tell him that he needs to buy a new shirt. I decided he was a salesman. They need to travel in suits, and they're skilled at driving a conversation until it crashes and burns at the bottom of a cliff. My cursory gaze provided all of the information I needed. The Salesman kept his money close to his chest—in his breast pocket to be precise. If it had been in a more accessible location, I might have engaged in conversation. As it was, he was no use to me.

The Salesman hadn't ordered his drink before he asked his first question. "What are you reading?"

I tried ignoring him, keeping my newspaper up like a riot shield.

He cleared his throat. "What are you reading?" he said again.

"Newspaper," I said. Sometimes being laconic will force your opponent to match your conversational style.

"My name's Howard."

"Uh-huh," I said because sometimes when you ignore people, they just repeat themselves.

"You got a name?"

I lowered the paper and looked him dead in the eye. "As a matter of fact, I do not." This *had* to be one of the greatest conversation stoppers that ever was.

But Howard would not be thwarted. "You reading anything interesting?"

"Nope."

The bartender approached the salesman and took his order. Whiskey from the well. The Salesman downed his shot and tapped the bar, his glass refilled just moments after it was drained. He cleared his throat again and turned to me.

"You got a whole newspaper—no, two newspapers—and you're going to tell me that there's nothing of interest in them?"

The laconic method was obviously failing. "You could get your own newspaper and find something of interest for yourself," I said, holding my gaze on the fuzzy black-and-white print.

"I was just making conversation, honey," the Salesman said.

"But I'm not interested in conversation," I said, "so this transaction seems pretty simple to me. You want to talk. I don't want to talk. I win," I said.

"Women these days," the Salesman said. "They don't have any manners."

"No, they don't. That's what the women's movement was all about. Not equal rights, but the right to be rude. We don't have to make polite conversation anymore. So you might as well find another way to keep busy," I said as I dropped the newspaper in front of him and left the bar.

In my brief reading time, I found no mention of me, but domestic crimes only get copy space when there's a new development. I had to get to a library one of these days and check on the inquiry into Frank's death.

I strolled under the grand arches of Union Station for an hour or so, stretching my legs in anticipation of the cramped journey ahead. Eventually I found a bench occupied by a teenager bobbing his head to the beat of whatever was blasting out of his earbuds. I sat down next to him. You can always count on the youth of the day to mind their own business.

17

Traveling at close to eighty miles an hour made it feel like the train was doing the running for me. I couldn't risk using Virginia's credit card again, so I had purchased only a regular seat on the Lake Shore Limited.

I found my way to the café car sometime after the lunch crowd dispersed. I ordered a turkey sandwich and found a table by the window, facing the cab. I looked around to see if anyone might give me trouble. I saw a teenager transfixed by her phone, a small family with children they were trying to quiet, and a stately, plump gentleman in an impeccable tweed suit who was snoring so loudly that the woman sitting across from him began to gather her belongings. She was an older lady, maybe seventy-five, tall, thin, but probably once a real beauty, judging from her bright blue eyes and pronounced cheekbones. Her hair was completely white and cut plain and short, probably by her own hand. The wrinkles on her face were heavy around her mouth and eyes, as if she got them all from smiling.

She gazed in my direction and rolled her eyes at the

snorer. I smiled; she smiled. She approached my table.

"Do you mind if I sit?" she said.

There were other free tables in the vicinity, but more passengers began to file into the car. On first glance her company seemed preferable to that of just about anyone else on the train, and I wasn't in a position to take my chances. I still had another ten hours to go.

"Please," I said.

She slid into the booth across from me and winked. On her it worked.

"For forty years I listened to my husband saw wood eight hours a night, seven days a week. I missed him when he died. I did not miss that sound," she said.

"Where are you headed?" I asked.

"Erie. You?"

"Buffalo," I said. It was the stop right after. I'd asked her first, so I wouldn't have to unnecessarily give away my final destination. Besides, if anyone had a Debra Maze or Tanya Dubois sighting and they said I'd landed in Buffalo, the general consensus would likely be that I'd hopped into Canada. Which was not a bad idea at all, if I could find a trunk in a car that would have me.

"Are you going on vacation or returning home?" I asked.

"Neither," she said drolly. "I'm babysitting my grandchildren for the weekend. My son and daughter-in-law think it's a vacation. But I've been to Paris. I know better. And you?"

"I'm visiting a friend," I said.

"A vacation?"

"You could call it that," I said. Sometimes I'd take in the landscape and try to trick myself that I was on a holiday. It never worked.

"My name is Dolores," she said. "Dolores Markham."

By providing a last name, Dolores was suggesting that I too should provide a last name. If I didn't, it would seem unfriendly and perhaps suspicious, although my heightened sense of paranoia might have been playing tricks on my sense of social conventions.

"Hi, Dolores. I'm Emma Lark."

I'd had the name in my back pocket if I needed to use one, but I was trying to stay as anonymous as possible on this journey. I'd never practiced saying it, so when I did, I paused. It was a brief pause, a split second, but I could tell from the shift in Dolores's gaze that she'd caught it.

"You look very familiar, Emma."

"I must have that kind of face."

"Maybe. Where are you from?" Her eyes locked into mine, scrutinizing, yet somehow kind. Her open smile didn't waver, but she was reading me as I answered her questions.

"Outskirts of Seattle. You?"

"Madison."

I was in trouble. Madison is just thirty minutes from Waterloo, where Tanya Dubois was a wanted woman. My mug must have been all over the papers there. If I had to guess, Dolores Markham knew exactly who I was. My travel itinerary through the Midwest was clearly a lapse in judgment.

My brain had been misfiring ever since I killed Jack.

"Madison," I said, as if it were the first time that word had rolled off my tongue. "I've heard good things."

"You've never been?"

"No. Never," I said.

I could change my hair, even my eyes, but you can't change your bones. Anyone with a good eye for faces would be able to pick me out of a lineup. I held onto Dolores's gaze, even as I felt my heart beating a hole in my chest. I kept my expression steady and warm as I tried to figure out a plan.

"Maybe one day," I said.

"That probably wouldn't be a good idea," said Dolores.

"Why is that?"

"You're the spitting image of a woman wanted for murder there."

The car seemed to have heated up ten degrees in the last five seconds. My brain felt like a corn maze. Each corner I turned, I'd find another dead end.

Dolores was forcing me to rethink all of my plans; I wasn't too keen on her at that moment. Still, killing Dolores was out of the question.

"How unusual," I said.

"Well, she's a person of interest. Husband was found at the bottom of the stairs and then the wife disappears. Why would she run, if she were innocent?"

"Maybe the real killer kidnapped her."

"There was no sign of a struggle, and she took her purse and at least one suitcase."

As far I could tell, Dolores was having herself a jolly good time chatting with a potential murderer. Well, a real one now. But did Jack really count?

It would have been suspicious and most certainly rude if I got up and left, so I let the conversation run its course.

"That is suspicious, indeed," I said.

"Interesting that you look just like her," Dolores said.

"They say everybody's got a doppelgänger," I said.

"I'm not convinced that the woman was guilty. Maybe he had it coming," she said.

"Maybe he just fell down the stairs," I said.

The loudspeaker whined before the conductor's voice cracked the rhythm of Dolores's educated interrogation.

"Next Stop: Erie."

Dolores sat perfectly still.

"That's you, isn't it?" I said.

"It is," she said, slowly gathering her purse and coat. "It's been nice chatting with you, Tanya."

If I had been standing, my knees would have buckled. "Emma," I whispered without any conviction. What was the point?

Dolores detrained, but I figured it would be a matter of minutes before she called the police with a Tanya Dubois sighting. I watched her walk along the platform into the station. I raced down the aisle and jumped off the train right before the doors closed.

I didn't dare go into the station until I was sure Dolores had departed. I strolled to the end of the tracks and sat on a bench for a half hour, breathing slow and steady, trying to calm my nerves. Then I walked into Erie's Union Station, bought a baseball cap and a pair of oversized black sunglasses, and left, strolling down Peach Street until I saw a sign for a motel that looked like it would take cash and forgo that pesky ID check.

Room 309 of the Dragonslayer Inn was about as medieval as my mother's bedroom circa 1985. If I had to hazard a guess at the age of the carpet and bedspread, I'd go with ten to fifteen years. The walls carried the grime of what I gathered was a Smoking Only policy, and the faucet in the bathroom sink was so caked with rust I tried to recall my last tetanus shot.

Yet, it felt good to be alone for a night, to have time to think. When I tried to count back, I realized I had been a killer for only four days, but it felt like forever. I took off my clothes, shucked the ancient duvet off the bed, and crawled between the scratchy sheets. I slept for as long as my mind would let me.

My conscience gave me only a three-hour reprieve. When I woke, the flip clock by the side of the bed read 9:09 p.m. I figured I might still have time to find an open drugstore, so I threw on my clothes and left.

Certain purchases can seem highly suspect. For example, if I worked in a hardware store I'd be inclined to call the cops on a customer who purchased only rope and duct tape.

However, if that same customer purchased rope, wood glue, lumber, hinges, a leveler, and duct tape, I wouldn't think much of it. At the drugstore I picked up scissors, hair color, a disposable cell phone, an assortment of makeup, and a scarf, and added mixed nuts, a new toothbrush, toothpaste, shampoo, and a multivitamin to my cart to throw the cashier off. It's quite possible I was overthinking the endeavor; the cashier didn't give me a second glance.

Back at the Dragonslayer Inn, I gazed into the mirror and thought about what I could do to make myself unrecognizable. I took the scissors from the plastic bag, grabbed a chunk of hair, and sliced it off right at the scalp. Then I sliced off another chunk and another chunk, until my head was the texture of badly mowed lawn. I had saved those blue contact lenses, just in case, and put them back in. I left the hair color alone. You never know when you might need another layer of camouflage. When I looked in the mirror I resembled a cancer patient, maybe one you wouldn't want to mess with. I figured I could roam safely looking like this, until I found a new place to land.

I cleaned up my shorn locks off the linoleum floor as best I could, having more sympathy for the hotel maid than your average guest. I set the alarm and went to bed.

I woke an hour later with my conscience in a vise. Domenic had seemed mostly okay when I left him, but head injuries are unpredictable. I began to fear that I had done more than just incapacitate a man who was probably pretty decent, on the whole.

I found his card in my wallet, took out the cell phone that I'd bought in Denver, and called his number. He answered on the third ring. At least, I was fairly certain it was him. I probably should have hung up, but I couldn't.

"Domenic?"

"Yeah, who's this?"

"How's your head?"

"Debra?"

"Don't call me that anymore."

"Okay, sweetheart. Just tell me where you are. Denver?"

"I'm not in Denver," I said. "What's your condition?"

"Concussion. Did you call to check up on me?"

"Yes."

"I'm touched. Where are you?"

"Do you have any other injuries?"

"A few stitches. Tell me where you are, sweetheart."

"As long as you're all right. Bye, Domenic."

It was three a.m. when I left the hotel. I dropped the phone in the bin and the keys in the slot at the front desk so no one would see me. I returned to the train station and bought another coach fare with my own cash on the Lakeshore Limited to Albany. I boarded the train at seven fifteen a.m.

As far as identities were concerned, Emma Lark turned out to be a layover. Even with the copy of her ID and passport that I'd stolen from the records room at JAC Primary, I wouldn't get any use out of her. I'd managed to chew her up and spit her out in less than three days, thanks to a sharp old dame named Dolores Markham. I wouldn't last long without a name, so I got straight to work.

As soon as I boarded the train, I began stretching my legs through the cars, noting all of the female passengers in my age range. Then I narrowed them down to the ones I bore some physical resemblance to. I had three promising choices. It would have been nice to take my time, to carefully study their bone structure, verify their height, maybe even be so bold as to engage in a brief conversation, learn her age, place of birth, point of departure, destination, before I made any more decisions. But opportunity knocked, and I answered.

A woman with long brown hair, whom I could definitely pass for after a cancer scare, left her purse in a virtually empty car as she went to use the restroom. I quickly reached inside, swiped her wallet, and shoved it into my bag. I found a restroom in another car and pulled her driver's license, several bills, and a credit card, with barely a glance. Then I casually walked back through her car. She hadn't returned to her seat, and she was less likely to notice a theft if her wallet remained in her bag, so I returned most of the stolen goods. Then I moved on to the next car. Every step went so fast I didn't even see the name on the ID.

My imprudent almost-lookalike got off the train in Syracuse, New York. It was only then I dared scrutinize my new identity. I plucked the driver's license from my bag with heady anticipation.

Sonia Lubovich from Bloomington, Indiana. Lubovich. Was that Polish, Russian? Maybe it was a name I'd acquired through a brief marriage to a man who never spoke much about his family. Lack of communication would certainly be a key ingredient in a failed marriage—although it might have been the ingredient that kept me and Frank together for so long.

I decided the ID could work. She was only two years older and one inch taller than I was, and we looked enough alike. The photo had been taken a few years ago, and the way I looked now could easily be explained away by life and illness taking their toll. I no longer had great expectations for my lives, but I figured I'd have a longer run as Sonia Lubovich than I did as Emma Lark.

April 17, 2015
To: Jo
From: Ryan
  Jo,
  Why did you call him, ask for his help? You could have called me.
  I would have helped you.
  R

June 22, 2015
To: Jo
From: Ryan
  Jo,
  It's been ten years since you left. People are talking about you again. Your face—god, I wish I knew what

you looked like now—has been in the papers. It made me miss you all over again.

    Be careful. Jason Lyons has come back to town. He's a prosecutor now. He doesn't care that you've been declared dead. He thinks you're still out there.

    R

SONIA LUBOVICH

18

I didn't know where I was going when I left Recluse. I don't know when the precise plan took shape. Perhaps it was always there, lost in pieces at the bottom of my luggage like a puzzle that I had to put together. My mother lived in Manhattan as a child, in a one-bedroom apartment with her mother. She had a paternal grandmother who didn't chip in much for the bare essentials but every summer paid for camp in upstate New York. For eight weeks my mom was shipped away from the steam box of that concrete island to run free among pine, maple, oak, cypress, and willow trees. She swam in lakes, canoed in rivers, engaged in leisure activities that were rarely afforded to her schoolmates back home.

These places sounded like such an adventure to my ear, I often asked my mother why I wasn't sent to camp. She pointed in the direction of the Waki Reservoir, where I swam every season except winter, and suggested I pitch a tent on the shore. It was only a partial joke. Our house was so small, I'm sure she wouldn't have minded the extra space.

Still, these majestic camps from her memory held court in

my mind and on occasion I'd ask her questions about her time there. Did she have her very own canoe? How many hours a day was she allowed to swim? Was anyone attacked by a bear? Did she stay in contact with any of her old cabin mates?

"No. We lost touch," my mother said as she took a sip of her third gin and tonic of the afternoon.

"Did anyone ever drown in the lake?"

"What's your obsession with drowning?" she asked.

I don't think I ever answered the question. In retrospect, it was a mild preoccupation of mine before it became an obsession.

"Did you have any boyfriends there?" I asked.

"Sure."

It was easy to tell when my mother was done talking. Her eyes would turn skyward, even if there was no sky worth seeing. I would always try to get one more morsel out of her.

"What would happen to the camp after summer ended?"

"Nothing," she said. "It was like Brigadoon until the children turned up the next year."

Only two hours were left in my journey when I sat down, looked out the window, and saw a glorious world passing me by. I realized that I'd found the perfect metaphor for my life. The color of the trees reminded me it was fall, now the middle of October. The leaves had changed and were starting to die, but the colors in the landscape were as extraordinary as anything I'd ever seen. For a little while I could forget all of the lives I was running from and gaze in awe at how beautiful this incredibly cruel world could be.

Before I knew what was happening, tears were running down my cheeks. I threw on my sunglasses and hoped no one had seen me. But the sunglasses dimmed the magic colors and I thought, *Fuck it, I want to see this*, because I wasn't sure how many more autumns I'd have left in my life, or how many I'd get to see as a free woman. I took the sunglasses off. I didn't care who saw me cry.

I got off the train in Albany sometime before three p.m. I purchased a ticket on the Empire Service, one stop to Hudson. I walked along Warren Street until I spotted in my peripheral vision the kind of motel to which I'd grown accustomed. I took a detour and checked into the Roosevelt Inn. I needed to clean up after being on the road, but I knew it was a luxury I couldn't afford much longer.

I paid cash so nothing would show up on her credit card, but I used the name Sonia Lubovich so I'd get used to it. I was surprised how easily the eastern European consonants rolled off my tongue. The clerk didn't give my pronunciation a second glance. Sonia and I were going to get along just fine.

"How long will you be staying?" the motel clerk said. He was heavily tattooed and looked like his ambitions far outreached his current station. Our exchange bored him immeasurably.

"Just one night."

I checked into my four-hundred-square-foot stopover, removed those stinging blue contact lenses, and took a long, hot shower. I changed into my other set of clothes and left the Roosevelt Inn to stretch my legs, enjoying a feeling that I could only describe as freedom. I picked up some practical items from a thrift store, washed my new and old hand-me-downs at the Laundromat, bought a couple of disposable cell phones, and checked the pockets of my new ten-dollar wool coat. It was a shabby, oversized checkered number, but one that looked like it might keep you invisible. I found a quarter in the pocket.

I located the library, which was closed for the day. I stopped in at an old-style diner, ordered a burger, and returned to the Roosevelt for my last night in a real bed.

In the morning, I took a hot shower and checked out of the motel, carrying all of my worldly possessions over my shoulder, and returned to the Hudson Area Library. Despite a gripping curiosity, I didn't check up on any of my past lives. Instead, I collected a list of summer camps in a thirty-mile radius and perused the classifieds for a used car.

After three hours, I had a list of five camps and three possible cars that were just a short stroll or cab ride away. After a few calls, I found an old lady who was selling her 1982 Jeep Wagoneer for $1,000. The price was steep considering my finances but a steal otherwise. I figured I'd be needing a vehicle with four-wheel drive and decent clearance on these country roads.

I made an appointment to meet with Mrs. Mildred Hensen at eleven a.m. I double-checked my finances, hoping that money had mysteriously appeared in my wallet, but things were as dismal as ever. After I purchased the car, I'd be down to just over five hundred dollars, and that wasn't much to live on without any source of income. I took a taxi to the seller's house in Red Hook.

Mrs. Hensen was a lovely old lady. Hard of hearing, which somehow facilitated our communications. She didn't bat an eye when she saw Sonia's Pennsylvania license, and she swatted her hand dismissively when I tried to explain that I needed to take the car registration papers and fill them out myself *after* I got my New York State driver's license sorted out. I'd contrived a whole long-winded story about an ex who was hanging on to my passport, but it was all unnecessary.

I took the Wagoneer for a spin. The shocks needed some work; it had the bounce of a horseback ride. The engine rattled more than it purred. But it worked and it was the right price and I wouldn't last long without a mode of transportation, so we made the deal over a cup of strong tea and homemade jam cookies.

When I left her house I drove through the windy, arborous roads trying to find my way to these camps that had no real landmarks or addresses one could discern under the thick awning of foliage. Eventually I came upon a maple sign adorned with the unremarkable name Camp Rodney. I followed an overgrown private drive past the NO TRESPASSING sign to a clearing with several cabins, painted white, evenly spaced apart, with one main building: white with blue trim, in the colonial style, but the structure appeared to be new.

I got out of the car, walked up the front step, and put my hand on the solid oak door. It was locked with a dead bolt that wouldn't budge. Curtains blocked the view through the window, so I walked around and peered through the side. I saw a room with several desks, like in a schoolhouse, and large steel closets in the back with more secure locks. I noticed a chart in the back of the room in binary code.

I took in the rest of my surroundings. One small badminton court, a tiny pond for a few rowboats, a fire pit, and a mess hall. My skills of deduction led me to the conclusion that Camp Rodney was a computer camp. With that kind of equipment on hand, I couldn't trust that they didn't have some kind of routine security. I moved on.

A few miles away, I explored the grounds of Camp Horizon. They had a lovely lake with rowboats, and their cabins were easy to trespass and seemed insulated enough that I could survive through early winter. But a pesky groundskeeper met me immediately, and I had to make up a story about vetting summer sleepaway camps for my finicky son next summer.

Camp Weezil had all of the amenities I required, but its grounds were too visible to the main roads, and I could easily be spotted.

It wasn't until late afternoon that I found Camp Wildacre, just north of Dutchess County and bisected by the Wildacre River. It was hidden one mile down a private drive. I didn't see any tire marks or signs of life. There was a short chain-link fence with a solid lock. I hopped the fence and explored the grounds. It felt like home right away. I just needed bolt cutters and a new padlock. I jumped back over the fence, got into the Jeep, and backed onto the main road. I stopped at a gas station and asked for directions to the closest shopping mall and followed the signs to the Rip Van Winkle Bridge. Travel on major roadways was generally something I would have to avoid. Every time I saw a state police cruiser, my heart would lurch. I could barely look at the road ahead of me, my eyes were so focused on keeping my Jeep in the sweet spot on the speedometer. The moment those lights whirled in my rearview mirror, my life would be over.

Perilous driving conditions aside, I made the journey across the bridge without any police interference. I stopped at a gas station to top off the tank and test whether Sonia's credit card had been reported stolen. I figured I had one final shopping spree left and then I was stuck with my minuscule nest egg. I found a collection of strip malls off the Kingston exit. I purchased four hundred dollars' worth of necessities, including a camping stove, carving knife, rope, can opener, padlock, bolt cutters, sleeping bag, nonperishable food items, and enough coffee to see me through the next few months. I tossed Sonia's card in a trash bin on the way out of the store. Maybe one day I'd write her a thank-you note.

I white-knuckled the return trip in the same fashion, my nerves clicking down a notch as I turned onto the dirt driveway of my new home. I felt like an eagle, my eyes so relentlessly darting about. At the hardware store I'd chosen the largest bolt cutters I could find, thirty-six inches. *It's all about the leverage,* I remember Mr. Parsons saying when I was a kid, as he used a wrench the size of six-year-old me to replace a rusted valve under his kitchen sink.

Turns out, fourteen-inch cutters probably would have done the job. I had the fence open and my new lock in place within five minutes. I drove onto Camp Wildacre, gave myself a brief twilit tour of the grounds, found an open carport to park my truck, and began to explore the cabins to choose my new home.

Wildacre, aside from the main building, had twelve satellite structures. As far as I could tell, ten were for the campers and two for the counselors. The main building probably had more amenities for the adults, but I didn't see any point in breaching security further than I already had.

What appealed to me about staying in these camps was living in a place that was there for the taking. The cabin doors had no locks. I wasn't hurting anyone. I was making use of something that wasn't being used. Kind of like recycling.

The cabins were all exactly the same. A-framed, wood-paneled, with green trim on the walls. Twelve built-in beds with plastic-covered mattresses remained in every cabin. Cubby spaces beneath the beds provided ample room for storage. The only thing that differentiated the cabins was the names graffitied on the rafters. I chose the structure with the girls' names and dropped my sleeping bag on the bed that was farthest from the door. I unpacked a few of my belongings inside a modest closet and stepped outside to check out the other amenities. There were two divided bathrooms and shower houses with running water, but cold only. I wished I had known that morning's hot shower would be my last for some time.

* * *

I didn't sleep a wink that first night at Camp Wildacre. During the day, I'd figured out how to go about my business without turning into a quivering ball of nerves, but nighttime presented a problem. While it seemed unlikely I'd have any visitors, one is most vulnerable at rest and I had to take measures in the event of unwanted trespassers. I found a shovel in the landscaper's shed and dug a few strategically spaced holes in the vicinity of my new home. It took a few afternoons to whittle branches into spikes, but eventually I had about twenty and I fashioned four Apache foot traps.

Booby traps aren't exactly my area of expertise and even I was surprised I would find a reason to use this skill. I'd made my first Apache foot trap more than fifteen years ago. Logan had taught me, back when I didn't know him so well. You dig a hole at least two feet wide and deep, then place several spikes of wood in the walls of the hole, the sharp ends jutting out of the dirt toward the center at a downward angle. If an animal (or human) steps into the trap, when he tries to pull his leg out, it gets caught on the wood daggers.

The day I helped Logan make his Apache foot trap, he told me he was trying to cut down on the deer population, which was becoming a menace to the community. There had been three deer-related traffic deaths in the past year. I'd read about it myself. Then a few days later this boy on the football team confronted Logan after he made some choice comments about the footballer's girlfriend. The footballer had forty pounds on Logan and looked like he was about to swing. Logan made a run for it, straight into the woods. The footballer gave chase and Logan led him straight to the trap. Logan jumped right over it. The football player didn't. He was out the entire season.

The cabins at Wildacre were organized kind of like the moons around Saturn. My cabin was at two o'clock. I set four traps in a semicircle about ten yards from my door. It might have been overkill, but the days were mine to do with as I pleased, and I figured it would give me peace of mind. I very much liked the idea of sleeping through the night. When I was ready to be on my way again, I would fill those holes right back up.

October 19 was the second night I spent in my new home. The air smelled so pure I couldn't help but breathe more than necessary. The moon was half-full. I couldn't make out all of the faces in the craters that I used to see as a child. I lay outside on the dirt and stared at the sky until my eyes couldn't stay open any longer. The sound of crickets was deafening. I tried not to think about all of the mosquito bites I'd find come morning. Well after midnight, I retired to my cabin and slept the sleep of the innocent. In the morning it felt as if I'd caught up on years of missed slumber.

I would never forget what I had done, the mistakes I had made, the innocent and guilty people I'd left in my wake. But when I weighed my crimes against the world, I still believed that I was owed a decent existence. I believed it was fair for me to find some small pleasure in life. In those few weeks I had at Camp Wildacre, I tried to find it.

In the morning, I'd wake and make coffee and oatmeal with my propane stove. I ate breakfast on the dock of the lake, as a few mallard ducks arrived and departed, paying me no mind. Sometimes in the afternoon, I roamed the campsite, found a hiking trail, and cleared my head with a good long walk. If the day warmed up just a bit, I took a dip in the lake. I swam every day I could, even though it left my fingers numb and my lips blue for a full hour afterward. It made me feel alive. And free.

My first thunderstorm at Wildacre reminded me that this was not a long-term solution to my housing problem. The temperature dipped twenty degrees, and I was wrapped in my sleeping bag in a cabin that could barely keep out the rain. Thunder rattled the entire bunk. It felt as if lightning could split the A-frame right in half.

Occasionally I'd venture out for provisions, but nothing more. I should have kept my head down, but after two weeks straight of admiring that glorious landscape, I wanted to see something else.

One day at the beginning of November, I walked straight out of camp and strolled along the road to this hamlet I'd spotted on my last journey out. Three Corners was basically a poor man's strip mall. It was home to a small grocery store, a post office, and a bar that had no name, as far as I could tell, but it looked as inviting to me as the crystal-clear lake had on my first visit to camp.

I picked up a town crier and sat at the bar. I was wearing

old jeans, a flannel shirt, and a wool coat. With my blue knit cap covering my shorn locks, no one paid me much mind. I remembered that night in Casper, when I first met Domenic—the way the heads turned for Debra Maze, doing her best impression of Blue. Now I was practically invisible. There was a time I wouldn't have gotten pleasure from being undesirable, but now I saw it as a superpower.

"What'll it be?" the bartender asked.

I ordered ale since I had a bottle of bourbon back at camp. I read an article about a local tree surgeon, detailing specific root rots and suggesting preventative measures to manage the forestry around your home. It seemed more like an advertisement for his services than news, but it held my attention until the next set of customers arrived.

When the door swung open, I heard a woman giggle over a man's deep, modulated voice, finishing up some story that must have been hilarious.

"So I gave him the money and said fuck it. You only live once."

I could have presented some serious arguments against his last statement, but I refrained. The city man was wearing designer jeans, a brown cable-knit sweater, and fashionable leather hiking boots that hadn't seen too many trails. The woman was bone thin, aside from her breasts. She was in a similar outfit, jeans and gray cardigan, and yet the pair looked as if they were from a foreign country.

A hush spread through the watering hole as soon as the duo arrived. It was as if their presence somehow sucked the life out of the room. Watching my fellow patrons, I observed a traffic jam of silent exchanges, followed by hostile sidelong glances at the new customers. None of this was lost on the city couple, who went mute as soon as they saw all of those scolding eyes on them. The duo sat down on their bar stools and looked like they were trying to shrink into themselves.

"What'll it be?" the bartender said to the city couple.

The man in the sweater ordered a beer to blend and the skinny woman ordered a vodka soda. They both said thank you and smiled and tried to ignore the eyes boring holes in the center of their backs.

"Do you want to leave tonight or tomorrow?" the man in the sweater asked. He kept his voice low, as if having a conversation in a bar is considered impolite.

"Tonight," the bone-thin woman said. "There'll be less traffic."

It was easy to feel a certain solidarity with the locals since I blended so well. But the city couple had inadvertently given me a gift so beguiling that I couldn't help but feel tremendous gratitude. Others like them were around—many of them, as far as I could tell. The few times I'd ventured out on the weekends, the town seemed to have doubled in size with moneyed folk from the city getting away from it all. Monday, they'd be gone. And in winter, they'd come less and less as the snow piled up. But their homes would remain empty for the taking. It was quite possible that I could find myself living in the lap of luxury at least five days a week.

The city couple departed, presumably for their country

home, which would soon be vacant. I waited a moment and heard some grumblings from the other patrons about how the likes of them were raising taxes and ruining the local economy. I stepped outside as they drove off in the Sweater Man's Mini Cooper.

I got into my Jeep, followed them two miles up the road, and saw the Mini turn into a private driveway. From the road their home was completely obscured by foliage. If they were leaving tonight, I could check back Monday. I drove back to Wildacre, made a can of beef stew on my propane stove. I sat on the dock bundled up in my hat and my scarf and stared at the stars.

I woke the next morning to the sound of rifle shots. The blasts seemed to be coming from a distance and I didn't hear any voices, so I let myself drift off again. It was hunting season, and I'd have to get used to the sound of buckshot. Guns I could learn to sleep through, but human sounds would always grip me awake.

It was a human sound that came next. It was a howl, a man's wild scream of pain right outside my cabin door. I heard footsteps approach and other male voices trying to discern what I had already figured out. One of the hunters had fallen into one of my traps. In retrospect, the Apache snares might not have been a genius plan. They were intended to alert me at night should someone be hunting me, not to ensnare any innocent bystander and inadvertently alert him of my presence.

I peered through the window and saw three men surrounding the unfortunate one caught in my trap. One man began to notice the strategically placed branches on the ground outside my bunk. He took a few cautious steps and then swept the branches away with the butt of his rifle. I watched him as he stared down into the giant toothy holes in the ground.

"Found another one," he shouted. "What the fuck is going on here? This a camp for kids, right?"

While the two other men helped dislodge their friend's leg from my trap, the fourth guy uncovered my third and fourth traps and began roaming the grounds looking for, well, me.

"Someone is living here," the most curious hunter said as he entered the cabin right across from mine.

The exit to my cabin was out of their line of vision, but to get to my truck, I'd have to run right in front of three men with guns—four, if we were counting the one just trapped in a hole. I took the sleeping bag off the bed and shoved it into a cubbyhole that was out of view, slipped on my shoes and coat, and grabbed a lighter and the keys to my vehicle. I ran as fast as I could behind the mess hall of the camp while the curious hunter was still in the first cabin. I found a clearing right behind the building, out of their line of view, and began to collect kindling. I started a small fire, added more kindling, waited for it to take, and added three logs in a triangle.

Through the window of the mess hall I could see the men with their guns shouldered, searching the cabins.

Once the fire was ablaze, I ran into the woods and followed a trail about two miles long in a drunken crescent shape. The trail would spit me out a few hundred yards from my cabin, but on the side of camp where my truck was hiding in that carport. I ran full speed through the woods.

Twenty minutes later, I was on the edge of the clearing, crawling along the tree line, searching for signs of the hunters. As I approached the campsite, I saw the injured hunter sitting on a log. I heard some commotion over by the fire and could still see a plume of smoke. I got into my truck with no time to spare.

I gunned the engine, pulled out of the carport, and drove right past the injured guy and down the dirt path that led to the main road. My chain-link fence was still locked; in front of it was their Ford truck, blocking my only passage out.

I unlocked the fence and checked the truck. The keys were inside. Three shots fired into the air. I figured it was the injured hunter calling his friends. I couldn't back their truck all the way along the road and still have enough time to run back to get my Jeep. So I just backed up their Ford about fifty yards along the cratered road until I found a small clearing. I put the car in drive and drove to the edge. There was a short drop into a creek below. I didn't want to inconvenience the men by messing up their car, but I needed to be sure they couldn't give chase. This truck had way more pickup than my old Wagoneer. I stepped on the gas and barreled forward, taking the truck on a nosedive into the creek bed. The bumper bent and caved under the weight of the drop.

I climbed out of their truck and up the rocky terrain. I booked it back to my old Jeep, climbed inside, and gunned the engine.

I could see the hunters in my rearview mirror. I put my foot to the floor and ducked as bullets pounded the metal of my tailgate. I made a sharp right turn onto the main road, cutting off a Subaru, which honked wildly in my wake. I made a quick left turn on a smaller artery to escape the Subaru and put as much distance as I could between me, those hunters, and my short-lived home at Camp Wildacre.

August 23, 2015
To: Jo
From: Ryan

I'm going to keep writing, even if you never read a word of it. I just learned what happened to you, who you became, who you married. It's in the papers. Everyone knows you're alive.

There's something that I need to know.

Did you kill him?

R

19

The hunters had stolen only a few more weeks of camp life from me. I wouldn't hold a grudge. I probably could have survived the cold nights with a better sleeping bag and a few more provisions, but once we had our first winter storm, I'd never have been able to travel that driveway without a snowplow. Besides, I already knew my next move. I was just making it a bit earlier than planned. For the first three nights after my run-in with the hunters, I slept in the bed of my Jeep at a rest stop off the Taconic State Parkway.

That Sunday I began my house hunting. I frequented all of the local establishments: diners, supermarkets—farmers' markets were best. They always stood out, the weekenders, even if they didn't want to. I noticed a preference for sweaters, turtlenecks, corduroy, and denim that had been strategically worn down by a day laborer in China.

They were couples, mostly, the ones I followed. They'd toss their provisions into the trunk of their brand-new Jeep, Mercedes, or Range Rover and drive down twisty country roads, now edged by dead leaves and denuded trees. I kept a notebook and jotted down the route after we reached our destination. County Route 7, right at Jackson Manor, left on Cyril Lane, drive two miles, and turn onto a dirt road leading up to a house that was more often than not obscured by evergreens.

Monday morning, I went to the getaway of the city couple I'd encountered at Three Corners, since they had been the inspiration for my adventure. I slowed my Jeep down as I approached their driveway and tried to catch a look at their house. There was no way up without driving or walking, and few people roamed those long, winding roads unless they were seriously out of luck or taking exercise.

I drove up the quarter-mile path and parked in a roundabout that had been beaten by tire marks in the front of their house. The A-framed cabin was modest and homey-looking from the front. Two Adirondack chairs rested on a porch in need of repair. A dead plant stood by the front door. I looked under the planter. At least they weren't that stupid. I lifted up the welcome mat: no key. I followed the line of shrubbery that led from the house to the driveway. Rocks framed the garden and gravel path. I turned over all of the rocks that had more or less shine than the others, kicked at a few to get a sense of their weight.

When I circled the house again, I saw another plant clinging to life. Right inside the planter was a key, jutting out of the soil. There were no signs for an alarm company, so I wiped the key off on my jeans and stuck it into the lock. It turned.

I opened the door and walked inside. Wooden beams hung across the ceiling, low enough to knock a six-foot-two man unconscious. The architecture might come in handy. The furnishings were spare and disjointed. A matching wood-framed sofa and love seat dominated the living room. A bright red Formica kitchen table was surrounded by green metal folding chairs. A frayed Oriental rug lay in the center of the adjacent living room, clashing violently with the flowered pattern that upholstered the couch. The overall décor gave the impression that the furnishings had been culled from a collection of yard sales without a moment's consideration. My first city couple were just visitors, trying to get away from it all. There was no way in hell those two had styled this house in this low-rent fashion.

Still, it was a house with a roof and a wood-burning stove and a working kitchen. I continued my inspection until I saw a laminated piece of paper with a calligraphed list.

House Rules

Make yourself at home.

Please do not leave any food crumbs out for the mice.

If you leave any food behind, please put it in the refrigerator.

Help yourself to anything in the house.

Please do not flush tampons or condoms down
the toilet. We have a septic system.

When you're ready to leave, please take the
sheets off of the bed and put them into the
washing machine. Our housekeeper will take
care of the rest.

I had already determined that this house wasn't a viable option. Unknown visitors mixed with an unpredictable maid were hardly a recipe for effortless squatting. I slipped out the back, locked the door, and stabbed the key back into the dirt. I got into my car and drove to the next house on my list.

The road leading up to the second house was about a quarter-mile long. When I reached the top of the hill, I practically plowed into an older gentleman on a John Deere riding mower. I slammed on my brakes and rolled down my window. He drove next to my truck and turned off his engine.

"Can I help you?" the man on the mower asked.

"I'm looking for the Bigelow house?"

"Who?"

"Don't the Bigelows live here?"

"Don't know the name. What's their address?"

"I didn't write it down, I was navigating from memory."

"Women should never do that," he said.

This got under my skin since I had an expert's grasp of

the US interstate highway system and an internal compass that failed me only on moonless nights. I probably shouldn't have engaged in any further conversation, but I couldn't help myself.

"Actually, I'm pretty good most of the time," I said. "But all of these private drives look the same. I must have overshot it."

"What town do the Bigelows live in?" the man asked. He wasn't going to let up, and answering any more questions was foolish.

"Sorry to have troubled you," I said. "I'll be on my way."

The man on the lawn mower remained parked in his spot, preventing me from making a U-turn. I put the car in reverse and backed the quarter-mile out of the serpentine drive as fast as I could.

Each house I went to that day presented its own set of challenges. The third house I visited shared a measly fence with neighbors, who seemed like locals based on the number of cars and bicycles in their driveway. No way could I come and go without their notice. The fourth house had several signs for a local security company perched in its yard. They might have been a bluff, but I didn't see the point in spinning the roulette wheel.

I was like Goldilocks looking for the bed that was just right. It was long past nightfall when I found it. A small but friendly looking stone cottage, at the end of a long private drive, entirely obscured by coniferous foliage. After a half-hour hunt by flashlight, I found the spare key nestled between two loose pieces of stonework under the kitchen window.

I opened the door and found a light switch by the foyer. The house was clean and simple and spare. Most of these country homes had accumulated a certain degree of clutter that cramped city apartments won't allow. I tried to remember what car/which people I'd followed to get to this place, but all of my marks had become a blur; they had no name, just a set of directions I'd jotted down on a cheap pad of paper I'd stolen from some motel.

It felt like the right place as soon as I turned on the lights. The air had a dampness, the way a house smells when it doesn't get much of a cross-breeze, which meant the owners weren't visiting all that often. I began looking through closets and cupboards. They were mostly empty, except for winter coats and canned goods. Some of the coats looked like they'd fit me. There was a television set but no cable, no Internet service. I picked up the phone and got a dial tone, but that was the only thing that linked this house to the rest of the world.

I checked the laundry room. It was clean, nothing left in the washer or dryer. The beds were made with military corners; there wasn't even a hint of a recent fire in the wood-burning stove; the dish rack was empty; the refrigerator held only condiments and baking soda. Perhaps I was being optimistic, but I had a feeling these people weren't coming back for a very long time. The thermostat was set to fifty-five degrees, which is a good number if you want to keep your pipes from freezing but have no interest in comfort.

Early November, the pipes wouldn't have much of a chance of freezing for at least six weeks. If they were planning on coming back before then, I couldn't see why they wouldn't turn off the furnace altogether.

I continued to scour the pantry until I found an open bottle of bourbon on a back shelf. I found a glass in the cupboard and poured myself a drink.

I roamed the house, trying to learn more about what I was beginning to conceive of as my new living arrangement. Despite the spare furnishings and general lack of decorative accents, a few personal touches were strewn about. A modest family portrait, taken on this very porch, rested on the fireplace mantel. A man and woman in their early fifties, who appeared both lean and vigorous, but without that shade of vanity that often accompanies the health-conscious. They both had gray hair, sun-lined faces, and warm smiles. Sitting between them were two boys, both in their early twenties. One was an exact replica of the father and the other, who looked about the same age, was a perfect composite of his parents. He had his father's high forehead and square jaw, his mother's big brown eyes, and the exact same gap she had between her two front teeth. Everyone had their arms around each other and they wore genuine smiles, as if they had just been laughing.

They looked happy in a way I had never known and probably never would. On the rare occasion my mother and I (and her man du jour) took a photo together, we'd all smile for the camera, but when you looked back at the picture, you never believed it. Even when I was young and had no concept of the limits that my future life would hold, whenever I'd see a happy family, a jealousy would overtake me that was so ugly, it felt like my soul was rotting. I had to train myself not to look at them. In stores, at the movie theater, outside schools, I'd avert my gaze.

I put the photo of my host family facedown on the mantel because it would break my heart whenever I saw it.

An old wooden desk stood in the hallway near the front door. A tan push-button phone, which looked like it had been stolen from an office, sat on the desk next to a calendar and a mug stuffed with an assortment of pens. I checked the calendar to see if they had marked the previous weekend's visit and saw two Xs over Saturday and Sunday. I looked ahead and saw a question mark over Thanksgiving and another series of Xs over Christmas. I finished my drink and poured another. I was settling in for the night.

Inside the desk were a few files with numbers for utility services and old bills. I looked at the name on the phone bill. Leonard Frazier. I wondered if he went by Len or Lenny. That might be important if a neighbor made a house call. I continued searching the desk to see if I could retrieve a name for the woman. In the bottom drawer was a small cardboard box containing a collection of letters and cards. Most of the cards were of the Christmas variety. Most were addressed to either "the Frazier Family" or "Mr. and Mrs. Frazier"; one or two were made out to only Gina Frazier.

The odd thing was that several, maybe a dozen, letters

were unopened. They appeared to be personal notes, judging from the feel of the envelopes. I eventually found one that had a clean slice along the rim. Since I had already invaded this family's home, invading their privacy didn't strike me as a significant detour.

I plucked the neatly folded rice paper from the powder-blue envelope and read:

> *Dear Len and Gina,*
>
> *We didn't know what to write or if we should, if words even exist that can bring you comfort. We've struggled with this letter for days. I'm so sorry about Toby. He was a beautiful soul and he will be missed.*
>
> *I can't imagine what you're going through right now, but let us know if there's anything we can do. It sounds so foolish to write that, but we mean it.*
>
> *Love,*
>
> *Tricia and Robb*

I returned the letter to the envelope and sifted through the rest of the stack. I found another opened envelope. A Hallmark card. *Many Sympathies for the Loss of Your Child.* Inside were a few lines about people mourning with them and finding strength with each other. The sender merely scribbled at the bottom: *My thoughts are with you, Diane.*

I had no idea they made greeting cards for such specific, tragic events, but they seemed like a bad idea, and Diane struck me as utterly tactless. There were more letters, unopened. Perhaps after getting the first few notes, Gina and Len didn't see the point in reading on. But I did. I found the letter opener in the middle drawer of the desk. I picked an envelope at random and sliced it open.

> Dear Len and Gina,
>   Please forgive me for taking so long to write. I was in such shock myself I didn't know what to say. I'm sorry for your loss. Toby was a sensitive, fragile soul. He will be missed.
>   Of course, if you need anything, I'm here. Always.
> Love,
> Lynette

It was odd, the emotional shift from my first steps into the Frazier home to the point where I currently found myself. After I glimpsed the photo of the perfect family with their quaint vacation home I gave myself permission to trespass into their unused space. I resented all that these people had. But knowing what they had been through, an unspeakable loss, made me more comfortable in their house, as if I belonged here because we shared the common ground of misfortune.

It would be days before I truly understood how extreme my violation was. At the time, I just thought, *I'm home.* I poured another drink and took a seat at the foot of the desk, searching the letters for one that might hold more than generic sympathies. I picked up a small, plain business envelope; the return address was from a C. Larsen in Oberlin, Ohio.

Dear Gina and Len,

I'm sorry. I'm so sorry.

I didn't know. Believe me, if I had any idea what he was going to do, I would have said something, I would have done something. I really thought he was getting better. He seemed happy just the day before. Please forgive me.

Damn it, this letter is stupid. It's about as useful as his suicide note.

Carl

I put the letters back into the box and closed the drawer. I crawled over to the corner of the room and sat there, listening to my heart beat so loudly I could hear it. For just a few moments, I didn't feel as welcome there anymore. It was like the house was expelling me on its own, begging me to leave, the walls practically giving me a shove out the door. Yet I remained firmly planted on the floor, the heels of my shoes digging in for traction. There was sickness in this house, and that part felt right to me. I was determined to stay.

That night I took a hot shower, my first in over three weeks. It felt as decadent as eating caviar. I looked through the drawers and found an old Yankees T-shirt. It could have been Leonard's or Gina's. It might have even been Toby's. I put it on and crawled into bed. I didn't sleep that night, but I was warm and comfortable and I wasn't sure what else I could hope for.

The next day I remained housebound. Most of my worldly possessions were marooned at camp, assuming those hunters hadn't pilfered all of my supplies. I didn't feel like heading back to retrieve them. Besides, the Fraziers had all I needed for a while. They had canned goods and dried goods and some frozen vegetables, at least three jars of tomato sauce, and the rest of that bourbon to consume. They had books and music, but it was their movie collection that was the most enticing in light of my recent television-free existence.

Their assortment of DVDs had no common denominator, nor were they in any discernible order. *Dr. Strangelove* sat next to *Better Off Dead*, followed by *The Philadelphia Story*, then *Die Hard*, *On the Waterfront*, *What About Bob?*, *Apocalypse Now*, *The Hangover*. The rest of the collection of fifty or so titles followed a similar lack of cohesion. I sat in front of that shelf for about an hour, trying to choose a film, until I realized that I had nothing but time. I picked the first disc on the top shelf on the left—*Dr. Strangelove*—put it in the DVD player, sat down on the couch, and watched.

Three days and twenty films later, I had barely moved from that very spot.

September 3, 2015
To: Jo
From: Ryan

I know you're on the run. How are you getting by? If you need money, don't ask him again. I have some put aside for you. I always had it. I never mentioned it to you, because I thought it would make you angry. You can have it any time you want it.

Maybe you think it's too dangerous to write back. I'm careful. I go someplace to do this and I've never told anyone.

I think you need help now. Let me help you.

R

September 16, 2015
To: Jo
From: Ryan

Look, there's this writer coming around asking questions, I think because of the ten-year anniversary. She says she's writing a whole book on the murder of Melinda Lyons and the disappearance of Nora Glass. She came to see me. I put her off. But she's renting one of Mrs. Carlisle's extra rooms. It looks like she's staying for a while.

Here's another thing, something that might make you happy. Edie left Logan. It's over. If you're still angry about that, about what I didn't do, maybe you can let it go and write me back.

Yours, R

20

The television in the Frazier home held me captive. I found myself incapable of doing much other than sitting on a couch and staring at a screen. By the fourth day, after I'd eaten plain oatmeal for ten meals straight, I thought I ought to venture out and retrieve my belongings from Camp Wildacre.

I left my car half a mile away tucked under an evergreen. I wore one of Gina's dresses and dotted my lips with a cherry gloss I found in the medicine cabinet. I didn't look right, I knew that, but I didn't look anything like the woman who'd had that run-in with the hunters. I could have just as easily been a worn-out mother looking for a sleepaway camp for her son or daughter. I found the camp just as I had left it, with the addition of the broken fender in the creek from the Ford truck I had crashed. The chain-link fence remained unsecured, and the hunters hadn't even bothered to fill in my Apache foot traps for the next unfortunate pair of legs to stroll in that direction.

I checked my bunk. Muddy footprints covered the floor,

but they hadn't noticed all of my supplies tucked away in the cubbyhole. Perhaps it had never occurred to the hunters that I had been settling in for a long stretch. I shoved my clothes and food into my backpack and gathered my camping gear. I refilled the foot traps with the same soil I had removed from them. I lugged all of my gear back to my Jeep, sweating hard in that cold fall air.

As I drove away, I already felt nostalgic. Even before I knew what was to come, I knew that Wildacre was the last place I'd find real freedom. Something was about to change. As the weather turned and my options narrowed, I might find moments of feeling safe, secure. But in general my life was like standing under a showerhead with the water heater on the fritz—ice-cold to scorching in two seconds flat.

I went to the store and purchased cheap produce, bread, peanut butter, and whatever was on special. I tried hard not to think about my dwindling savings. I tried not to think about the kind of work that the likes of me could get in this town, or any town in which I might remain anonymous. I wouldn't need much to survive in the way I was planning, but I'd need *something*.

I thought about calling Ryan, but pride deterred me for the time being. It was easier to keep my distance. Besides, I still had $228 to my name and a roof over my head.

On my way home from the store, I drove past the no-name bar. I felt like company even if I wasn't planning to talk to anyone. It was happy hour and drafts were only two dollars. The bartender nodded, as if he remembered me from last time. I decided this ought to be my last visit.

Someone had left a newspaper on the bar. I picked it up to avoid conversation.

"What'll it be?" he asked.

"Draft," I said.

As he poured my pint, he decided to make friendly conversation. I wondered if I'd ever be able to engage in small talk without feeling like there was a lit stick of dynamite in the vicinity.

"You a local?" he said.

"Just passing through."

"From where?"

"Everywhere."

He looked at me, right in the eye, and then averted his gaze as if something about me troubled him. He served me without making eye contact again. I wondered what he saw. Would I see it if I looked in the mirror? Improbable thoughts bubbled to the surface. Could he see who I was, what this life had made of me? I hadn't let myself linger much in the past. The best part of running full speed is not having time to look back. But even if I didn't think about it much, I had felt a seismic internal shift after I had killed Jack Reed.

If I had to do it over again, I probably would. But I would do it knowing that the person I used to be, the person I dreamed of returning to, was completely gone. It wasn't as simpleminded as a shift from good to bad. I wasn't evil. But some kind of disease was spreading in my gut, and eventually it would take over my entire body. I hadn't yet realized anyone could see it from the outside.

"Did you hear about Earl?" a customer with a handlebar mustache asked the owner.

"No. What?"

"Got caught in some kind of animal trap at Camp Wildacre."

"What was he doing there?"

"Hunting with Gary and Lou and I think Mike."

"Who set the trap?" the bartender asked.

"They say a teenage boy, probably a runaway, had set up camp there. When Earl got caught, the kid made a run for it. They got a partial license plate number, but Mike doesn't want to call it in because you ain't supposed to be hunting at Wildacre."

"Do they think the kid set the trap?" the bartender asked.

"That's what Gary figures. He might be one of those paranoid kids, the kind that blow up schools."

"Sounds like he just set a trap," said the bartender. "Maybe he was hoping for some venison for supper."

"Who the hell knows? Kids today."

My Jeep was parked outside, with the partial license plate right on display and dotted with bullet craters. I didn't think I looked like a teenage boy up close, but I finished my beer and got out of there.

As I drove back to the Frazier home, I pulled onto the shoulder of the road a couple of times to let cars pass me by, even slow ones hauling tractors. There wasn't a single witness as my car pulled into the private drive of my secret home.

After two and a half weeks of keeping house in the Frazier cottage, I'd come to feel as if I knew them, knew the whole family. Subtle clues were strewn about—organic cleaning supplies, the denuded garden beds in the backyard, and of course their incoherent movie collection. A woodshed stood behind the house. It took me five hours to find the key for the padlock. It was a small art studio where Mr. or Mrs. Frazier painted amateur landscapes. They weren't half-bad to my eye, but what I found intriguing was that none of them had been hung inside the house. There was humility to that, which I respected. Behind a stack of paintings I found an aborted attempt at a portrait of Toby.

I went to the library one day and searched "Toby Frazier suicide." I read an article in his college paper about his death. Friends and family described Toby as a reserved but kindhearted young man. Sensitive. His suicide happened on the heels of a breakup with a girl. She was unnamed. He was survived by his fraternal twin brother, Thomas, a Yale sophomore, and his parents, Gina, a math teacher in Manhattan, and Leonard Frazier, an investment banker.

That was the last time I looked into the private lives of the Fraziers. I left the rest of the letters unopened in their box, although I felt them calling to me every night.

Sometimes I thought I could feel the sadness in the house,

as if I knew the Fraziers personally. After two and a half weeks of living in their home, I no longer felt like an intruder. I was simply a houseguest staying for an indeterminate period of time. I treated the home with respect. I washed dishes after every meal, dusted on occasion. Washed the floors and cleaned the bathroom at least once a week. I even scrubbed down the windows, which I was fairly certain they would notice once they returned. But it seemed like the right thing to do.

As with anything, I adjusted. I'd adjusted to being on the run; I'd adjusted to a new name, and another new name; I'd adjusted to being a liar; I'd adjusted to being a thief; I'd even adjusted to being a murderer. It wasn't that hard to adjust to a new home. I had even begun sleeping through the night. I was sleeping as if this life I led was perfectly ordinary. I was Sonia Lubovich, houseguest of Gina and Len Frazier, until I woke up one night and I was someone else.

PAIGE

21

"Hello? Hello? Is anybody in here? Hello?"

I didn't wake as the car traveled up the winding driveway; the Prius might have stirred some gravel, but the engine was as quiet as a mouse. I didn't wake when she put the key in the lock; I didn't wake when she quietly shut the door behind her. But when her foot hit the floorboard in the entryway, I shot straight up in bed, adrenaline pumping too fast for my lungs to catch up.

The bathroom had a window without a screen. If I ran right then and crawled outside, she wouldn't see me. My bag with my wallet and cash was at the foot of the bed, but the keys to my Jeep sat on the desk in the front hallway. I wouldn't make it far on foot, and I was at least ten miles from any form of civilization.

"Hello?" she said again.

"Hello?" I said.

I was still working on the next thing I would say when Gina Frazier entered the bedroom. She resembled her photo in so many ways—the same practical haircut, the strong bones of her face, the sturdy physique—and yet she also looked like someone else. Her eyes had deep pools under them. In the dim glow of moonlight, she looked haunted. For a brief moment I found her terrifying.

"Paige, is that you?"

"I'm sorry," I said.

She stepped closer, her eyes adjusting to the dark, trying to make me out in the dim light. She wasn't afraid. She knew me, or thought she knew me.

"I thought you were coming next week," she said.

"No. This week."

"Did you get all of your things?" Gina asked.

"I think so. Thank you. Should I go?"

"It's late, Paige. Where will you go?"

"A motel. Anywhere," I said.

"It's fine," Gina said coldly. "You can stay the night."

"Thank you, Mrs. Frazier."

"*Mrs. Frazier?* Really?"

"Gina," I said hesitantly as I crawled out of bed. "I'll take the couch. You sleep here."

"That's very kind of you," she said unkindly. "But I'm not quite ready for bed. I'm going to make some tea," Gina said, leaving the bedroom.

I followed Gina into the kitchen and living area, where she turned on the kettle. She wrapped her coat tightly around her body and strolled over to the thermostat.

"It's freezing in here. Why didn't you turn up the heat?"

"I wanted it to be like I had never been here," I said.

"Interesting," she said as she cranked up the thermostat.

I could hear the boiler kicking on in the basement, sending vibrations through the entire house, matching the thrumming of my nerves.

I was standing aimlessly in the middle of the room. These days I saw every challenge in the form of a map, my mind traveling different routes to find my way out. With Gina, I kept hitting dead ends.

"Sit down," she said. "You're making me nervous."

I sat on the couch.

"I'm surprised you don't have hypothermia," she said.

I was cold. But it was always warmer than the camp. And the Fraziers had hot water.

"I was fine," I said.

Gina kicked off her shoes and curled up on the other end of the couch. She looked at me again, tilting her head at different angles.

"You look different. I guess it's the haircut," she said.

She had seen this Paige before, I guessed. I was fairly certain that if she turned on an overhead light, she'd know immediately that I was a fraud. I tried to modulate my expression, but I had so many other things to keep in mind, like gathering my cash and my keys and making a run for it, that I doubt I had much control over my facial muscles. I must have looked confused, because she clarified.

"I made him show me a picture once. Your hair was long."

I'd gotten pretty solid at being anyone other than myself,

but Paige was proving more difficult than the others. Who was Paige?

"I cut it," I said.

"You sure did," Gina said knowingly. "Women do very strange things over men."

"I was drunk," I said.

"Ah," she said.

Gina spotted the family photo facedown on the mantel. She got up from the couch and righted it. She sat down, lifted her eyes to mine, and gave me an inscrutable gaze. I turned away.

"How have you been?" I asked because it was the kind of question I thought Paige, or someone who knew something of Gina's life, might ask. I also asked because I wanted to know.

"How do you think I am?"

"I guess that was a stupid question."

"It was an especially stupid question for *you* to ask," she said.

"I assume you came here to be alone," I said.

"I came here to get away from my husband."

"Why?"

"I can't manage his guilt and my own," Gina said.

The constant edge to her tone was chipping away at all those friendly feelings I'd felt toward the woman before I knew her. She had looked kinder in the photos.

The kettle whistled. Gina jumped, startled. Her nerves might have been as raw as mine. She walked over to the stove.

"Would you like a cup of tea?" she asked in an oddly professional tone.

"Okay."

"Peppermint or chamomile?"

"Peppermint."

She poured two mugs of tea, passed me my cup, and sat back down in the same spot.

"I wanted to meet you," Gina said. "Len didn't think it was a good idea."

"I wanted to meet you too."

"Liar."

I didn't know what to say to that. I sipped my tea and burned my tongue.

"Where are you going for Thanksgiving?" she asked.

For the last eight years we'd had an "orphan dinner" at Dubois'. That was always the worst day of the year for me, including Christmas and my fake birthday.

"I don't know," I said. "You?"

"We'll be at my sister's," Gina said.

"That sounds nice."

No one said anything for a while. We drank our tea and I tried to look for an excuse to depart in the middle of the night.

"Do you feel guilty?" Gina asked.

"All of the time," I said.

"Good."

The radiator made a clanking sound, like an out-of-tune musical instrument. I could feel the heat coming into the room, but her response sent chills through me. My best guess was that Paige was the unnamed girlfriend of the dead son, the girl who broke up with Toby right before he killed himself. I stared blankly at Gina.

"It wasn't all your fault. I know that," she said.

"Wasn't it?" I said.

What reason did Paige have to visit the cabin?

"How did you two meet?" Gina asked.

"He never told you?" I said.

"I never inquired."

"Right."

"So how did you meet?"

The woman in front of me had a darkness and cruelty that I hadn't seen in a long while. Being the recipient of this kind of grief and anger reminded me of things, of people, I'd just as soon have forgotten.

How *did* Paige meet Toby?

"In a bar," I said. I could have said a party, but she might have asked whose party. I could have said class, but then I'd have been foiled by specifics.

"In a bar," Gina repeated as if it left a bad taste in her mouth.

"It's a cliché, I suppose."

"The whole thing is a cliché."

Her voice was as sharp as the tip of a sword. Her eyes narrowed into dark crescents as she looked at me searchingly.

"What did he see in you?"

I didn't know why she was asking that question, but it

felt all too familiar. I used to ask myself what he saw in me. Later I had to ask the more important question: what did I ever see in him?

"I don't know," I said.

"You must have amazing tits," she said.

"What?"

Her words felt like a whiplash. I didn't know who I was supposed to be anymore.

"There's nothing else to you, besides youth. You're just a shell. You seem empty inside, as if your personality has been hijacked."

I felt like I was being clawed from the inside out. My face flushed deep crimson and my eyes welled with tears. I went into the bedroom and began to dress. I could no longer impersonate a real human being without carving out the last chunk of my old self and leaving it behind. Everything Gina said to me was true, even though she was talking to someone else. She followed me into the bedroom and watched me dress.

"Are you leaving?" she said, as if surprised.

"Yes."

"I said you could stay."

"It's all right. I should go."

I shoved all of my clothes into my bag, searched the house for anything incriminating that I might have left behind. Two words repeated over and over in my head. *Get. Out.* I took the key to the cabin off of the ring and left it on the desk. I turned and looked back at Gina as I opened the front door.

"I'm sorry about everything."

"What are you sorry for?" she said, this time with genuine curiosity.

"I'm sorry about your son," I said.

"My son? Why? You didn't know him."

Was she speaking figuratively? Maybe I wasn't who I thought I was. I stepped onto the porch. My Jeep was only a few steps away. All I had to do was walk ten paces and I'd be free.

"I'm sorry for your loss," I said as I stepped off of the porch.

"That's what you're sorry for?"

"I'm sorry for so many things," I said.

"Are you sorry you fucked my husband?"

I tripped on the last step. Once I got my legs under me again, I turned back to Gina. Her face was as still as the stonework around her home. She saw me as her enemy, but I couldn't return the favor. I had stolen her hospitality for over three weeks. I figured I owed her, and I didn't have much to give. So I gave her all I had.

"I'm sorry I fucked your husband," I said.

"Thank you," she said as she stepped back inside and closed the door.

JO

22

The clock in my truck read 3:05 a.m. as I pulled onto Maple Lane. I had no place I needed to be or wanted to go. I was awake now. Wide awake. I had to keep moving, keep driving. My hands needed something to grip or they'd turn into fists looking for a target to swing at. I followed the country road until it spat me out on Route 9. I turned right, heading north. Plenty of miles stretched ahead of me before I'd hit the Canadian border.

By morning, I was in the foothills of the Adirondack Mountains. I'd stopped just once overnight at a gas station to fuel up, use the restroom, and buy a bottle of water. I drove another two hours. When dawn broke, the glare on my windshield blinded me. I pulled into the parking lot of a small grocery store, Walt's Market. I leaned the seat all the way back, covered my eyes with my jacket, and tried to sleep.

Three quick raps on the window woke me. I pulled the jacket off my head and saw a police officer standing by the truck. He motioned for me to roll down the window. I did.

"Good morning," he said. His eyes were hidden behind aviator sunglasses.

"Good morning," I said as I tilted the seat upright.

"How are you doing this morning, ma'am?"

"Fine, thank you."

"Do you know how long you've been parked here?"

The clock on the dashboard read 11:24 a.m.

"I'm sorry. I just stopped to rest my eyes."

"I got a call from Walt. That's his store over there. Walt wanted to make sure you were okay. You've been parked here for four hours."

"I didn't realize it was that long. I'll be on my way."

"Where are you headed?"

"I was just taking a drive, seeing the sights."

"You from around here?"

"No," I said, in case he asked for ID. Where was Sonia Lubovich from again? "Indiana."

"What brings you to New York?"

"I'm visiting an aunt in Red Hook," I said, in case he asked for registration. The car was still registered under the name Mildred Hensen of Red Hook, New York.

I was plain fucked if he asked for proof of insurance.

"I hope you enjoy your stay," he said.

"Thank you."

He started to walk away, then turned back.

"Sure you got enough shut-eye?" the officer asked.

"I'm awake now," I said.

The officer returned to his squad car. He made a right turn

out of the parking lot onto Route 9. I took a left, beating a return path on the same road I'd traveled all night long.

My run-in with Gina had left my mind jumbled and confused. I felt like I was roaming unfamiliar grounds in a blackout. My only plan was the same old plan: find another mark with a vacation home and remain an uninvited guest until circumstances caused my eviction. I didn't have a plan for money, which was running dangerously low; I didn't have a plan for becoming someone else, someone who could exist in a real way in this world. I most certainly didn't have a plan for how I was going to live the next forty or so years of my life.

With the way things were going, though, a full life seemed unlikely. As I drove, even knowing the exact road I was on and where it would lead, I felt more lost than I had that first time I left anyplace, so many years ago, without any idea of what the future might hold.

I decided to take a detour to Saratoga Springs. The air outside was cold and wintry. I roamed the town for a while, pretending to be a regular tourist. I didn't turn any suspicious heads. Christmas lights were strangling street signs and dangling across roadways. When I figured out what day it was, I realized it was only five days to Thanksgiving.

I was so homesick I could have drowned in it. I fought that feeling hard because you shouldn't pine for a place that spat you out so cruelly. I had ignored my past for a long time. I'd been ignoring all of my pasts as I attempted this shadow of a life. As I strolled past the main library, homesickness overtook my whole body, and I walked inside determined to take a stroll down memory lane.

I felt that aching slice across my back the moment I sat down at the computer banks. The library was mostly vacant this time of day, so I didn't feel that constant prickly need to look over my shoulder, and yet I felt this internal thrumming, my heart beating on overdrive. I stared at the blank screen, not sure where to begin, which life to check on first, which crimes to fear the most. I began with Tanya. Headlines, photos, fragments of my life flashed across the screen.

Then I checked in on my life before that. I had mistakenly thought I'd be old news by now. I figured that was the one benefit of being declared legally dead. Now I was worse than dead. My old lives were beginning to coalesce like a primitive dot-to-dot sketch. I scanned the headlines but didn't bother reading the stories.

Who is Tanya Dubois?
Tanya Pitts Dubois, Lived 8 Years Under Assumed Name
New Leads on Melinda Lyons Murder Ten Years Later
Prosecutor Jason Lyons Says Nora Glass Is Still Alive

I thought about walking into a police station and turning myself in, begging for the mercy of the court. It seemed unlikely that they'd believe anything I'd have to say, but at least I'd be done running and I wouldn't have to worry about where I was sleeping that night. Every morning I woke up, remembered my predicament, it felt like getting a shot of adrenaline.

I scanned the library to see if anyone was looking and then I thought back a few years, trying to remember my old e-mail password. I had tried to forget it so many times in the hopes that I could never look back.

But now it was time to go back to where all the trouble began.

I remembered the login and password on the second try. I could never forget it because I could never forget him. I'd managed to ignore him for a while, that's all. It had been two years since I'd last checked this e-mail. I figured Ryan might have given up after a while, but he didn't. I found seven new messages. I was ashamed at how happy it made me, sickened that he still had some power over me. I opened the oldest message, from back in 2014, when I was still safely locked in my life with Frank.

March 3, 2014
To: Jo
From: Ryan
    Where are you? Are you still alive?

I continued to read the messages he had sent while I was running, when I wasn't looking back too often, at least not to him.

August 23, 2015
To: Jo
From: Ryan

I'm going to keep writing, even if you never read a word of it. I just learned what happened to you, who you became, who you married. It's in the papers. Everyone knows you're alive.

There's something that I need to know.

Did you kill him?

R

I wanted to write back. I wanted to call him and scream and ask him if he really thought I could kill a man. But then I remembered that I had—just not *that* man. What he was really asking was how much I had changed over these ten years. I'd changed more than he could imagine. He wouldn't recognize me now.

I read the final two e-mails, dated just four weeks apart.

September 16, 2015

To: Jo

From: Ryan

Look, there's this writer coming around asking questions, I think because of the ten-year anniversary. She says she's writing a whole book on the murder of Melinda Lyons and the disappearance of Nora Glass. She came to see me. I put her off. But she's renting one of Mrs. Carlisle's extra rooms. It looks like she's staying for a while.

Here's another thing, something that might make you happy. Edie left Logan. It's over. If you're still angry about that, about what I didn't do, maybe you can let it go and write me back.

Yours, R

October 21, 2015
To: Jo
From: Ryan

Jesus, Jo. Where are you? You need to be careful. Things have changed. They know who you are and what you became. You're not dead anymore. They're looking for you.

R

I had so many things I wanted to write, so many things I wanted to tell him. Sadly, Ryan was still my best friend, even though he was the reason I was lost. I wanted to trust him, but I wasn't sure I could anymore. It seemed unwise to trust anyone. But I had to write back.

November 22, 2015
To: Ryan
From: Jo

I'm here. Sorry I was gone for so long, but it seemed best. I'll keep this brief.

No, I didn't kill Frank. He fell down the stairs, but I didn't know what would happen if the police started looking at me, really looking. And you know they would have. So I left. As for going to Mr. Oliver, it was a choice made from necessity. I didn't need just cash. I needed something only he could get me. Did he tell you he tried to kill me? He did. So I didn't bother him after that.

What do I need to know? Tell me more about this writer. Is she getting close to the truth? That would be bad for everyone, wouldn't it? Except me.

I need money.

Jo

I logged out of the e-mail account, erased my search history, put on my coat, and left the library. I took a walk under a light drizzle, trying to clear my head. Then I heard thunder rumbling and saw a flash of lightning. The rain battered the town. My wool coat was soaked through within minutes. I shuffled along the sidewalk, taking refuge under shop awnings and scaffolding until I found a tavern. I opened the door and walked into complete darkness.

23

It took two whiskeys to get my bearings. It wasn't until I'd downed the third that I started to think clearly again. My past lives would hold for the moment. It was the present I needed to sort out. My identity was weak, I was almost out of cash, and I needed to find a roof over my head sooner than later.

No one paid me any notice other than to suggest I hang my coat by the fireplace so it might dry off. My wool cap, cropped hair, hollow eyes, and menswear kept me mostly invisible to the opposite sex.

I ordered another whiskey and decided to stay. Maybe a customer would drop a line on a vacant home. The desultory conversations yielded no leads beyond football picks, some petty neighborhood crime, and a marriage on the verge of divorce. I already knew I wouldn't be able to drive that night, so I ordered one more drink and I left.

I slept in the back of my Jeep as a storm battered the roof. In the morning when I opened up the tailgate, the sky was still sulfurous, but the rain had cleared. The air was fresh and damp, and the blast of cold felt like an ice pack for my hangover. I strolled over to a café, used the restroom, brushed my teeth, splashed cold water on my face, and bought a cup of coffee for the road.

I got into my truck, put the keys in the ignition, and the engine sputtered and died. I turned the key again. The battery light blinked on the dashboard, but my Jeep was quiet as a mouse. I pumped the gas pedal and tried again, because that's what you do, you keep trying even when you know the effort is in vain.

As I prayed for my car to start, someone knocked on my window. He could have punched me in the face and I might have been less alarmed. I looked over. A man stood there, maybe fifty, sixty years old, with a full brown beard speckled with gray and a mop of unkempt salt-and-pepper hair. I rolled down the window.

"Sounds like your battery is dead," he said.

That was what it sounded like.

"Think so," I said.

"Pop the hood," he said. "I got jumpers."

I wasn't one to turn down the assistance of a Good Samaritan. His car was parked a few spots over in the lot. He drove a bright red Chevy truck twice the size of mine. Leaving the engine on, he attached the jumper cables and made a swirling motion with his finger, telling me to start the engine. My Wagoneer sputtered more heartily but never seemed to get any ground. The Good Samaritan told me to shut it down. He walked over to my window.

"It's toast. You need a new battery. There's an auto shop just a few miles up the road. I can give you a lift."

I nodded, already thinking of excuses and explanations. He shut the hood of my Jeep, then his, and returned the cables to a toolbox in the bed of his Chevy. I got out of my vehicle as he opened the passenger door to his.

I thought maybe I could do it just that one time, ride two miles in the passenger seat without the paralyzing fear and nausea kicking in—but standing there, with the door open, I couldn't.

I looked at the Good Samaritan and smiled. "You mind if I hop in back? I got a wicked hangover this morning, and I wouldn't want to lose my lunch in your pretty new truck."

The Good Samaritan looked like he was about to rescind his offer, not for my lack of gratitude, but because it occurred to him that my entire head might be a jangling mess of loose screws. He narrowed his eyes, as if a deeper focus on his subject might reveal whether my character had any dangerous faults. I jumped in the back of the truck and sat down, giving him the thumbs-up sign.

"It's very comfortable back here. Thank you so much for your kindness."

The Good Samaritan shrugged and drove. When we reached the auto parts store, I jumped out of the truck. The Good Samaritan got out of his vehicle and continued to study my demeanor as if I were bouncing around in a padded room.

"I can take it from here. Thank you," I said, shuffling off.

"You know what kind of battery to get?" he shouted after me.

I turned around and said, "I figured I'd just tell them the make and model, and go from there."

He nodded his approval. "Do you know how to replace the battery?" he asked.

I hadn't thought that far ahead. When Frank and I were married, every time we heard an unusual squeak or rattle in the engine, we called Otis, who was such a regular at Dubois' we often didn't need to call him at all.

"I guess I don't know about that," I said to the Good Samaritan.

He made an excellent point, but his generous spirit was making me uncomfortable. In my experience people don't go far out of their way for a complete stranger unless they want something.

"I can probably figure it out," I said.

The Good Samaritan took a deep, cleansing breath and walked inside of the store ahead of me. He made a beeline for the aisle with the car batteries. I followed him. He pointed to the one I should get. I picked it up and took it to the register. We walked back to his truck. This time, he didn't even bother opening the passenger door. I dropped the battery on the truck bed and climbed in after it. We drove the two miles back to my car, the cold breeze continuing to tame my pounding skull.

Within fifteen minutes, the new battery was swapped for the old and I was sitting behind the wheel, my engine purring. I reached into my wallet, pulled out a twenty-dollar bill that I really couldn't spare, and extended my hand through the window.

"Thank you so much, sir. What do I owe you?"

I'd offended him. He approached the car, shoving his hands in his pockets to make it clear he wasn't accepting any gift of gratitude.

"Got a daughter about your age. She can change a tire and swap out a battery and she never goes anywhere without jumper cables. But say she didn't have a daddy who taught her these things. I would hope someone decent would do the same for her."

I felt terrible for thinking the things I thought he might be. It had never occurred to me that he might be a pure soul, that there were any of them left. I nodded and said thank you again—a real thank you, not one with guardrails all around it.

He was about to leave and turned back. "I understand why you didn't want to get in the vehicle with a complete stranger, but it's not safe to ride in truck beds. Don't make a habit of it. And don't make a habit of driving around in an old car without jumpers, a spare, and a jack."

When I got back on the road, I headed north in the general direction of Canada, although I stayed off of any main highways. In a few hours, I was in Saranac Lake, stopping for fuel and provisions at a small grocery outlet. Inside was a Western Union office. I took fifty of the eighty dollars I had left and put it on a prepaid credit card. The clerk asked for my social security number and ID. I wrote down a random number that was a few digits off from my social as Debra Maze and left with instructions for making an online transfer to my card.

I went to the main library, sat down at the computer bank, and logged in to my old e-mail. Ryan hadn't written back yet, but it had only been twenty-four hours. I sent another message, marked "Urgent." I gave Ryan the account number and told him that it would be deactivated in five days. I had no idea if or how he could track me, but I had to cover my bases.

I was just about out of cash and my back was aching something fierce. I didn't think I could spend another night sleeping in the Jeep, so I commenced a wholehearted attempt to find a new home.

I began driving around the foothills searching for overstuffed mailboxes along the roadside, figuring one of them might turn up a vacant vacation home. There were a few candidates that seemed promising, but one stuck out in particular. It was a one-bedroom A-frame cabin nestled on at least five private acres. The house had everything I required. It was hidden behind a stable of evergreens, and the closest neighbors were at least a mile down the road. It even had a generator, which seemed odd, considering the bare-bones nature of the property. When I checked the mailbox, it was swelling with fliers and junk mail, not a single bill, letter, or anything one might consider time-sensitive.

Despite the simple construction, the house was trickier to breach than I'd expected. There was no spare key tucked away, as far as I could discern. But one window was cracked just enough that I managed to wedge it open with my pocketknife. I took an old rocking chair from the porch and balanced precariously on it as I hoisted myself inside.

I had hit the squatter's jackpot. Every inch of that home was covered in dust. It's hard to describe the smell that had been trapped inside: a mixture of dirt, mildew, and stale air. The spare, unadorned furnishings told me it was a bachelor's very occasional retreat. According to his mailbox, his name was Reginald Lee.

I got to cleaning right away since the cloying combination of odors caused a sneezing fit that I recovered from only when I stepped outside again. I finished dusting in an hour. There was no washing machine, so I gathered the bedding and towels I found in the bathroom and drove to the closest Laundromat.

While the linens churned in the centrifuge, I worked out a story that might fly should Reginald Lee decide to take a holiday and find a strange woman sleeping in his bed. I chose to mix a bit of truth in with a hearty serving of fiction.

My husband died. He left me nothing. I had no source of income and couldn't pay the mortgage. My house was in foreclosure and I was evicted. I'd been living out of my car and the occasional motel room, but I had no money left and it was too cold for the car. I came upon your house, Reginald—Reggie?

I saw that it was empty. The window was open and I was just looking for a warm place to stop for the night. Please find some charity in your heart during this holiday season.

I pictured Reggie as a soft-spoken, simple man not unfamiliar with the plight of the impoverished. I truly thought he would take pity on me. When I looked in the mirror, I had to own how pitiful I looked. There was no fixing this hair of mine, and I'd lost fifteen pounds in the last month. Reginald would show me some mercy. And I certainly doubted he would accuse me of fucking his wife.

24

Reggie's home took some getting used to after the comforts of the Frazier cottage. He had no other form of heat besides a wood-burning stove. At least a cord of lumber was stored under a tarp on the back porch, but I still hadn't any notions about the vigilance or curiosity of his neighbors. If they saw a plume of smoke coming from Reggie's house, would they drop by to investigate?

That first night, I slept in a wool cap and thick socks under every blanket I could find. In the early hours of morning, when one would expect to hear only the whistling of wind and critters crawling across the roof, looking for trespass and shelter, I heard something else. It was a low humming sound. It could have been a furnace, but Reggie didn't have heat. It wasn't the refrigerator or any other household appliance. I shrugged off the mysterious noise and attempted sleep. I woke with my joints achy and my head still in a dreamy fog. I had bought basic provisions the first time I ventured out. I made coffee and a peanut butter and jelly sandwich for breakfast. I prayed that Ryan would come through for me since I didn't have many more peanut butter and jelly sandwiches in my budget.

Reginald didn't have much in the form of entertainment. He had an old TV and a DVD player, but no movies, which surprised me. His bookcase was primarily dedicated to Clive Cussler and stacks of *Guns & Ammo* magazines. He also had a copy of *The Anarchist Cookbook*, *The Turner Diaries*, *I'm OK—You're OK*, and *Who Moved My Cheese?* Reggie was hard to figure from his bookshelf, but I had to guess he wasn't the laid-back soul I had imagined.

There were no other personal touches to the cabin—no photographs, no artwork, no decorative accents beyond a dusty old rug, a plaid La-Z-Boy chair, a boot rack, and some tea towels with daisies on them. He did, however, have a shockingly extensive supply of canned goods, freeze-dried meals, and bottled water, as if he were anticipating the end of days. Out of respect for my missing host, I tried to limit my use of his stash to one can of soup a day. That humming noise I heard came and went. I didn't pay it much mind at first. Every home I've ever stayed in had its own kind of chatter.

The following morning, I returned to the library and checked the balance on my Western Union card. Ryan had deposited one thousand dollars. That might last me a few months in my current condition, but it was by no means a long-term solution. I logged in to my e-mail and saw that he had written back.

November 23, 2015
To: Jo
From: Ryan
    I'll send more, if you call.

He left a number and three different time frames over the course of the week in which I could make contact. I wrote back.

November 24, 2015
To: Ryan
From: Jo
    If this is a trap, I won't spare you. I won't spare anyone.

I remained in the library for a few more hours researching other matters. First I looked up the property records in Saranac Lake for the address of Reginald Lee's cabin. The previous owner was named Jedediah Lee. It was obviously family property, deeded to the son fifteen years ago. I ran a search on Reginald's name, but it was fairly common, so it was impossible to determine his current residence. I had to hope that he was content wherever he was and not planning a private getaway any time soon.

The library had central heat, so I was reluctant to leave. Beyond the more than ample supply of reading material, I couldn't resist the lure of the computer, the way it connected me to a world I was no longer part of. It seemed that the further away I moved from civilization, the more I was drawn to this false sense of community. I had resisted many things over the last several years. I didn't look back much, with the exception of my correspondence with Ryan. But it was the holiday season, and I was lonelier than I'd ever thought possible.

I typed the name "Edie Oliver" into a search engine. The first link was her profile page on a social media website that became popular right around the time I began running. The photo she used to identify herself was that of a little girl who mostly resembled her, with a little bit of *him* thrown in. Her privacy settings were weak, so I got a glimpse of the milestones in the last decade of her life. Married. Birth of daughter. Divorce. A few pictures of her. She looked the same as I remembered her, maybe a bit plumper with a few more wrinkles, and she'd grown out her bangs. I wanted to write, to say hello, but I remembered the way she'd looked at me the last time I saw her and I felt the betrayal all over again.

I read some of the comments people had left on her page. After her divorce announcement, some guy I thought I remembered from math class wrote: *Call me!* A few female names that rang a bell wrote things like *congratulations*; *hang in there*; *love you, baby*. I wondered if those words of encouragement brought her any real comfort. I imagined that she was a reluctant participant in this world, signing on because it was all part of the social fabric. That's how I think I would have been, if I'd stayed.

I scrolled down the posts on her page until one struck my curiosity. Someone named Laura Cartwright, no photo, had left a message:

Please contact me. I'm writing a book about Melinda Lyons. Looking for interview subjects.

I clicked on Laura Cartwright's profile page. That name. I knew that name, but I couldn't place it. Her personal details were spare and cryptic. She worked for *Self*. Her birthday was on April 1. She "liked" nothing. Her online existence, as far as I could tell, had begun only six weeks ago. Her life seemed to revolve entirely around the case of Melinda Lyons.

I created a profile for myself under the name of Jane Doe. It was just a name, after all. She wasn't supposed to be real. I began to compose a message to Laura Cartwright, offering my anonymous assistance with her investigation and inquiring whether she'd uncovered any new clues about the case.

As I was about to click the Send button, I thought better of it. She could also be a trap. Everywhere I turned, I saw potential land mines. I had to weigh all of my options before I proceeded.

The library was about to close. I checked my e-mail one more time and saw that I had a new message from Ryan.

November 24, 2015
To: Jo
From: Ryan
   Why would it be a trap? How would I benefit if you came home?

Something about his phrasing hurt my feelings. I guess I'd always believed that he wanted me to come home.

I returned to Reginald's cabin and opened a can of soup. That night we had our first snow of the season. When I woke up the next morning the world was blanketed in white. Icicles dangled from the trees and awnings like chandeliers. The world looked pure and peaceful and as perfect as I'd seen it in a long time.

I threw caution to the wind and built a fire in his wood-burning stove. Within an hour, the cabin was toasty. I took off my hat and my sweater. I made a cup of tea and let myself be hypnotized by the burning embers of the fire. How wonderful it would be if I could stay all winter.

The snow kept coming down, I wasn't sure for how long. I had failed to check the weather report when I was at the library. Reggie probably had a radio around somewhere. Based on his supplies, he was a practical man.

I had already made a cursory search of the house. There was no obvious door to the cellar, but I eventually determined that the humming sound generated a small vibration on the floor. I knew there had to be a cellar somewhere. I started at the front of the house and worked my way back, crawling along the floor looking for some kind of door. I found nothing, but I could feel the quiet vibration under my feet. I started at the front of the house again. The second time around, I moved the coffee table out of the way and lifted up an old threadbare rug. Then I saw the cellar door. I lifted it from a notch in the wood and saw a stepladder leading down to a cement foundation. I fetched a flashlight from the pantry and shone it into the cellar. The humming sound came in full volume.

I had nothing better to do, so I decided to explore. I kicked away a mass of cobwebs as I went down the ladder. There were five oil drums against the wall. I tapped on one, which resonated like a gong. I knocked on the rest—all empty. A giant metal cabinet stood right below the kitchen; at the other end of the room, right below Reggie's bed, was a thick latched door. From what I could tell, the humming sound emanated from there.

I approached the door, my mind getting creative about what I might find inside. Maybe this was just where Reggie kept extra meat or beverages, frozen perishables. Plenty of people keep refrigerators in their basement. Only, from the outside, this looked like a walk-in model, which seemed suspect considering the modest condition of the rest of the house. I felt a cold chill wash over me, which couldn't be explained by the temperature of the cellar. I thought about climbing back up the stairs and taking off. But this life doesn't offer much. Sometimes fear and dread are superior to tedium.

I opened the door. The refrigerator lit up, a light brighter than anything I'd seen for days. Inside were over a dozen bags of fertilizer. The bags had warning signs on them. *Contains Ammonium Nitrate. Combustible.* I counted the bags. Fifteen. They gave off a faint smell, but the fifty-degree refrigeration kept that in check. I closed the door, strolled over to the metal cabinet, and tried the handle. Locked.

I went upstairs and rifled through my bags until I found two paper clips at the bottom of my purse. I lifted up the metal spine of one, making a hook, and opened up the other into a straight line. Frank liked locks, so I'd learned how to pick them. I returned to the basement and stuck the hook edge into the bottom of the lock, keeping pressure on the left side. I used the other paper clip and stabbed at the tumblers until the lock gave way and I heard that satisfying click. Queasy adrenaline surged through me as I opened the door.

Inside were handguns, rifles, and semiautomatic weapons. On the bottom shelf were boxes of ammunition. There was enough artillery in that basement to wipe out a small town. Once I saw the guns, the purpose of the fertilizer clicked into place. Reggie wasn't the affable man I had hoped. I think Reggie was planning to blow some shit up. A man like that wasn't likely to leave his bunker for too long a stretch.

I climbed back up the ladder, gathered my belongings, and tried to restore the cabin to the exact manner in which I'd found it. I rushed to my car and drove for three hours from Saranac Lake to Burlington, Vermont. There was no direct route, so I had to pull over a number of times and consult my map. Once I made it to Burlington, I purchased two disposable cell phones at a drugstore and took a stroll along Main Street until I found a pay phone. I dialed the Saranac Lake police department and asked to speak with a detective.

"This is Detective Webb."

"I have an anonymous tip," I said.

"Okay. What have you got?"

"I have information on an individual who I think is planning to blow something up."

"Is that so?" Detective Webb said.

"His name is Reginald Lee, and he lives or has property at 333 Church Street off of Lake."

"May I ask to whom I'm speaking?" he said.

"Like I said, this is an anonymous tip."

"I see. Do you know what he's planning on exploding?"

"I don't know. Whatever fifteen or so bags of fertilizer could detonate."

"May I ask your relationship to this person?" Detective Webb asked.

"I don't know him," I said. "But if you go to his house and then lift up the rug in his living room, you'll find the hatch door to the cellar. You'll find all of the evidence you need in there."

"May I ask how you're connected to this man?"

"I'm not."

"You must know him somehow, ma'am."

"Are you planning on doing anything about this?"

"Unfortunately, under the circumstances, I can't."

"Why not?"

"Because you could be anyone with an ax to grind. I need a warrant to search a man's home. Without probable cause and a legitimate complaint from a real human being, not an anonymous source, there's nothing I can do."

"But you have to do something. He's not keeping that fertilizer to garden in spring. He has a whole walk-in refrigerator where he's storing it. Also, he's got an arsenal down there. At least twenty weapons."

"That's a Second Amendment right, ma'am."

"Tell me you're going to do something."

"If you want to come in to the station, ma'am, and make an official statement, then we might look into the matter. I see you're calling from Burlington, Vermont—"

I disconnected the call.

Roaming the street in a daze, my brain worked like a web of intersecting roadways. I'd take a turn, follow one direction a ways, hit a dead end, hit reverse, try a different offshoot, and hit another dead end.

If it were something else—human remains, perhaps—I might have let it slide. I've let many things slide in my lifetime. But it seemed to me that Reggie was planning on taking out a lot of people all at once, and I wasn't sure I could live with that on my conscience.

I checked my watch. I had about an hour until my prearranged phone call with Ryan. I stopped into a bar to fortify myself. I drank two whiskeys and left. I returned to my car, picked up one of the cell phones, and dialed.

"Hello?" he said.

Just that one word, loaded with all of the anticipation that I felt, sent me back ten years. I thought I'd hear his voice and feel all the rage of a decade at once. Instead, I felt heartsick and nostalgic. I missed him more than I hated him.

"Hello," I said, trying to sound professional, as if feelings weren't part of my current repertoire.

"Is that really you?" he said.

"Who else would it be?" I said.

"I've missed you," he said.

"Is that so?"

"How have you been?" he asked.

I hung up. Waited five minutes and called from the other phone.

"What happened?" he said.

"I really hope you're not tracing this call," I said.

"Why would I do that?" he said.

"Why do you do anything?" I said. "Because somebody tells you to."

"Fair enough."

"Are you alone?" I asked.

"Yes. I'm alone. I'm in a hotel room in Everett on business."

"Do you have a mistress?"

"Why?"

"Just curious what kind of marriage you have."

"If I had a mistress, I'd want to tell her things."

"That's a no?" I said.

"I don't have a mistress."

I hung up, waited five minutes, and dialed again from the other phone.

"I wish you'd stop doing that," he said when he answered.

"I can't take the risk of a long, drawn-out reminiscence. What have you got to tell me?"

"Your mother is sick."

"She's always been sick."

"Dying sick," he said.

"I see. What is she dying of?"

"Lung cancer."

"Well, thanks for letting me know."

I always believed I would see her again, that my last words to her would be replaced with new last words. It never occurred to me that my mother would leave this world before I had a chance to forgive her. I must have been silent for a while.

"Are you still there?" Ryan asked.

"Yes."

"I think you should get out of the country," he said.

"What makes you think I'm still in this country?"

"I can help you with a passport, if you need it."

"Good to know," I said. There was no point in providing any details of my life.

"I just put another thousand dollars on your card. I'll send more when I can."

"You're a man of your word," I said.

"I'm sorry," he said.

"You've said that before."

"Be careful, Jo, they're looking for you. And that writer is like a dog without a bone."

"Would that be Laura Cartwright?"

"Yes. How do you know her name?"

"She's been soliciting interviews online. Have you talked to her?" I said.

"She came by my house once. I told her I had nothing to say. Then I saw her again at the hospital when I was visiting your mother."

"Not talking to her might come off as suspicious," I said.

"I can't. I can't even look at her. She's got these blue eyes. On anyone else, I might think they were beautiful, but they just look cold to me."

"Blue eyes?" I said.

"Ice blue."

25

With all of the phone calls I was making and cell towers I was pinging, I had to keep moving, even if it was only around the Eastern Seaboard. After I ended my earthshaking phone call with Ryan, I tossed my two cell phones and cashed out a thousand dollars from my Western Union card, lest someone decide to freeze my assets. I drove to the Amtrak station in Burlington. The next train wasn't until the morning, so I found yet another cheap motel and lay low for the night. I woke up at dawn, gathering all my worldly possessions in that tiny backpack, and drove to the station, parking in the long-term lot. I won't deny that Blue's appearance in my past life was of immediate concern, but I felt obliged to first deal with the Reginald Lee matter.

Only one train served the Burlington region. I bought a ticket from Essex Junction to Philadelphia. It all felt like a hell of a lot of work, more than ten hours and back on a train, just to make a phone call, but I'd had a few too many close calls in the past year. I was running out of luck. The ticket cost me $150. I slept on the train so I wouldn't have to get a room for the night. When I woke I felt that familiar slice across my back.

I arrived in Philadelphia around nine p.m. I strolled down Market Street until I found a drugstore that sold disposable cell phones. I purchased two and continued on my way until I ran straight into the Liberty Bell. For just a few minutes, I was a sightseer, reading about the history of the bell and its poor construction. I thought about Andrew and how he would have memorized the details of the bell. Like the clapper was forty-four pounds and it was made of copper, tin, and some other metals, including arsenic. I wished I could send Andrew a postcard.

After I played tourist, I continued downtown and found my way into the lobby of the Ritz. I stepped into the bathroom and tried to clean myself up so that the hotel staff wouldn't ask me to leave. I didn't have to look like a guest, but I definitely needed to look like someone who might intermingle with a guest. I powdered my face, wrapped a scarf around my shorn locks, and put on bright red lipstick. My winter coat was a bit ratty, so I stuffed it in my bag. I returned to the lobby and found a quiet seat in the corner. This was as good a place as any to make the phone call.

"Sheriff Lowell," he said.

"Domenic?"

"Speaking."

"I need your help."

"Where are you, sweetheart? I'll come get you."

"Are you alone?"

"Yes."

"Tracing this call would be a waste of time and resources," I said. "I traveled hundreds of miles to phone you."

"You sure know how to flatter a guy."

"Let me ask you a question," I said. "Can you think of any benign reason why a man would store over a dozen bags of fertilizer containing ammonium nitrate?"

"You called to talk about fertilizer?"

"Among other things," I said.

"Less flattered now," Domenic said.

"He keeps the bags in a temperature-controlled vault. The basement also holds a decent-size arsenal, plenty of ammunition, and several empty oil barrels."

"Who is this man?"

"I'd rather not say."

"How'd you end up in his basement?"

"I was house-sitting."

"Does he know you were house-sitting?" Domenic asked.

"No."

"Then it's not house-sitting."

"Aren't you concerned about what this individual might be up to?"

"I'm extremely concerned," Domenic said. "I'm also concerned about what you might be up to."

"I just want to get him caught. That's all."

"You need to stay away from this individual. He sounds dangerous to me."

"I know that. That's why I called the police. But they just think I'm a bitter ex-girlfriend."

"Darling, tell me where you are and I promise I will help you."

"This is how you can help me. Tell me what I can do to stop him."

"What you need to do is keep your distance from that man."

"So you have no other suggestions for turning him in to the police?" I said.

"You could go to the police. Identify yourself. I suppose you could tell them you were homeless. That you broke into the house for warmth and then inform them of what you saw."

"That's all you've got?" I said.

Twenty hours and $150 for nothing.

"I'd like to help you. Let me help you."

"I have to go now, Domenic."

"Whatever you're thinking about doing, sweetheart, please don't."

"I'm not going to do anything."

"I don't believe you," Domenic said.

"We never had a chance to build any trust," I said.

I was about to sever the phone call when he spoke again. "A body turned up at Dead Horse Lake about a week after you left. He hasn't been identified yet, but it's just a matter of time."

I could still hang up, I thought, but that might look even

more suspicious. "How unfortunate."

"You wouldn't know anything about that, would you?"

"No. But good luck with your investigation. Take care—"

"Wait. Remember when you left me on the side of the road?"

"I apologized for that already."

"I'm not asking for an apology," he said. "It could have been worse."

"I could have done something with the peanuts," I said. It had crossed my mind.

"You left me a bottle of water," Domenic said.

"I did."

"That was thoughtful."

"I thought so," I said.

"I pulled your fingerprints off of it."

I couldn't speak. I could barely breathe. The last thing I needed was Debra Maze linked to my first two past lives. She was the guiltiest of all.

"Did you run them?" I said.

"No," he said.

"Why not?"

"What if I got a hit? Then I'd be the cop who let some criminal mastermind get away."

"Mastermind. Now you flatter me. Is that the only reason?"

"No, it's not."

"Good-bye, Domenic."

* * *

The concierge at the Ritz started giving me the eye around two a.m. I took a taxi back to the train station and killed six hours contemplating my next move. By morning I was groggy and dazed and could barely keep my head upright as I waited in line for the Vermonter train. I didn't even notice the police officers until they were right in front of me.

"ID and ticket please," a female officer said.

I just stared blankly back at her.

"ID and ticket," she said again.

I reached into my wallet and showed the officer Sonia Lubovich's driver's license.

The officer looked at the photo of the vibrant and healthy Sonia in the photo and returned her gaze to me. He brow furrowed as she studied the photo again.

"Are you aware that your license is expired?" the officer said.

"It is?" I said. "No, I was not aware."

She looked at me for a moment with sympathy and then shifted back to professional.

"Take care of that as soon as you get home," she said.

"I will," I said.

For the first four hours of the train ride, I slept with my head rattling against the window. One could hardly describe it as a restful sleep, but it was enough shut-eye to get my wits about me. When I woke up, the train had just departed the New Haven station.

It was time to start hunting for a new name. I traveled

from car to car, shopping for a new identity, the way some women pick out shoes. I found a promising option in her early thirties with long brown hair. Her nose and jawline resembled mine, but her lips were pumped with fillers and her forehead was as frozen as a clay sculpture's. I couldn't predict whether the natural or fake version would be on her driver's license photo, so I moved along to the next car, searching for a more viable option.

It wasn't until we passed the border into Connecticut that I found another person who might do. She was younger, maybe twenty-three, and she had at least fifty pounds on me. Our height and coloring, however, were about the same. As Blue once said, sometimes the best disguise is a thick layer of fat. At least this time I wouldn't have to go on an all-doughnut diet. You never know what someone might look like if they drop fifty pounds.

The plump woman, however, sat in a crowded car with her arm looped around her purse. I took a seat two rows away from her and waited for an opportunity. None arose. When the train conductor announced the next stop, Wallingford, my new name shrugged on her coat and shouldered her bag. She joined a knot of passengers by the exit door as I shoved my way into the fold. I took off my coat and threw it over my arm. My hand was grazing the plump woman's bag. As the train jostled into the station, I rummaged through her purse. When my hands felt a fold of smooth leather, I clutched her wallet and hid it under my coat. I shoved my way past the departing passengers and moved to the next car.

I stepped into the lavatory and locked the door.

As I caught my breath, I opened the wallet and checked the ID. Her name was Linda Marks. A perfectly respectable name. I gazed at the photo and it's quite possible I was being overly optimistic, but I thought I could pass as Linda Marks.

The train came to a stop and the doors whined open. As I slid the restroom door into its pocket, a rough-looking middle-aged man blocked my passage out and shoved his way into the bathroom with me, locking the door behind him.

"I saw you," he said.

"What did you see?" I said.

"Hand it over," he said.

The thing about being a criminal is that it hinders your ability to call out other criminals, as I had just discovered with Reginald Lee. I took the wallet from my bag and handed it to him.

"It's yours," I said.

He shoved the entire billfold, ID and all, in his backpack.

"Now your wallet," he said, holding out his palm.

I had eight hundred and eighty dollars in my wallet and my Western Union card that I was not inclined to hand over. I sized up my opponent and couldn't see a promising end to any physical altercation. I pretended to be fishing around in my backpack as I freed the Western Union card from its pocket and let it fall to the bottom of my bag. Then I handed over the wallet, cash and all. The man whistled with pleasure when he saw the wad of cash. He plucked forty dollars from the stack and offered it to me.

"Travel money."

"Fuck you," I said, although I took it. "Now if you'll excuse me, I don't want people thinking we're having a rendezvous in here."

"Next time wait until the conductor hits the brakes. Passengers are too busy getting their footing to notice a misplaced hand."

"Thanks for your advice," I said as I shut the door behind me.

I strolled to the end of the train and tucked myself into the last seat. I gave up on identity hunting for the day. I never saw the thief again. I arrived in Burlington at night. I drove to a motel, used my Western Union card, and checked in under Sonia Lubovich's name. I was wide awake after my journey, and my conversation with Ryan was still fresh in my mind.

The motel had a low-rent business center furnished with a photocopy machine and a computer. I logged on to the computer and created a profile under the name Amelia Lightfoot. I sent Laura Cartwright a single-word message.

Blue?

Five minutes later, Laura Cartwright wrote back.

What took you so long?

We exchanged a few more messages before Blue sent me a phone number and wrote, *We have some business to discuss.*

I performed a reverse lookup of the number she gave me. It was a prepaid phone, just like mine. I returned to room 209 and tried to figure out whether this was some kind of trap. Last I'd checked there was a thirty-thousand-dollar reward for information that led to my arrest, but I just couldn't see Blue playing me like that, especially with all of the dirt I had on her. I tried to be rational about the whole endeavor, but frankly, curiosity got the best of me.

I called.

"Laura Cartwright," she said, but it was most definitely Blue.

I didn't say anything at first. I listened for any background noise that might be suspicious.

"Is that you?" she said.

"Yes," I eventually replied.

"How has Debra Maze been treating you?"

"Not so great."

"I'm sorry to hear that," she said. "Would you like to talk about it?"

"I wouldn't mind discussing Jack Reed."

"Oh, him," she said, sighing with boredom.

"He came after me, Blue. With a gun."

"Shit. My apologies," Blue said.

"Did you plan it? Did you know it might happen?"

"To be honest, I considered it a distinct possibility."

"What if he killed me?"

"But he didn't, did he?" Blue waited patiently, as if the question were worthy of a reply.

"No, he didn't."

"Did you tell him anything?" she asked. I could sense she was nervous, and I wanted to keep her off balance just a moment longer.

"I told him *everything*," I said.

She was quiet for a spell and then she spoke.

"I understand. He can be very persuasive. But I'm not going by Amelia Keen anymore, so it seems unlikely he'll be able to track me."

"I think it's very unlikely," I said.

"And why is that?"

"Because I killed him."

"How?" she asked. I'd never heard a single word loaded with so much delight.

"With the gun you gave me."

"How magnificent. That was *his* gun, you know. Did you make it look like a suicide?"

"Nope. I'm pretty sure it looked like plain old murder."

"Tell me everything, and please don't spare me a single detail."

"I've said enough. You talk."

"What do you want to know?" Blue said.

"For starters, who the hell was the guy we buried in that state park?"

"You haven't figured that out?" Blue said, disappointed.

"No. Care to enlighten me?"

"Lester Cartwright. Laura's husband, the widower."

"Wait, you killed Laura Cartwright's husband? The guy we met in the funeral home?"

" 'He's no longer with us' is the phrasing I prefer."

"Why?"

"Because you said he killed her. Don't you remember

talking about that?" Blue asked.

"I don't remember talking about killing him."

"Do I have to clear everything with you?" Blue said.

"Not everything. But I would love it if you told me what you're doing in my hometown."

"I'm writing a book about the murder of Melinda Lyons. She was quite a girl, wasn't she?"

"She was."

"I can see why you were jealous of her."

"I wasn't that jealous."

"You were a little jealous. I better run. I've got an interview in fifteen minutes."

"No one is going to talk to you, Blue."

"Your mother already did. In fact, I have an almost-confession on tape. I doubt it would hold up in court, though. She was clearly drunk."

"I heard she got sober," I said.

"She did. But I had to get her un-sober to get her to talk."

"Blue, what is it that you're doing?"

"I'm trying to clear your name," Blue said.

"So far it looks a lot more like you're trying to set me up."

"Then you are misunderstanding my motives. After what you've done for me, I owe you this. I'm going to fix everything. Trust me, Nora."

I felt a shiver so deep, it was like being frozen in an ice cube. It was the first time anyone had called me by my real name in ten years.

26

Whatever moral compass Blue abided by eluded me. So far as I knew, she was living this life by choice; it wasn't thrust upon her. I had witnessed her heartlessness, but there was some part of me that also believed in her loyalty, believed she really was trying to clear my name.

When we parted ways in Austin, with her gun in my glove compartment and her ID in my purse, she had already calculated the most likely course of events that my life as Debra Maze would take. She knew Jack would track me down. She might have even clued him in to my whereabouts. She knew that Jack would be thrown off his game when he saw me and not her. She took a gamble on whether I'd shoot him or not. She probably figured her odds were fifty-fifty on me or Jack. She was willing to risk my life, but now she owed me a debt. And Blue's debt might be the one thing that could save me.

I wondered what Blue was like before all of this happened. Was her trigger finger as quick at the beginning of her run as it later became? I didn't want to end up like her, but I could see how my situation was like an ax, chopping away at the decent, upstanding citizen I used to be. I was now capable of doing things I would never have considered when I was young. I had my own debt, a debt to the world I felt I had to pay before I could justify any attempt at starting my life over again. Because my crimes prevented me from going through the proper channels to apprehend Reginald Lee, I had to adopt a different tack.

I checked out of the motel late the next morning. I drove back to Saranac Lake and picked up a bottle of bourbon and lighter fluid along the way. I checked the mailbox to 333 Church Lane: still untouched. As I drove up the driveway, I saw no sign that Reginald or anyone else had visited his property since my departure.

I had my Thanksgiving feast in Reginald Lee's home. It was turkey-and-rice soup and pumpkin pie filling out of a can. I had a couple shots of bourbon to clear away the cobwebs. It was one of my saddest days on record, but I just reminded myself that I was in transition. I didn't think Reggie could stay away too long, but I decided he needed an incentive to come home.

I wasn't sure if Reggie knew any of his neighbors, but if he did, I'd make it known that someone was making use of his home. I lit a fire in the wood-burning stove and waited. Three hours later there was a knock at the door. I didn't answer. There was another knock and then the sound of a man's voice.

"Reggie! Reggie, you in there?"

The man kept knocking for maybe five or ten minutes. I was worried he might have a key, but he eventually departed. I looked at the clock. It was 3:34 p.m. I figured Reggie wouldn't live more than a few hours' drive from his arsenal. I got to work. I crawled down to the basement and moved several bags of fertilizer out of the refrigerator. I took the propane tank from his backyard grill and lugged it down the steps. I returned to the main floor and fed a few more logs onto the fire. I put on three sweaters, one of Reggie's winter coats, a skullcap, and mittens over gloves. I stole one of his guns from his arsenal—I didn't think he'd miss it—and shoved it in his coat pocket. I hunkered down under the porch, as if it were a bunker.

One hour and forty-five minutes later, I heard a pickup truck barrel up the snow-covered driveway. He parked right next to my Jeep and searched the perimeter of his property. I had extinguished all of the lights inside his house, minus the fire. He treaded cautiously up the steps. The door was slightly ajar. It squeaked on its hinges as he slowly swung it open. I took off my gloves, curled my hand around the gun, and crawled onto the porch as he stepped inside.

He turned on the light and saw the hatch door to his cellar wide open and on display.

"Fuck," he said.

"Take a seat," I said with the gun aimed at his back. "We need to talk."

Reggie turned around and saw me. He had a full beard and long brown hair. I guessed his age was around forty-five.

He wore a flannel shirt, a hunting jacket, and a skullcap. The gun didn't seem to scare him. It just made him angrier.

"Who the fuck are you?"

"Sit down," I repeated.

He took a seat on his scratchy plaid couch. He couldn't take his eyes off the hatch door.

"Who are you with?" he said. "FBI? Nah, you look too fucked for that. DEA?"

I thought it best not to answer.

"Reggie, why don't you tell me what you were planning on doing with all of that combustible material in your cellar."

"What combustible material?"

"Those fifteen bags of fertilizer containing ammonium nitrate that you keep in a temperature-controlled vault."

"I like to garden, come spring."

"And all of those guns?"

"Deer hunting."

"You don't need a semiautomatic weapon for deer hunting," I said.

"Sometimes you do," Reggie said.

"Tell me what you were going to do."

"I ain't telling you shit," Reggie said.

I could almost feel the heat of his anger. He looked me dead in the eye, challenging me. It was as if he couldn't even see the gun I had trained on him. I took a cell phone from my pocket and tossed it on the couch next to Reggie.

"I want you to call 911 and tell them you have dangerous chemicals in your house that you wish to dispose of."

Reggie gave me a scrutinizing gaze. He glanced over at the phone but didn't pick it up.

"Why haven't you called for backup yet?" Reggie asked.

"I thought we could work this out on our own."

Reggie looked puzzled. He scanned his house, noticed a bag of trash in the corner, piled high with spent canned goods.

"You been staying here?"

"Pick up the phone, Reggie."

He didn't.

"You're no one, aren't you?" he said.

He had that right.

"I'm no one," I said.

Reggie smiled. His teeth were yellow and gray. The last traces of fear left him. I shot out the window to get Reggie's attention. He didn't even flinch, while my entire body vibrated from the blowback.

"Why don't you get the hell out of here and we'll call it a day?" he said as he got to his feet.

I picked up the lighter fluid and doused the couch with it. Then I got the butane lighter by the stove and held it over the couch.

"Make that call," I said. "Or I'm going to burn this place down."

Reggie charged toward me. I shot him in the arm. He stumbled a few steps back, righted himself, and glanced over at his bloody arm. I didn't bother giving him a second warning. I clicked the lighter. Within a few seconds the entire couch was engulfed and smoke had filled the room. I could see Reggie weighing his options. I tried to steer him in the right direction.

"It's over, Reggie. Why don't we get out of here?"

It seemed like some of the fight had left him. He stared at the blaze and then nodded his head. He turned around and slowly walked to the front door. I followed him, maybe a little too closely. He suddenly spun around and backhanded me. I fell to the ground. Reggie landed a solid kick to my ribs.

I pulled the trigger. The second bullet hit him in the gut. He looked surprised. He took a few steps forward and crumpled to the ground moaning in pain. My eyes were watering from the smoke and fire. I got to my feet and headed for the door. Reggie tried to get up, but he kept falling down.

"Show me some mercy," Reggie said.

"What do you want?" I said as I turned around.

"I'm already dead. So shoot me right this time. You owe me that."

I thought that maybe I did. I raised the gun one last time.

"God forgive me," he said.

I pulled the trigger. The bullet hit him in the forehead. His head tipped to the side like he was taking a catnap. I ran out of the house, guzzling air when I stepped outside. I jumped into my Jeep, backed out of the driveway, and floored the gas until I was at the mouth of Reggie's driveway. I stopped for a second and looked through the rearview mirror. The tiny house had been transformed into a wildfire.

I hit the gas and pulled onto the main road. I drove maybe a quarter of a mile and then I heard the angry thunder and felt a series of small earthquakes. I pulled onto the shoulder and looked through my rearview mirror again. Reggie's house was gone; just the fire remained, a fire as bright as day. It was then I realized it was over. I'd used up at least eight of my nine lives. I doubted I had much time left as a free woman. I thought I should see something beautiful.

I drove to the Albany train station, parked my car with the keys in the ignition, and checked the departure board. There were no more trains that night. I bought a ticket for the ten a.m. Empire Service and checked into a cheap motel.

I didn't sleep. For seven hours, I stared at the stucco ceiling and saw Reginald's face again and again—first that look of defiance and then resignation.

If you murder someone once, even with a tenuous argument for self-defense, you can blame it on chance, being at the wrong place at the wrong time with the wrong name. But the next time you kill someone, you have to start asking the hard questions. Is it really self-defense or a lifestyle choice? When you kill another human being in cold blood, you kill part of yourself. Until that moment I had always hung on to a shred of the old me. I knew who I was deep down. It was different now. Ten years on the run, and I was finally the cold-blooded murderer they'd always said I was. My conscience would haunt me like a shadow. I would never be able to close my eyes again without seeing Reginald Lee's face.

*   *   *

The next morning I boarded the train to Niagara Falls. I held my gaze on the landscape for the entire six hours, trying to forget who I was and who I had become. When I detrained, I quickly checked into a lodge under the reliable, but expired, Sonia Lubovich name. I dropped my bags in my room and strolled straight to the falls.

The sound was deafening. The mist felt cleansing. It was impossible to think of anything ugly standing before so much power and beauty. This would have been as good a place as any to throw in the towel. But I wasn't quite ready for that. I took the gun out of my pocket and threw it into the falls. If that wasn't the best place to dispose of a weapon, I don't know what is.

As it turns out, most people don't visit Niagara Falls in winter. I had the luxury of walking the cold streets alone. All of the things you see in movies—the *Maid of the Mist*, the Cave of the Winds (that long wet walk along those red stairs)—were closed for the season. I remembered them from watching *Niagara* with my mother as a child. Mom idolized Marilyn Monroe. They were nothing alike, aside from unfortunate choices with men. Still, getting to see that giant frozen waterfall made me feel like an average tourist. I stayed outside as long as I could manage the cold. Then I strolled back to town, found a motel with a bar, and ordered an Irish coffee to warm my bones.

I tried hard to sit quietly and enjoy the comforting burn of hot whiskey in my throat. I tried hard not to think about what the next day would bring, even though I had a clear and concise plan. I tried hard not to steal the wallet of the woman at the bar flirting with a man who paid her no mind. For her, the evening would provide a double insult, but I had to do it. Sonia Lubovich's expired ID might not get me where I needed to go. The flirting woman, who would wake up alone and without her wallet, looked just enough like me, and I had found that that was all it took. I left the bar and stepped out into the cold air.

You could hear the falls even back in town. I opened up her wallet and checked her ID. Moira Daniels was her name. She was an inch shorter than me, twenty pounds heavier, with long brown hair and blue eyes. I didn't bother to say it out loud, or practice introducing myself, or conjure up a complete identity. Moira was just an ID in my pocket until I reached my final destination.

On my way back to the hotel, I stopped by a drugstore and picked up some hair bleach, contact lens solution, and a new toothbrush. In my room I dyed my short brown hair blond. I've found that the more different you make yourself look from the photo, the more it's chalked up to cosmetics. The smell of bleach lingered in the room and burned my nostrils as I slept. In the morning, I took a long shower since it would be the last one for a while. When I looked in the mirror, I still recognized myself. So I rinsed those terrifying blue contacts in solution and spent a good half hour shoving them back into my eyes. My lids were rimmed with a traumatized red by the time I was done. But I wouldn't have known me anymore.

I packed up and checked out of the motel. There was bus service to Buffalo, so I bought a ticket to avoid a ten-hour layover before my journey even began. I found a coffee shop with a view of the falls and made myself invisible for a while, downing one caffeinated beverage after the next. I took out one of my mobile phones and made a call. There was no answer, but I left a voice-mail message.

"I can't do this anymore. I don't care what they do to me. I just want to come home. I want to be me again."

The next morning I boarded the Lake Shore Limited. I sat across from an older gentleman with the cloudy eyes of glaucoma. He smiled at what I imagined was the shadow of me. There was something comforting in knowing that I couldn't really be seen. Although no one had seen me in a long time.

"Good morning," the old man said.

"Good morning," I said.

"Heading home?" he asked.

"Yes," I said.

"It's always good to go home," he said.

I didn't bother arguing with him.

NORA GLASS

27

When I began the first leg of my journey home, I decided it was time to shrug off all of my other lives. I was going to be me again. The problem was I had spent so many years trying to tamp down the memory of me that it took some time to resuscitate it.

Nora Jo Glass was the name on my birth certificate. I was born in Bilman, Washington, on March 15, 1987. I had two parents for a while. Naomi and Edwin Glass. Then I had one parent, after my father committed suicide. There were all kinds of speculation about why that happened. Some people thought he did it because he couldn't provide for the family. The Glasses had had a grocery store in Bilman for as long as there were Glasses in Bilman. But that went under on my daddy's watch. Some people think he offed himself because his wife was having an affair. I think he did it just because he was sad.

At the time my childhood seemed far from ordinary— dead father; drunk, neglectful mother. In retrospect, it was the most ordinary part of my life. In light of the present, it was easy to revisit the distant past through a rosy filter. My early memories began to flood back as I gazed through the train window at the Ohio landscape drifting past me. My countdown began. I would be home in fifty-six hours.

I had freedom as a child and a teenager that I would never know again. My mother was either at work, drinking at the Sundowners, or out cold in bed, recovering from a hangover.

I found places to go and things to do to fill my time. My best friend was Edie Parsons. She lived on the other side of town, in a four-bedroom, two-story house, the kind of home that families live in on television. It was just a three-mile bike ride from my house, but many nights I didn't bother making the trip home.

Freshman year of high school, I joined the swim team on a lark, just to escape. Edie joined at her parents' insistence, to pad her college application. I discovered I had a talent for it. Freestyle and the backstroke were my races. I was more of a distance swimmer than a sprinter, but I always finished strong. My coach once told me that he thought I had more mental than physical strength. I knew what he meant. I could see the way my competition gave up. I watched Edie give up every day. She wasn't like that in class, but she hated that desperate need for air. I didn't mind that feeling you got underwater, when your chest felt like it was about to burst. Edie quit the team at the end of the year and started dating a guy in Everett. I no longer had her home as an escape, so I stayed at the pool as late as I could or rode my bike through town until the occasional police cruiser sent me home.

I was okay in class, but all I really had was the water. It was the first time in my life I thought I might be better than average. Maybe great. It was the first time I found ambition. And then I fell in love with Ryan Oliver.

I'm getting ahead of myself.

Roland Oliver owned most of Bilman. He ran a construction firm, Oliver and Mead, and that was where my mother worked, as a receptionist. Roland was also the man my mother was sleeping with. Roland had two sons, Logan and Ryan Oliver. I can't remember a time when I didn't know them. Logan was a year older, a few inches taller, and he had a shine on him that's hard to describe. He made you want to look at him, even when you tried your hardest not to look. It was his smile that killed you. Maybe because he wouldn't give it up all that often.

It wasn't just his good looks and the effortless way he could throw a football that drew me to him. Once, when I was eleven, I saw Logan beat the shit out of Mike Miles after Logan caught Mike bullying a local boy who had Down syndrome. I worshipped Logan after that. He seemed good and thoughtful. It was such a clichéd crush. My knees got weak and my tongue got tied whenever Logan was around.

I got over it fast one afternoon when I followed Logan into the woods by the Waki Reservoir. I followed Logan often, I'm ashamed to say. I remember that afternoon. It was a warm, muggy day in May. I trailed Logan like a spy down to a place called Wildcat Alley, named for its feline infestation.

I slipped behind shrubbery every time he looked over his shoulder. He never knew I was there. He never knew I saw him. Afterward he wondered what had changed, why I was the only one who could see beneath his shine. Simple. I was the only one who saw him pick up that stray cat and snap its neck. When I watched him do it, I first thought there had to be a solid explanation. Maybe the cat was sick and needed to be euthanized. It was the look on his face that told me otherwise. Logan enjoyed it. I didn't mention the incident to anyone. I kept my distance after that.

But Ryan Oliver was different. He was shy and quiet. He watched people as if he was trying to figure them out. Sometimes I caught him gazing in my direction. He'd always look away. Ryan never said much to me back then. He never spoke to the girls he saw lingering by his older brother. I think he felt embarrassed for them.

Ryan was softer than Logan. If anyone messed with Ryan, Logan made sure they paid for it. There was no sibling rivalry, because Logan was better at everything—school, sports, girls. Ryan figured out at a young age that there was no point in competing. Besides, Logan never drew attention to his achievements. He was satisfied with winning quietly.

The first time Ryan and I spent any time together was in the ninth grade. We were partners in a chemistry lab. We made a battery from a lemon and lit up a tiny Christmas-tree light, using zinc and copper nails to conduct the electricity. The class was accustomed to dramatic volcanic experiments; no one cared about the tiny light, except Ryan. I still remember that goofy grin he made when our bulb flickered on.

Later, during a class kayaking trip to the Tacoma Narrows, we paired up again. As we rowed through Puget Sound, I remember hearing Ryan say my name over and over again with different inflections, testing the sound by emphasizing different syllables.

"NO-ra, N-ora, No-RA. It just doesn't sound right."

"You feeling all right, Ryan?" I asked.

"My grandmother's name is Nora. We call her Grandma Nora. It's just weird calling *you* Nora. Do you have a middle name?"

"Jo," I said. "It's short for Joseph, my granddad's name."

"Jo. Jo, how's it going, Jo? See you around, Jo," Ryan said, testing it out. "I like it. If it's all right with you, I'll call you Jo."

Back then I liked the idea of being called something else. It never occurred to me that one day I'd pine for my old name.

"It's all right with me," I said.

For the teenagers of Bilman, the reservoir was the focus of our social life. On weekends you'd find a knot of inebriated students loitering on the rocky shore of the Waki Reservoir in a clearing called Stonehenge because of a few unusually placed boulders. I began supplementing school practice with my own workouts at the reservoir.

Ryan showed up one afternoon. I found him on the

shore as I climbed out of the water.

"What are you doing here?" I said.

"Making sure you don't drown."

"I won't drown."

"Probably not, but you shouldn't swim unsupervised."

"That's what you're doing? Supervising?"

"Yes."

Ryan supervised the next day and the day after that. Then it was a regular thing. Some days he'd watch me swim and sometimes I wouldn't swim at all. We'd go for walks along Wildcat Alley or just sit against a giant boulder and smoke weed. People talked, people asked questions. I never had a need for a solid answer. I didn't know what Ryan was to me. He was just someone I knew would be there. Because he was always there.

Then one day he wasn't. I went to the reservoir for my swim, and when I came out of the water, it felt like I was on an abandoned island. Ryan didn't show up the next day, either. I called his house and his mother told me that he was "unavailable." The third day, when I arrived at the reservoir, Logan was there instead. He put his arm around me and tried to sound all big-brotherly. He said things, things I'd remember only in fragments.

You're getting too attached.

Boys are different.

He can't be with you.

You're not the kind of girl . . .

I asked Logan why Ryan couldn't tell me any of those

things himself. Before I could stanch the flow, a single tear fell down my cheek.

"Because he doesn't like to see girls cry," said Logan.

"Do you?" I said. "Do you like it?"

It looked like he did.

After that day, I kept my distance from Ryan, even when he tried to breach it. One day he had the nerve to ask me what was wrong. He asked to meet me at the reservoir. My answers were always *nothing, no.* Never more than a single-word response. He gave up after a while. He even gave up saying hello to me as we crossed paths in the hallways. Sometimes, I liked to pretend he was invisible or that I was.

A swimming scholarship was the only way I was getting out of Bilman, and I wanted out. There were a few decent swimmers on the team, but no real competition, no one to challenge me. Not until Melinda Lyons moved to town.

The first time I swam the freestyle against the new girl, Melinda beat me by a full body length. The days of taking it easy in practice were over. I doubled my practice time, now that Ryan was out of the picture. The next time I swam against Melinda in a meet, she won by just a hair. We became fast friends.

In those days, I spent most evenings at the Lyons household. Melinda had an older brother, Jason. One night when I couldn't sleep, I went out on their back porch and smoked a cigarette. Jason came outside and confiscated it.

He pointed out a few constellations. I pretended I could see the patterns he insisted were in the sky, and when he caught me shivering, he put his arm around me. As I was trying to decide what I felt at that moment, Jason kissed me. It was nice. It was easy with him. It was my first real kiss. I thought I might feel more, but then I figured that maybe I wasn't the kind of girl who had those kinds of emotions. I thought it was the universe creating a balance with my mother, who could fall in love with a mannequin.

For three months I would sneak into Jason's room at night and pretend I was feeling more than I was. After a few weeks, Jason thought we were together. Everyone at school thought we were something. I thought nothing at all.

One day, as I finished my supplemental training at the Waki Reservoir, Ryan was waiting for me again. As I climbed onto the rocky shore, he held out my old beach towel. He had something to say. I could always tell when too many ideas were crowding his mind. He would start a sentence a bunch of times, as if he wasn't sure where to begin.

"What?" I said impatiently.

"Do you love him?" Ryan asked.

"Who?"

"Jason."

"What do you care?" I said.

"I care."

"You disappeared."

"They made me stay away from you," Ryan said.

"Why?"

"I don't know."

"You know," I said, even though I wasn't entirely sure myself.

My mother's reputation probably had something to do with it, and maybe my father's suicide, and maybe the old forty-two-inch television sitting on the brown lawn of my house.

"What difference does it make?" he said.

"Did you send Logan that day to break up with me?"

"What?" he said.

"You didn't know?"

He didn't know.

"I'm sorry," he said.

"What are you sorry for?"

"Being a coward," he said.

"It's been nice catching up."

I started to walk away. Ryan blocked my path, put his hands on my shoulders, leaned in, and kissed me. The kiss felt different from Jason's, but I still shoved him away, maybe because I felt something. Maybe I was worried that there was something in me that was like my mother. I started to dress.

"Jo, I miss you," Ryan said.

"What do you miss?" I said as I threw a sweatshirt over my swimsuit and shoved my damp feet into a pair of sneakers.

"You were my best friend."

"You don't kiss your best friend," I said, and I picked up my schoolbag and started on my way.

"Sometimes you do," Ryan said, stepping into my path.

He kissed me again. It *was* different. I was lightheaded, warm, and scared because I thought maybe it was just a prank. Maybe Logan was hiding in the bushes, egging on his brother.

"I have to go," I said, walking along Wildcat Alley, remembering that day, the look on Logan's face.

Ryan followed me.

"Didn't you miss me?"

"A little," I said.

"I want to be with you," he said.

"You're not allowed. Remember?"

"We're sixteen. We only have to hide it for two years."

I broke up with Jason the next day.

For almost two years, Ryan and I hid our relationship like two married people having a scandalous affair. We met in the woods by Stonehenge most afternoons, always with a solid alibi in place. Sometimes we'd drive to a different town, park in a remote location, and have sex in the backseat of his car. We became so skilled at car screwing, we once joked about writing a book together. When the weather allowed, we'd spread a blanket in the woods and check ourselves for ticks when we were done. A few times, Ryan sprang for a motel room. Those nights we imagined what our future might be like. I never imagined a future without Ryan. Even after what happened, even when I became someone else, I still hung on to the hope that one day he'd be my future.

We were caught a few times and aggressively punished. Ryan's car was taken away and sold. He had to hitch rides from his brother and friends after that. My mother tried to ground me once or twice, but she always passed out too early to enforce her punishment.

It was at a swim meet when Logan first noticed Melinda, really noticed her. At a party later that night, he brought her a beer and asked her to go for a walk with him, an invitation rarely refused. She refused. The next day at school, he found her by her locker and asked her again. She said no. He persisted, doing things that in the past would have never occurred to him. He picked flowers, left her sweet notes, waited for her after swim practice with a mug of cocoa. Melinda's resolve began to weaken. She thought perhaps she was the one woman who could tame him.

They went out one night to a drive-in movie in Everett. He figured he'd at least get to third base that night. Most girls put out on the first date. He rarely had a need for a second. Melinda let Logan kiss her, and that was it.

After that night, Logan could think of no girl but Melinda.

Melinda agreed to a second date and then a third. I told her to be careful. I told her what I knew, what I had seen that one afternoon in Wildcat Alley. Melinda thought there had to be a logical explanation. She didn't break up with Logan. Not then.

A month later, after their relationship status was cemented, Melinda saw the side of her boyfriend that I had told her about. Logan caught Melinda talking to Ben, a boy from her French class. They were speaking in another language and Logan assumed that Ben was making a move on his girl.

After school, Logan broke Ben's nose. Melinda figured her nose might be next. She broke up with Logan that evening. She quickly got herself another boyfriend. Hank Garner. I heard he was a chemistry major, a college boy, and a gentleman. He held doors and walked on the right side of the street. Melinda cared about those things; I never did. All you really need to know is that Melinda moved on. Logan didn't. He graduated and stuck around Bilman the next year, working odd jobs for his father and keeping tabs on Melinda.

When senior year rolled around, we began to make plans. Ryan would turn eighteen in January; I would in March. Ryan applied to several colleges back east. He had the grades for them. I thought maybe I could still get a swim scholarship.

One night, after a statewide swim meet, where Melinda got first place in the freestyle and I got second, we celebrated by getting tattoos. Melinda got a dolphin; I decided on the Chinese nothing. We kept training after school, but I'd start to miss a practice here and there. While Melinda kept her eyes on the prize—a swim scholarship—I had lost my focus.

Ryan and I made more plans. Many young girls make that mistake at one time or another—they lose themselves in a boy. But I doubt any girl paid more dearly than I.

"Next stop. Chicago."

I had a four-hour layover. In the restroom I got a good look at myself under the unforgiving fluorescents. No one would ever have seen an old picture of Nora Glass and thought it was the same person. I only hoped that one day I might look in the mirror and recognize myself again.

I stopped into a bar for a drink. No man paid me any mind. I sat down at the bar and ordered a beer. The news was on, but the sound was muted. I stared in a daze at traffic and weather reports. Then I stared in a daze at a familiar face. The picture had been taken outside a police station. The woman was emaciated and wearing a scarf to cover her bald head. She looked like death was beating on her door and she was just about to answer.

The headline on the screen said, *Naomi Glass confesses to fraud and obstruction of justice.*

I spilled my drink. The bartender cleaned up the mess and poured me another.

"Would you mind turning up the sound?" I said.

The bartender unmuted the TV, just as a picture of me from ten years back flashed on the screen, all flesh and lightness and eyes bright and clear and full of hope, with a stupid school-photo grin.

The newscaster, standing in front of a familiar Craftsman house, said, "Mrs. Webber claims that her daughter, Nora Glass, was the victim of a criminal conspiracy involving a prominent family in her hometown of Bilman, Washington. She insists that Miss Glass is innocent of all pending charges. Authorities have recently discovered that Nora Glass has been living for eight years as Tanya Dubois. Tanya is currently a person of interest in the suspicious death of her husband, Frank Dubois."

The bartender asked me if I wanted another. He looked me straight in the eye without a hint of recognition.

"Yes," I said, still riveted by the television screen.

Chief Lars Hendriks of Bilman, Washington, the caption read. He wasn't chief when I lived there. He stood at a podium outside the police station and read from a piece of paper.

"Nora Glass, if you're out there, please come home. We have new information on your case. I think it's time we put these crimes to bed."

The news cut back to the Craftsman house again, my old house. The door opened and my mother, looking as thin and fragile as a glass doll, stepped onto the porch. The reporter asked her a question. She answered it. I couldn't make out the words, I was so stunned to see her after so long. Too many emotions were vying for attention. My eyes watered and burned as the reporter signed off and the weatherman took over the screen. My bartender poured my drink and tipped his head in the direction of the TV.

"Do you know she was living for ten years under another

name?" the bartender asked. "What do you reckon? You think this Tanya/Nora is guilty?"

"I think she's probably guilty of something," I said.

28

I bought a ticket to Everett, Washington, on the Empire Builder. It followed the Lewis and Clark trail for part of the journey. I looked at my watch. I would be home in forty-eight hours.

Snow-covered mountains made every window look like a landscape photograph on the move. I tried to enjoy the view, but the memories kept flooding back. My mother's face was lodged in my mind. Not the woman I saw on the news, but my mother on the last night I saw her. She was drunk yet sober. Her eyes glassy and clear. She said, *I told you to stay away from that boy.* I remembered the smell of hair color stinging my nostrils as my mother's shaky hands massaged in the dye. And I remember thinking that none of this would have happened had I not wanted to be with him.

I leaned my head against the cold train window. It felt nice against the heat of my anger. I let myself go back to that night, the moment when I took a battle-ax to my entire life.

It was prom night. Ryan and I went separately since he was still on close watch by the Olivers. We danced once that night. Afterward, a knot of students changed clothes and congregated at Stonehenge. We had dozens of oil lamps, two kegs, and hard liquor that was passed around and drunk straight from the bottle. The reflection of the lights on the reservoir made it look like the water was on fire. I was stupid happy in that way you can only be when you're young.

I remember Logan turned up later. He had hitched a ride with some locals, kids who'd graduated a few years back but still hung with the high school crowd on weekends, buying them booze and lurking around jailbait. I saw Logan out of the corner of my eye, drinking from his private bottle of bourbon as he roamed the grounds searching for Melinda. I remember catching a glimpse of her with Hank, making out behind a boulder. They were there and then they weren't there. I only learned that they'd left when Logan asked for my car keys.

"No. Go catch a ride with one of your townie friends."

"Give me your keys or I'll tell them I saw you two fucking in the woods," Logan said.

"Fine," I said, getting to my feet. "I'll drive."

Ryan and I followed Logan toward the clearing where all the cars were parked, including my mother's beat-up 1986 Datsun. Impatiently, Logan circled back and snatched the keys from my hand and beat a path through the woods.

When Ryan and I caught up with Logan, he was standing like a statue, staring at Hank's Volvo. The radio was playing, the dome light was on. You could see their silhouettes inside the car.

The booze loosened my tongue. I said all of the things I

had wanted to say ever since I figured out he wasn't as shiny as everyone thought.

"Get over it," I said. "She doesn't love you. She'll never love you. There's nothing you can do to change that."

"Shut up," Logan said.

"No one good, no one decent, will ever love you. You might fool them for a little while, but then they'll find it, that thing inside of you that you hide so well. Anyone can see it if they look hard enough—"

"Nora, stop," said Ryan.

I didn't stop.

"You're dead inside. You need to find a dead girl—"

Logan wrapped his fingers around my throat. *This is what drowning feels like*, I thought. Ryan tried to wrestle his brother off of me. Logan shoved Ryan to the ground. I heard the Volvo's engine turn over, the lights blink on. Logan released his grip on my neck. I sucked in air. Logan unlocked the driver's-side door of my mother's car and got in.

I wasn't thinking ahead. I had no notion of what Logan might do. I just thought my mother would kill me if I came home without her car that night. I raced around the car and jumped into the passenger seat and Ryan hopped in back.

The Volvo pulled out of the driveway onto the two-lane country road. The Datsun spat dirt charging in the wake of the Volvo.

"What are you doing, Logan?" Ryan said.

Logan said nothing. He just followed the car as Hank and Melinda traveled the foggy two-mile stretch of Reservoir

Lane. Logan lead-footed the gas until he was only a few feet away from the bumper of Hank's car. Logan started honking the horn.

"Slow down," I said.

Logan said nothing.

"What are you doing, Lo?" said Ryan.

Logan said nothing.

"Make him stop," I said to Ryan.

Logan tapped the bumper of the Volvo. I knew then that something horrible was about to happen. Hank picked up speed, but not enough. He was scared, I guess. Logan wasn't scared.

Hank made a sharp right turn on Skyline Road, heading north toward Everett. Maybe he was heading home. Logan followed. As they reached the Skyline Bridge, a one-mile stretch of road that crossed a fingerlike extension of Moses Lake, Hank slowed down. It was a narrow bridge with low guardrails that would invite caution in any other circumstance, but slowing down at that moment was the biggest mistake of Hank's life.

When I looked over at Logan, his eyes were fixed, his jaw clenched and pulsing.

"Please stop," I said, but he had already done it.

Logan put his foot to the floor and rammed into the back left fender of the Volvo.

Hank's head slammed against the steering wheel. He never had time to hit the brakes. The Volvo jumped the guardrail and dove headfirst into the water below. Logan kept his foot on the gas; he never straightened the wheel. Our car plunged into the lake, landing just shy of the Volvo.

I smashed my head against the dashboard but came around when bone-chilling water began spilling into the car. I couldn't see Melinda or Hank. I couldn't see much of anything other than Logan rolling down his window and crawling out into the water.

In the sinking Datsun I felt a sharp stabbing on my forehead. I touched my hand to my head and came back with blood. I turned around and saw Ryan sitting in the backseat, buckled up, gazing forward in shock, frozen with fear. The water rushed into the car and had risen to his nose. I unbuckled my seat belt and took one last gulp of air. I swam over the seat and unbuckled Ryan. He began to panic as the water rose above his head.

I wrapped Ryan's arm over my shoulder, opened the back door, and pulled him out of the car, pumping my legs until we reached the surface. I held Ryan above the choppy water as he gasped for breath. We swam to shore. Ryan coughed and wheezed on the rocky beach.

I fell on my back and looked up. I remember the sky and thousands of stars. And then it all went black.

I woke in the hospital. A doctor or a nurse told me I had a concussion. I was kept another day for observation. My mother sat by my bed but refused to look me in the eye. When I asked her what happened, she said that her car was at the bottom of Moses Lake and left the room to get a cup of coffee.

The doctor informed me that Ryan still had some fluid in his lungs and Logan was suffering from mild hypothermia. The Oliver boys were expected to be released in the next day or two.

Aside from my mother, the only visitors I had were two detectives. I can't remember their names. A man and a woman. I asked them what happened to Hank and Melinda. The female officer told me they were dead. The way she said it was strange, without any sympathy. The man told me not to go anywhere, which I thought was an odd thing to say to a girl in the hospital.

I cried for an hour when I got the news. No one tried to comfort me. I didn't notice that at the time.

The phone calls, text messages, and online taunts began shortly after I came home. I felt like a ghost. My mother could barely look at me or speak to me. Those same detectives dropped by our house to take my statement. They kept asking me if I was sure that's what happened. My mother went outside for a smoke. I told the cops everything I remembered. They nodded their heads, made notes, and told me again that I shouldn't go anywhere. I wondered where they thought I wanted to go.

Ellen, an acquaintance from math class, sent me a text: *Why did you do it?*
John, from English: *I hope you get the death penalty.*
Bitch

Sociopath
I hope you die
Murderer

I called Ryan's mobile number. He didn't pick up. I called his house phone, and his mother, Sarah, answered. She sounded heavily sedated. Her words slurred like they were slipping down a slide.

"Heeesss not abailable to talk," she said.

I asked where he was. Sarah mumbled something I couldn't make out and hung up. I called Edie. She didn't answer, so I dropped by her house. I went straight to her bedroom window and knocked quietly three times.

Edie opened the window and said, "What do you want?"

"I want to know what's going on," I said.

"You should know that better than anyone," Edie said.

"Why are people calling me a murderer?"

"Because you are one."

"I don't understand."

"Melinda and Hank are dead. Has no one told you?"

"I know that, but it was Logan who was driving."

"No. You were," said Edie. She looked at me as if I weren't even human. I would get used to that look, but I wasn't just then.

I returned home to my mother, who was chain-smoking and drinking a bottle of cheap bourbon on the porch. I asked her what was happening.

"Five people were in that accident. Three survived. Two say you were driving."

"But I was the passenger," I said.

"I told you to stay away from that boy," my mother said.

After dark, I rode my bike to the Oliver mansion. It was a tacky three-story showpiece with four Greek columns and a twelve-foot wrought-iron door on eight acres of land. Ryan once told me it took the gardener an entire day to mow the lawn. I circled the house in the shadows and found my way to Ryan's window. I threw tiny rocks up to the second floor, like I had done many times before. Ryan had always answered. Not that time.

"Why don't you use the front door," Mr. Oliver said from the edge of the porch.

I thought about running but couldn't see the point. I followed Mr. Oliver back inside the house. The foyer was about the size of my mother's entire home. Mr. Oliver walked past the main staircase into a parlor. Sarah Oliver sat on the couch, flanked by Ryan and Logan. She had a clear drink sweating on her knee.

Sarah stared at something in the distance. Ryan focused on his shoe. Only Logan had the balls to meet my gaze. I couldn't find remorse or regret in his eyes or anything else that might have been right for the moment. He looked defiant, as if I deserved what was coming.

"Have a seat," Mr. Oliver said, gesturing to a plush leather chair in direct opposition to his family.

Roland paced back and forth behind the couch as he spoke.

"It is my understanding that the police will come to your house tomorrow morning with an arrest warrant," he said.

"An arrest warrant for what?" I said.

"For the vehicular murder of Melinda Lyons and Hank Garner."

I didn't really believe it until then, until Roland said it. My lungs felt as empty as they did at the end of a race.

"Logan was driving," I sputtered.

"No," Mr. Oliver calmly said. "*You* were driving. Logan and Ryan were passengers."

"Ryan," I said, trying to wake him up.

He wouldn't look at me.

"Ryan," I said again. "Tell them who was driving. You remember, right?"

Ryan looked up for a second. "You were driving," he whispered.

My tears ran so hot they burned. Ryan looked away so he wouldn't have to see them.

"Logan, you know what happened," I said.

"You killed her. You killed my girl," Logan said.

If I didn't know it was a lie, I might have believed him.

"I'd like to help you, if you'd let me," Mr. Oliver said.

"Help me? I don't want your help."

I stood up, but the floor didn't feel as solid as floors should feel. I snaked a path to their front door, feeling dizzy and queasy and murderous all at once. Mr. Oliver caught up with me at the foyer. He gently took me by the arm and spoke in a smooth, soothing tone. He offered me his handkerchief. I wiped the tears away with my sleeve.

"I'll drive you home and we can discuss your options," he said.

I got into the car. I remember feeling lightheaded and seeing spots. As Mr. Oliver drove me home, he presented my options in his practical manner.

"You could stay and have your day in court. You would likely be charged with second-degree murder. The sentencing guidelines require a minimum of ten years in prison, but you could get out in seven—"

"I didn't kill anyone. Logan did."

"Nora, listen to me. It was your mother's car, and the only two living witnesses say that you were driving."

"What was my motive?" I asked.

"You were jealous of Melinda. She was better than you at everything."

"That's a stupid motive."

"You don't need a motive when you have two eyewitnesses."

"Why have you always hated me?"

"I don't hate you," Roland Oliver said. He said it in a way that was almost believable. "I care for you. That's why I'm trying to help you."

"Ryan won't do this to me."

"Do you think Ryan would choose you over his entire family?"

"Pull over," I think I said.

Mr. Oliver pulled over just outside the deserted high school. I spilled out of the car and vomited on the asphalt. Mr. Oliver waited patiently as I doubled over, convulsing.

When my body stopped gutting me, I staggered to my feet and started walking home. Mr. Oliver didn't say anything. He followed me all the way home, driving in short five-mile-an-hour segments in his Mercedes.

At home, Mr. Oliver and Naomi sat me down to discuss my option. The only one that didn't involve serious jail time.

"You don't belong in prison," Mr. Oliver said.

"Logan does."

"Your mother and I think you should run. I can help you. But you have to leave tonight. We'll hide you in a motel outside of Tacoma. In a few days I'll return with a new driver's license, social security number, and birth certificate. You can start a life somewhere else. You can be anything you want to be," Mr. Oliver said.

"I want to be Nora Glass."

Mr. Oliver stood and buttoned his blazer. "You need to make a decision by midnight. I'll leave you two to discuss it in private."

Roland let himself out.

I looked at my mother, searched her eyes for something real. She was sober enough in that moment.

"Mom," I said. "They can't do this, right?"

She walked into my room. I followed her.

"I packed your bag," she said.

A small suitcase sat on top of my bed.

"No," I said.

But I didn't say it with much conviction. It was over. I had three options: I could live free on the run; go to prison; or die now, like my daddy did. I chose to run because I figured that would give me the best chance at something like living. And that's exactly what it was. Something like living.

My mother took me by the hand and led me into the bathroom. Her hand felt clammy and cold and unfamiliar. I couldn't remember the last time she had touched me. Naomi sat on the edge of the tub, took a pair of scissors from a drawer, and cut my long, sandy brown hair in a straight slice across my chin and then she gave me thick uneven bangs. When I looked in the mirror it was the first of many times I wouldn't recognize myself.

I remember my mother prepping the hair color and realizing that she had made the decision to send me away hours ago. I remember the smell and the cold burn of the chemicals on my scalp and inside my nose.

As we waited for the color to process, she said only one thing: "I know you won't ever understand, but this is for the best."

The black hair color didn't suit me. It made my skin look yellow. Vanity should have been the least of my concerns, but it still cut to feel so plain.

"You can change it later," Naomi said. "Just never go back to what you used to be."

Mr. Oliver returned right before midnight. My mother tried to hug me. I let my arms hang to the sides.

"I love you, Nora," Naomi said.

"Fuck you, Mom," I said.

Mr. Oliver took my bag and walked me to his car. I got into the backseat straightaway. We drove for two hours. Oliver pulled his car into the lot of a Motel 6 in Tacoma. He went to the front desk, got a room, and returned to the car.

He passed me my room key, got my bag out of the trunk, and handed me a plastic bag.

"Room 3C. Don't leave. That food and water should hold you for two days. I'll knock four times when I return."

I waited two days in room 3C. I thought about running to the police and telling them the truth, but when I watched the evening news, I saw that I had already been publicly convicted.

When Mr. Oliver returned, he knocked four times. I opened the door; he handed me an envelope.

"Your name is Tanya Pitts. You were born April 3, 1985, in Mesa, Arizona, to a Bernard and Leona Pitts, both deceased. There's ten thousand dollars in cash in that envelope, a birth certificate, and a social security card. You should have no trouble becoming gainfully employed."

"Where am I supposed to go?" I said.

"Go as far away as you can and never come back."

When the Empire Builder reached Everett, Washington, I thought about getting right back on the eastbound train.

After revisiting my old life, the end of it, I wasn't so sure that coming home was the wisest notion. I'd lasted a decade on the run. Maybe I could last another. But then I remembered all of the things I'd had to do to remain a free woman and decided I didn't want to do them anymore. I detrained, leaving my bag of secondhand clothing behind.

I bought a bus ticket to Bilman, Washington. Two hours later, when the bus stopped in my old hometown, my ten-year journey was almost complete. I strolled the two miles to Main Street. I walked up the brick steps to the Bilman Police Station.

The man at the front desk looked up and gave me a quizzical gaze. "Can I help you?"

"My name is Nora Glass. I'm here to turn myself in."

29

The officer on duty gave me a quick glance, sighed like bored teenager, and picked up his phone.

"Chief," the officer said. "We got another Nora Glass i town."

The officer listened, nodding his head, saying *uh-hu* a few times, and then placed the phone back in its cradle "Ms. . . . ," he said, leaving a blank space as if I hadn't jus told him my name.

"Glass. Nora Glass. I believe there's a warrant out for m arrest."

"I'll never understand you people," he said.

"The chief these days, he's called Lars Hendriks, right Why don't you call Chief Hendriks out here and we'll sor this thing out."

"Listen, Ms. . . ."

"Glass. Nora Jo Glass. The real one."

"Listen, Ms. Glass, we've been through this about dozen or so times before. Why don't you save me the troubl of writing up a three-page report and enjoy the freedom tha this country has fought centuries to provide for you."

I could have stood there arguing with the man, but he had handed me another get-out-of-jail-free card, and I thought I should take it. Besides, I owed someone a visit. I could take care of a few social niceties before they put me behind bars.

I strolled down Main Street to get my bearings, but everything I'd known had changed. Only the post office remained in its original spot. My family's old grocery store, after a brief interlude as a thrift store, was now an upscale market, everything organic and marked up 300 percent. I bought a two-dollar banana because I was starving. An Italian restaurant had taken the place of the diner that I used to frequent post–swim practice for chocolate shakes and burgers. Parsons' hardware store had doubled in size, shoving out Art's Deli & Pizza; in place of the shoe repair store was a boutique clothing shop. The Sundowners now had a swanky new sign, as if shunning its past clientele.

I walked through town just as I had ten years ago, although no one waved or said hello. I recognized a few faces with the years and/or the pounds packed on. I saw Mrs. Winslow, my old English teacher, shopping at the fancy market. She was probably retired by now. I spotted the old postmistress, head bent over her walker, taking a stroll. I saw Edie chasing after a blond boy, maybe three, who was the spitting image of Logan. I wanted more than anything to run up and give her a hug, hold her child. But then I remembered how she'd looked at me the very last time I saw her and I didn't want to see that face ever again.

I thought about walking into the Sundowners or the post office and making my presence known, but it didn't seem like the right time and I was hardly in the mood to argue over whether I was a wanted woman or an impostor.

I kept walking until I arrived at 241 Cypress Lane, the address I used to call home. Only it wasn't home. Home, in my mind, resembled a sepia print of a house during the deep depression—chipped paint, broken steps, missing shingles. This house was in impeccable condition. The lawn was bright green and recently cut, the smell of fresh grass cloying in my nose. The house was repainted light blue with white trim around the windows. The second stair on the porch, which had been broken most of my life, was now solid like the rest. The windows were scrubbed clean, the roof replaced. The yard wasn't cluttered with a single item meant for disposal. There were two rocking chairs on the newly painted porch, and that was it.

I rang the doorbell. A man in his sixties with a gray beard and a small belly, wearing blue jeans and a well-ironed plaid shirt, answered.

When he saw me, his eyes widened and watered just a bit. I could hear him gasp as he took a step back to steady himself.

"Nora?" he said.

I didn't know if I'd ever get used to being called by my old name. It didn't fit like an old sweater; it was more like putting on a pair of someone else's shoes.

"Yes," I said.

The man's eyes crunched into a warm, sad smile, as if he was genuinely happy to see me. He held out his hand and said, "I'm Pete. Pete Owens."

"Hi, Pete," I said.

We shook hands.

He stood there, still smiling, looking sad and a bit lost. "Excuse me," he said. "I forgot myself for a moment. Please, come in."

Pete walked back into the house. I stayed put.

"Pete," I said, still standing on the porch, "who are you?"

"Oh my," Pete said, turning around and shuffling back to the front door. "I'm your mother's fiancé."

He extended his hand again. I shook it.

"Nice to meet you, Pete."

Pete stepped away from the door and offered a silent invitation. I entered my old house, but it felt like my old house in an alternate universe.

"I guess you're here for the funeral," he said.

Tears I never thought would fall for my mother began to drip down my face.

"When did she die?" I said.

"Two days ago," said Pete.

I sat down on the couch and tried to stanch the flow. I wasn't going to cry for one of my traitors.

"She was sorry about everything. She was trying to make amends near the end," said Pete.

"I heard she's been talking to the police."

"She made an official statement. Told the truth."

"On her deathbed," I said. "When she had nothing to lose.

"Would you like some tea, coffee?" Pete asked.

"Got anything stronger?"

"This is a dry house."

Just my luck. The one time I needed booze in my childhood home, it wasn't there.

"Tea is fine," I said.

"I'll be right back," Pete said as he retreated to the kitchen

I expected that feeling you have when a memory take hold and your whole body shifts back in time. *But I neve lived in* this *house*, I thought. *I could stay for a little bit withou the wrong memories shaking me by the shoulders.*

But then I opened the door to my old bedroom and memories flooded back. That old flowered duvet I'd hated; the posters of bands I hadn't listened to in years; the bookshelf my father made from planks of wood and cinder blocks pilfered from a junkyard; my swim medals gathering dust on the walls That room had stayed the same, like a shrine to the old me.

I quickly shut the door on my past and sat down on Pete' couch.

He brought me a cup of tea.

"The writer is on her way over," said Pete. "She told me to call her as soon as you came."

The doorbell rang. Pete answered it. Blue entered my childhood home. She looked the same, but different. He hair was cut in a sharp bob and she wore black-framed glasse

hat I was certain she didn't require. Over her shoulder was
heavy canvas bag that seemed weighed down with papers.

"Nora Glass, as I live and breathe," she said with a thick
outhern drawl. "I'm Laura Cartwright. I'm the writer
esearching your case."

"Nice to meet you, Laura," I said as I got to my feet.

We shook hands, playing strangers.

"Have you heard the news?" she said.

"What news?"

"You're a free woman."

"How is that possible?"

"Ryan made a statement. So did your mother. It was
nough evidence to convince the prosecutor, Jason Lyons.
n fact, we're supposed to meet him at the police station in a
ew minutes. I'll give you a ride."

Everything felt like a trap, but Pete looked so honest and
ight, I thought maybe it was true.

"I hope you understand the debt of gratitude you owe
his woman," said Pete. "It was Laura here who convinced
our mother and then Ryan to make their statements."

"Really?" I said.

"It was nothing," said Blue. "I just appealed to their sense
f honor."

"Well, I'll have to find some way to repay you," I said.

"I think we're even," Blue said.

I had to agree.

* * *

"Is this really her?" Chief Hendriks said to Blue.

The three of us were standing in an awkward triangle i[n] the waiting area of the police station.

"It's Nora," I said. "I'm Nora."

"It's her," said Blue.

"But you never met the real Nora Glass, did you?"

"No," said Blue. "But I've seen dozens of photos, and sh[e] has her mother's nose."

Chief Hendriks gave me an inscrutable gaze and spok[e] slowly and clearly, as if English might be my second language[.]

"Let me explain something," he said. "In the last ten year[s] we've had exactly fourteen Nora Glass impostors. About hal[f] of 'em you could rule out on first sight. One was in her lat[e] sixties and another was clearly a transvestite. It's a drag, n[o] pun intended, on police resources every time. And it used t[o] be very traumatic for Naomi when she'd have to come dow[n] to the station to identify, or deny, the impostor."

"Well, she's dead now," I said.

"Jason Lyons will be here shortly. I suppose he ca[n] confirm."

I sat for an hour with Blue in the interrogation room, facin[g] a one-sided mirror.

"Some weather we've been having," Blue said.

She nodded her head in the direction of a camer[a] mounted in the corner. We were likely being recorded.

The police officer, the one at the front desk who'd sent m[e] away, brought us both a cup of coffee.

"You don't look like her. Not like any of the pictures I've seen. That's why I sent you away."

"People change," I said.

"You changed a lot," he said as he departed.

A few minutes later, Jason Lyons walked into the room followed by Chief Hendricks. Jason wore what looked like a new suit and carried a battered old briefcase. He looked nothing like the boy I remembered, and yet I could still see that boy somewhere inside of him. He wasn't lost completely like I was. He looked like a prosecutor. I can't say why, but it fit him. It was hard to gather my thoughts with my past and present clashing as they were. I remembered Jason's clumsy kisses in his bedroom, but now his expression was implacable.

"Is this her?" Chief Hendricks asked.

"Hi, Nora," he said.

"Hi, Jason."

"Glad that's finally settled," Chief Hendricks said. "I'll leave you to it."

Hendricks left. Jason sat down across from me and opened his briefcase. He glanced over at Blue, silently hinting for her departure.

"Nora, when you're done, meet me at the Sundowners," Blue said. "I have a few more questions before I can turn in my article."

"I'll see you later."

As soon as she was gone, Jason said. "Why did you run?"

"Because I didn't want to go to prison for something I

didn't do. I was eighteen. I wanted to be free."

Jason slid a document in front of me. "That's a signed statement from Ryan Oliver corroborating your story."

"When did he do this?" I said.

"He called me last night. He said you were coming home and it was time to tell the truth. I took his statement this morning. We had a very interesting conversation."

Before I knew it, tears were streaming down my cheeks. In the last twenty-four hours I'd cried more than I had in the last decade.

"I'm sorry," I said.

I had nothing else to offer. For the first time in years, I thought about Melinda. Not about what Melinda's death had done to me, but the life lost. I'd started running so soon after her passing, I never had the chance to mourn it. The things people said, some of it was true. I *was* jealous of her. She *was* better than me—not just a better swimmer or student, but a better person. If the tables had been turned, I knew for a fact she wouldn't have run.

"Thank you," Jason said. "I remember you were close for a time."

"What happens now?" I asked.

"We're dropping all charges. I also talked to the authorities in Waterloo. They'd like you to go home in the next few weeks and answer a few questions. But the warrant has been withdrawn. You're a free woman. You can do whatever you want now."

I have to admit, it was a bit of a letdown. Running so hard

for so long only to learn I was free. It was like gearing up for a championship fight only to have your opponent take a fall. I still wanted to fight. I had lived for so long with my options narrowed into a foxhole, I wasn't sure how I would proceed now that the real world was open to me.

"What about Logan and Mr. Oliver?" I asked. "Have you made any arrests?"

"We're reviewing the old case for any physical evidence. A man like Roland has every kind of lawyer on speed dial. I'm not bringing them in until the case is airtight."

"Three witnesses isn't airtight enough for you?"

"Never underestimate your enemies."

"I don't," I said.

"There's one thing I don't understand. It's been nagging at me," Jason said.

"What?" I said.

"Your mother. Why did she keep quiet all of these years?"

I had debated whether I should shield my mother's memory and keep her secrets intact. But there had been so many lies already, I didn't see a problem in speaking the truth. Besides, the woman had sold me out for ten years.

"Because she was in love with Roland Oliver," I said. "They had a thing for as long as I can remember."

Jason remained still. I could see his brain putting pieces of a puzzle together in his head, only there was still a piece missing.

"So she chose him over you?" he said, not quite buying my theory.

"Yes, she chose him."

"I think there's more to it than that," Jason said.

"Maybe," I said. But I figured we'd never know.

"You've led quite a life in the last decade," Jason said.

"You have no idea."

Jason and I hugged awkwardly as we said our good-byes. As I walked out of the police station a free woman, I thought I might feel different, released. But, really, I felt even more like an impostor answering to a name that was no longer mine. I put on my sunglasses and strolled to the Sundowners.

Blue was sitting at a table in the corner. She waved me over with a cheery smile.

"Tell me *everything*," she said, like we were two gossiping schoolgirls.

I noticed she had a giant rock on her ring finger.

"You're married?"

"Just for a few months. I normally go by Laura Bainbridge, but I use my maiden name for my literary career."

"You work fast," I said.

"It was a quick courtship, I must admit. But he's running out of time."

"Is he sick or something?"

"No, nothing like that," said Blue. "What are you drinking? Gin?"

She smiled wickedly, as if she always knew that drink order was a disguise.

"Whiskey," I said.

Blue went to the bar and got our drinks. It was kind of like old times, drinking with Blue. Only she refused to cut out that Southern drawl no matter how many times I asked.

We exchanged travelogues and compared notes about our relative successes being each other. As Amelia Keen, she'd managed to bilk twenty grand out of Roland Oliver before he closed the bank. She moved to Colorado and met Eugene Bainbridge. She didn't offer too many details on that engagement; I didn't ask. There were some things that I felt better off not knowing. I regaled her with a few stories from my teaching stint in Recluse. She liked the idea of my geography lessons revolving around road maps. I wondered how Andrew was doing.

"Did you know that I always wanted to be a writer?" Blue said. "You're like my good luck charm."

I couldn't quite say the same for her, although she did right by me this one time.

We ordered another round. Blue held her glass of whiskey aloft in a toast and said, "To Naomi Glass, rest in peace." She looked me right in the eye.

"What was she like?" I asked.

"She was your mother. You should know better than me."

"I hadn't seen my mother in ten years. What was she like in the end?"

"The way most people are at the end. Scared and full of regret. The way you are all of the time."

I felt like she was digging tiny graves in my conscience. I couldn't look at her. The town of Bilman had turned me into a fake criminal, but Blue had turned me into a real one.

Blue smiled. Not the way most people smile, when

prompted by laughter or joy or a fond memory. She smiled with satisfaction. She knew more about me than she had five minutes ago. She asked me when I decided to come home, and I told her about Reginald Lee.

"You blew up his entire home?"

"It was either that or let him murder dozens of innocent people."

Her eyes lit up. "Did you take any video?"

"Of the explosion?"

"Yes."

"No, I didn't."

"Not even a picture?" The light in her eyes faded just a bit.

"No."

"Oh, well. I'm still proud of you."

"What's next for you, Blue? Are you going home?"

"Not until I write the last chapter of the Nora Glass story."

"You can't be serious," I said.

She was.

Blue dropped me off at my childhood home and said, "See you tomorrow?"

Time had lost some meaning for me. When you're not sure what the future holds, you choose to stay in the present.

"Tomorrow?" I said.

"Your mother's funeral."

"Right," I said.

It felt odd knocking on the front door of 241 Cypress

Lane yet again. I wondered if the key was still hiding under the fake rock.

Pete opened the door. He smiled nervously. "Welcome home," he said.

All those years I wanted to hear those words. Now they just got under my skin.

Pete cooked me a meat-and-potatoes dinner, which we ate in awkward silence. He made a ceremony of giving me the keys to my mother's two-year-old Toyota. Naomi had left the house to Pete, since he'd paid off the mortgage, but there was some money in a bank account. Pete gave me the paperwork.

"I know you don't have any family left. You can think of me as family, if you want."

Pete was a nice man, but I didn't have the same notions of family that other people had. It wasn't something I was looking for.

I excused myself from the table and went to bed. I fell asleep fast. I slept in that deep careless way that children do, as if I were making up for all of those years I spent on guard.

At some point in the night, I woke. Someone was rapping on the window outside.

I opened the window and there he was. My best friend, the man I loved for far too long, and the person who betrayed me more than any other. Seeing him made me happier and sadder than I could ever remember. I climbed outside. We stood there just looking at each other. We didn't hug or shake or anything.

He'd changed over the years. Lost a bit of hair, put on a few pounds. Worry and sorrow had burrowed highways on his brow.

"You don't look like you," Ryan said.

"I wasn't allowed to be me."

"I mean, you don't look like I thought you'd look."

"It's the hair," I said, hoping he wasn't seeing right through to my conscience.

"Are you planning on staying?" he said.

"I'm not planning anything."

"I have a family," he said, taking a few steps closer.

"I know."

"I have a daughter."

"I heard."

He closed the distance between us. Up close I could only see his eyes, the same eyes I had stared into thousands of times. They were sad now, but they were still Ryan's and they still made me ache.

He kissed me. His lips felt more familiar than my own reflection. I felt seventeen again, as if anything were possible. And then he pulled away, and I was reminded of every cruel trick that the world had in store for me.

"You ruined my life," I said.

"You ruined mine," he said.

"I'm not staying," I said.

"Good. I don't ever want to see you again."

He never did.

30

The morning of my mother's funeral, I decided to dye my hair back to brown. I was growing tired of the stares that my bleached, chopped locks were drawing. After I rinsed out the dye and dried my hair, I looked half-normal again, even if I didn't feel it inside. I picked an old dress from my closet to wear to the funeral. It hung loose on me. It was the same plain black dress I'd worn to my grandma Hazel's funeral. Only three people had attended Hazel's service.

My mother drew a bigger crowd—or rather her notorious daughter did. Half the town seemed to have packed into Bronson & Sons mortuary to get a glimpse of the infamous Nora Glass. It was a closed-casket service, so there wasn't a whole lot to look at besides me.

When Edie came through the door, I averted my gaze. She approached me cautiously, like I was a stray dog. Then she hugged me. Not tight, like a real hug, but a tentative hug you might give a fragile old relative.

"I'm sorry," she whispered. "I should have known you didn't do it."

"I'm glad you left him," was all I said.

Pete stood by the door and welcomed the guests, even the ones he knew were attending just for the show. He shook everyone's hand until Roland and Logan Oliver arrived. Pete turned away from the door as if they were invisible. An audible gasp came from the crowd and then a quiet murmur, like a still ocean.

Guilt hadn't aged Logan as it had his brother. He was still lean, handsome, and looked like he could fool you into believing he was a good man. As Logan sat down in a pew, Roland walked right up to me.

"I'm sorry for your loss," he said.

"Which loss are you referring to? My mother's life or mine?"

"I tried to help her, you know. I put her in rehab. I gave her money whenever she asked."

"You're good at paying people off."

"You may never understand, but I really thought we were doing what was best for everyone."

"If it's absolution you're after, I'd see a priest."

Roland retreated and took a seat in the back row. As the service was about to begin, Blue stepped inside. She was wearing a sleek black dress, pumps, and a veil.

"You're a bit overdressed," I said.

"Nice turnout," she said. "Oh good, the Olivers are here."

"*Why* are they here?"

"I suggested that if they didn't attend the funeral they'd look guilty," she said.

"They *are* guilty."

"That's neither here nor there, Nora. Excuse me, I can't finish my book until I get an exclusive interview with Logan. I'm going to try to steal him right now. I doubt he wants to sit through a boring funeral service."

From a distance, I watched Blue work her wicked charm on Logan. After just a few words passed between them, Logan was following Blue out the front doors of the mortuary. I swear that Blue could talk her way out of a lion's den.

Pete gave a lovely eulogy about redemption and tried to convince the cynical crowd that Naomi had truly made amends for a life riddled with misdeeds. I stood in the back of the mortuary, hoping to keep as many eyes off of me as possible, but I still caught rubbernecks trying to catch a glimpse. I wondered if people were hoping for tears. They would have been disappointed. My eyes were dry as the desert. I had lost my mother ten years ago. I'd shed all of my tears back then.

I slipped out of the mortuary as the service came to a close. I didn't need any more false mourners paying me their respects. Outside, sulfurous clouds loomed low in the sky. A light drizzle began to fall. I spotted Blue and Logan chatting intimately in the parking lot. They were standing by a black Range Rover.

As I walked over to them, Blue clocked me out of the corner of her eye and said something to Logan. He looked in my direction and opened the passenger door for Blue. Then he got into the car and drove out of the lot.

* * *

My mother's Toyota was parked at the far end of the lot. Blue and Logan had a head start, but it didn't matter. I knew exactly where they were going. I started the engine and pulled out of the lot. I turned right on Buckwheat Lane, made a left on Route 47, and took the exit for Skyline Road. The speed limit was forty; I was going sixty.

After ten minutes on a two-lane road, I had the Range Rover in my sights. I hadn't been on Skyline since the night Melinda died. We were at least four miles from Lyons Bridge. I remembered reading years ago that they had named the one-mile viaduct after her. I picked up my phone and dialed Blue's number. She answered after the third ring.

"Now's not a good time," she said.

"I know what you're doing, Blue. Please don't. It's not what I want."

"I'll call you when I'm done interviewing Logan."

"Blue—" I said.

But she had already disconnected the call.

I was driving seventy miles an hour, just to keep them in my sights. We were only two miles, less than two minutes, from the bridge. But time had lost all meaning. I was in the past, the present, and the future all at once.

I saw Logan's car swerve, right itself, swerve again, and then jump the rail of the bridge, bending steel. The windows were tinted, so I couldn't see what happened inside the car, but I knew that when the Range Rover jerked wildly to the right, Blue had her hands on the steering wheel. There was no skidding or braking. The Range Rover barreled into the guardrail and dove twenty feet down, right into Moses Lake.

I hit the brakes, put on my hazard lights, and jumped out of the car. The black SUV was slowly being swallowed by the lake. I sighed in relief as I saw Blue climb out of the passenger window. I couldn't see Logan through his window tints, but I knew Blue wouldn't help him escape.

I threw off my shoes and coat and dove off the bridge into the murky water. I swam past Blue, dove under, and climbed through the open window into the car.

Logan was still alive, struggling with his seat belt. His face was bright red from holding his breath. I reached for the belt and pressed down on the button, but the buckle wouldn't release. I tried again. It wouldn't budge. I was running out of air. I tried the belt one more time. I needed oxygen.

Logan watched the bubbles rise as I expelled the last air I owned. He grabbed the collar of my shirt and held it around my neck like a noose. I tried to pull him off me, but I guess he had decided that if he was going to die, so would I.

My lungs felt primed to explode. I looked Logan in the eye, silently begging for mercy. I should have known that he didn't have any. Then he took a breath of water, convulsed, and released his hold on me. I turned around and dove out of the car, kicking to the surface, where my lungs were finally able to feast on air. I treaded in the cold lake as I got my fill of oxygen.

I spotted Blue on the shore. I swam over to her and

climbed out of the water, still gasping for breath.

"He's gone," I said.

"That's what I figured," said Blue, shivering, blue-lipped, but calm. "I was worried he was taking you with him."

"What did you do?"

"I didn't do anything," Blue said without any conviction. "He realized that his days were numbered as a free man, and he wanted to go out on his own terms."

"So he just drove off the bridge all on his own?"

"It seemed like a poetic end. He dies on the same bridge that first made him a killer. I do love symmetry, don't you?"

"I prefer justice," I said.

"Sometimes you get both."

Blue and I hiked up the embankment back to the road.

"Give me a ride to my motel," said Blue.

"We should go to the cops."

"Why?"

"Because you were in the car with him."

"Was I?" Blue said. "I don't remember that."

I didn't argue with her. I didn't see how it changed anything in the end. I drove Blue to the Super 8 on the outskirts of town. She told me to wait in the car. I had the heat on full blast, but I was still shivering from being soaked through.

When Blue returned to the car, she was carrying a large manila envelope.

"You should have this," she said. "I thought Logan's death was the ending I was looking for, but this is the Nora Glass story, and that's not over yet. I can't publish it as it is. You probably know most of the stuff that's in there, being Nora Glass and all. But there's one thing about Nora that you might not know, and it would clear a few things up."

"I don't want it," I said.

"Take it anyway," she said, dropping the stack of papers on the passenger seat. "Be happy, Nora. Justice was served."

"You and I have a very different idea of justice."

"Do we?"

"Good-bye, Blue."

"This isn't good-bye," Blue said as she walked away.

I went back to my old house and took a hot shower. Later Pete came home and asked me where I had been. I said it was all too much for me and I had to leave. I crawled into bed and slept until my conscience woke me. All I could see was Logan bucking against his seat belt, awaiting death. I turned on the reading light and picked up the pages from Blue's damp manuscript.

As I leafed through the papers, I had to laugh. They were all blank except the title page and the last page, which was a report that took me some time to understand.

Blue was right. There was one thing about me that I didn't know, and it did indeed clear up a few things. At least now I knew why my mother and Mr. Oliver were so determined to send me away. Still, I think there had to be another way.

* * *

I stayed two more days in Bilman helping Pete clear my mother's things out of the house. I was standing right next to him when the phone rang and he got the news of Logan's demise. The police were calling it a vehicular suicide.

I packed up my mother's car and said good-bye to Pete. I drove to Roland Oliver's house. I had one final piece of business before I'd leave Bilman forever.

I found Mr. Oliver sitting on his porch drinking a whiskey. It clearly wasn't his first of the day.

"I'm sorry for your loss," I said.

"Are you?"

"A little. I suppose I think of Logan differently now."

"You know?" he said.

"I know."

"Now do you understand?" he said.

"I understand why you and my mother wanted to send me away. I don't understand why you tried to have me killed in Austin."

Mr. Oliver sighed and closed his eyes.

"That wasn't me. Logan found out you made contact and he—" Roland didn't finish that sentence.

"I see."

"Ryan can never know."

"I agree," I said.

"Forgive me," he said.

"I don't think I can," I said as I passed an envelope to Mr. Oliver.

"What's this?"

"It's the money I borrowed. I'm paying you back."

"I don't want your money, Nora."

"I don't want yours."

I stood up and looked down at the old man one last time.
I tried to see him differently, but he was still the same.

"Good-bye, Dad."

EPILOGUE

I got into my car and drove. I took I-5 South to 405 South and exited onto I-90 East. I drove until midnight. I stopped at a cheap motel in Missoula, Montana, woke up the next morning, and kept driving. By dusk I was in Wyoming. I took I-25 South toward Casper. I got a room at the Friendly Ghost Inn, where I took a hot shower, changed my clothes, and put on a bit of war paint.

I strolled down the street and into the establishment called Sidelines. I ordered a top-shelf bourbon. I was celebrating my innocence. I sat and nursed my drink as I waited for him to notice me. My drink was almost empty by the time he took a seat next to mine. He cautiously looked in my direction but didn't say a word. I brushed the hair away from his forehead and touched the scar I had given him when I'd slammed on the brakes.

"You seem to be healing all right," I said.

"Just on the outside," he said, winking.

"You'll be fine."

"So what brings you to town, sweetheart?"

"Domenic, do I have to keep looking over my shoulder?"

"I don't know," he said. "Do I have to keep looking over mine?"

"I just want to be free. Am I?"

He looked me in the eye and seemed to mull the question over. "Will you promise to be a law-abiding citizen?" he said.

"I'll do my best."

"That's all any of us can do," he said.

"How about we start over," I said.

"I like the sound of that. Can I buy you a drink?"

"I think I owe you the drink."

"I think you do," he said as he extended his hand. "My name's Domenic."

We shook hands.

"Nice to meet you, Domenic."

"And you, darling? You got a name?"

ACKNOWLEDGEMENTS

As always, I must first thank Stephanie Kip Rostan and Marysue Rucci. I am ridiculously fortunate to have an agent and an editor who had faith that I could write a whole book based on a two-sentence pitch in a bar.

At S&S I must thank Carolyn Reidy and Jon Karp. You both have been extremely generous and supportive. I am in your debt. Also at S&S: Richard Rhorer, Laura Regan, Amanda Lang, Sarah Reidy, Marilyn Doof, Allison Har-zvi, Kristen Lemire, Ebony LaDelle, and Maureen Cole. You are all fantastic. Last but not least, Jonathan Evans. Thanks to you I will never have to master the English language.

To all of the amazing people at my literary agency, Levine Greenberg Rostan! (I added the exclamation point, but I think it works): Jim Levine, Dan Greenberg, Melissa Rowland, Beth Fisher, Miek Coccia, Monika Verma, Tim Wojcik, Kerry Sparks, Lindsay Edgecombe, and Shelby Boyer. Thank you will never be enough.

Clair Lamb and David Hayward deserve some kind of ward for having to suffer through my writing in its lowest form. They are remarkable at finding the right words that keep me going. I love you both.

And friends: Morgan Dox, Steve Kim, Julie Ulmer, and Julie Shiroishi. I'd be lost without you. Diego Aldana, thanks for the catch in the last book and the idea for the hideout in this one. Hopeton Hay and Tim Chamberlain: Thanks for the scoop on Austin and for the years of great interviews.

Thanks to David at Camp Scatico for the tour.

Family: Aunt Bev, Uncle Mark, Uncle Jeff, Aunt Eve, Jay, Anastasia, Dan, and Lori.

Thanks to all my criminal friends who make me feel like I'm part of something. There are too many to list, but you know who you are. Since I have to turn this in now and I know I'm forgetting someone:

Thank you, _____.*
You are like my favorite person ever.

* Insert your name here.

ABOUT THE AUTHOR

Lisa Lutz is the *New York Times* bestselling author of the Spellman Files series, *Heads You Lose* (with David Hayward), and *How to Start a Fire*. Lutz won the Alex Award and has been nominated for the Edgar Award for best novel. She lives in upstate New York.

RIVER ROAD
CAROL GOODMAN

Driving home in a snowstorm, Nan Lewis hits something
with her car. She's sure it's a deer. What else could it be? Then
one of her students is found dead, the victim of a hit and run.
And there is blood on Nan's tyres. As friends and neighbours
turn on her, and she starts finding disturbing tokens that
recall the killing of her own daughter, Nan begins to suspect
that the two deaths are connected…

*"Emotion-charged twists and turns that
you won't see coming"*
TESS GERRITSEN

"An intense psychological thriller"
PUBLISHERS WEEKLY

"An engrossing mystery"
BOOKLIST

THE DEVIL YOU KNOW
ELISABETH DE MARIAFFI

Rookie crime beat reporter Evie Jones is haunted by the unsolved murder of her best friend Lianne. Now twenty-two, Evie is obsessively driven to find the killer. She leans on childhood friend David Patton for help, but every trail seem to lead back to David's father. As she gets closer to the truth, Evie becomes convinced that the killer is still at large – and that he's coming back for her.

"[An] artful first novel"
PUBLISHERS WEEKLY

"Evie is a tough, wisecracking narrator worthy of the greatest private-eye pulp novels"
BOOKLIST (STARRED REVIEW)

"A totally riveting novel"
NEW YORK JOURNAL OF BOOKS

TITANBOOKS.COM

For more fantastic fiction, author events, competitions,
limited editions and more

VISIT OUR WEBSITE
titanbooks.com

LIKE US ON FACEBOOK
facebook.com/titanbooks

FOLLOW US ON TWITTER
@TitanBooks

EMAIL US
readerfeedback@titanemail.com